PLAIN JANE

PLAIN

Jane

Eve Horowitz

RANDOM HOUSE
NEW YORK

Library of Congress Cataloging-in-Publication Data
Horowitz, Eve
Plain Jane/Eve Horowitz.—1st ed.
p.   cm.
ISBN 0-679-41261-1
I. Title
PS3558.06935P57   1992
813'.54—dc20   92-3991

Manufactured in the United States of America
98765432

The text of this book is set in Bembo

Book design by Oksana Kushnir

To my husband, David Leibowitz,
and to our families.

ACKNOWLEDGMENTS

I wish to express my gratitude to all my friends at Sterling Lord Literistic, particularly my agent, Philippa Brophy.

I am deeply indebted to my editors, Kate Medina and Jonathan Karp.

PLAIN JANE

1

$\mathcal{E}$verything was fine until my sister Caroline graduated from Barnard last May and announced she was going to marry Jonathan. My parents loved each other, my sister loved my parents, and I loved Eddie. My father still yelled at my mother all the time and had temper tantrums the likes of which you can't imagine—"There are bones in this fish!" he'd scream at the dinner table and then storm out of the kitchen, shrieking, "I can't eat this!" One time he even threw an overdone hamburger across the table at her. My mother was a sport, she'd just laugh and go into the kitchen, and I'd follow her to make sure she was all right. She always was. "What a nut, huh?" she'd say, and she'd see if she could find a burger that wasn't quite so well done. Then she'd go coax him out of his bad mood, tell him he *liked* well-done burgers.

Then there were the times when he'd tell her how beautiful she looked in a certain dress, when he'd take her hand and give her that admiring look of his, when he'd give her just the right birthday present with a little white card tucked inside that said no more or less than that he loved her.

We'd all agreed that my mother was the prettiest, the kindest, most wonderful person, the very best cook and hostess in the whole world, and my father was the funniest, most charming, moral, handsome, intelligent man in the world. We had great Thanksgivings and Passovers; everybody came, even my brother William was flown into Cleveland from Connecticut. Connecticut was where the Winthrop School for Boys was, a special boarding school for boys whose older sisters had screwed them up for life.

Grandma and Grandpa didn't believe in the "religious" part of the seder, but they knew just how to harmonize when we were singing "Dayenu" or "Adir Hu." We'd eat so much, we'd barely be able to move when dinner was over—chicken soup (with the fat skimmed off the top, of course, to avoid a blast from my father), gefilte fish, brisket with Grandma's homemade horseradish, and those delicious little Passover cookies filled with jelly. After we ate, Caroline and Willy and I would look for the *afikomen*—the piece of matzah which the fathers were supposed to hide from the children—and whoever found it would get a silver dollar, enough of an incentive to get us moving. At the end of the seder, we would sing "God Bless America" and "Next Year in Jerusalem" and be done with it; I mean, we weren't fanatics or anything, we didn't feel we needed to read every single word in the Haggadah.

But now that's all changed. Caroline's not even going to come home for Passover this year, and when she tells me why,

I don't believe her; she says Jonathan wouldn't feel comfortable eating in our home on Passover because my mother doesn't change the dishes in the pantry or get rid of the All-Bran in the cupboard or the beer in the refrigerator. She says our seders are "incomplete at best," a fancy way of talking she must have learned at Barnard. She says that my father doesn't even do the *afikomen* right. The right way, she says, is the way Jonathan's father does it. He doesn't hide it from the kids, the kids hide it from him, and if he can't find it, he rewards them with bicycles or trips to Israel, not measly silver dollars. She says it's all a charade, the way our family sings "God Bless America" and "Next Year in Jerusalem"; she says God didn't get the Jews out of Egypt only to have them sit in their big suburban houses singing about next year in Jerusalem. I'm surprised she hasn't started going by her Hebrew name, Chana, since she's so Jewish all of a sudden.

The hardest thing about all this is the shock of it. If anyone was going to marry an Orthodox Jew, it should have been me, not Caroline. I'm the one who had a Bat Mitzvah. I'm the one who used to shush my friends during Saturday morning services so I could utter The Silent Prayer with complete and total concentration. I'm the one who went to Camp Ben-Gurion and accompanied the singing of "Thou Shalt Love the Lord Thy God" with my guitar. While I was lighting Sabbath candles on Friday nights, Caroline was going to Joni Mitchell concerts with one of her thousands of boyfriends who, I might add, had no trouble getting her into bed.

I only mention this last detail because now that she's Orthodox, it's as if she was the greatest virgin who ever lived. Caroline was far from being a virgin when she got married, I can tell you, and I probably don't need to add that her boyfriends were far from being Jewish. She was very open-minded back then: she didn't even discriminate between black and white, or married and single, never mind Protestant or Buddhist or Catholic or any other category. Now she probably votes Republican, even, and calls black people *shvartzes*. But back then she was an equal-opportunity lay.

The summer before she went off to Barnard, she came to me crying and asked me if I could lend her two hundred dollars. The next day, I sat in the waiting room of the Planned Parenthood clinic on Prospect Avenue, not one of Cleveland's loveliest neighborhoods, and drove my sister home while she clutched her stomach and cried. I was only fourteen, but I'd developed early and easily passed for sixteen. Caroline had taught me how to drive long before that, and that day she didn't even complain about the way I passed in the right-hand lane.

Caroline barely even looks Jewish, except for her slightly crooked nose. She's got long blond hair and no boobs at all. I, on the other hand, have curly brown hair, and wear a 34D. My boyfriend Eddie practically worships my chest, and I actually think it's even possible that he still enjoys putting his face in my cleavage as much now as he did when he first started. He acts like he does, but I'm a little bored with it. Long gone are the days when all he had to do was brush his hand lightly over my shirt and I'd be having twelve orgasms. Now even his mouth between my legs isn't enough; if I want to come, I close my eyes and summon forth the image of Dr. Stevens going down on me in his office. That usually does it, unless I happen to run my fingers through Eddie's hair at the same time and realize it's Eddie down there, not Dr. Stevens.

Eddie and I do some pretty intense fooling around, but we've never gone all the way, so *I* wouldn't have had to pretend to be a virgin. Not that Caroline pretended, I shouldn't imply that. I mean, I have to give her credit—she was pretty honest with Jonathan, if not with the rest of her new family, about her sordid past, and he was pretty understanding, considering the cloistered world he grew up in. Jonathan had gone to Jewish day schools all his life, and then one day, he told Caroline, he doesn't know what got into him, but he decided he wanted to go to a secular university for college. If he hadn't, he never would have met Caroline, never would even have considered someone like her but, according to Caroline, he'd had a few sexual experiences of his own at Columbia. Let's just say, he was a virgin the way I'm a virgin. Everything but. I guess he was saving himself for his wife; I guess I'm saving myself for Dr. Stevens. Anyway, now you see why I say if anybody was going to marry a Jonathan, it should have been me.

Not that I would have. I mean, Jonathan's a great guy, if you like the mature, responsible, cute, funny, interesting type—but if you get him, you get his family, and you wouldn't believe what that means.

Jonathan and Caroline's wedding, for instance. First of all, everybody knows that a wedding takes place in the bride's hometown, not the groom's, but not this wedding. My parents took me with them to New York in May when the engagement was announced, and you should have seen the look on Mrs. Klausner's face when my parents suggested having a fall wedding in our backyard. "You mean, in *Cleveland?*" Mrs. Klausner said, as if Cleveland were Akron or something. "And besides, you can't have a wedding this fall. September is only five months away."

The only one who looked more disgusted that evening than Mrs. Klausner was my father, when Jonathan's younger sister Shira brought out a tray of cheese puffs to go with the kosher Asti champagne. My father can't stand greasy, fattening food, especially cheesy food (I think it reminds him of fat women with fat white breasts, he's also indicated he's not so crazy about them), and seeing it there must have confirmed all his theories about Orthodox Jews, even though Mrs. Klausner and her daughter Shira were anything but fat. All I ever saw them consume was diet Coke and Sweet'n Low.

Anyway, the wedding ended up taking place in December at this tacky hotel in New Jersey. Don't get me started on why Mr. and Mrs. Religious Couple of the Century didn't object to getting married in a hotel. Apparently, only Conservative synagogues and Reform temples were large enough to hold five hundred people, and the Klausners' rabbi refused even to step foot in one of those. Can you believe it, a rabbi who'd rather pronounce a Jewish couple man and wife in a Holiday Inn.

My parents were great about the whole thing. Even though they'd wanted no more than a hundred guests, they gave in and let the Klausners invite as many people as they wanted. "A hundred people?" Mrs. Klausner had said. "I meet a hundred people I know on the way to the butcher!"

My parents said they didn't care enough about the wedding one way or another to upset my sister's in-laws. They said they found the whole thing rather amusing, considering that their own wedding and the weddings of their friends' children never involved more than fifty people, a clarinetist, a rabbi, priest or justice of the peace, and a light salmon dinner. Now they found themselves at their own daughter's wedding, among five hundred people, a five-piece klezmer band, a video-camera team, tuxedos and huge bridesmaid dresses made out of navy taffeta and velvet. Caroline was wearing a four-thousand-dollar Carolina Herrera dress, which her mother-in-law found for her half price at Kleinfeld's, a discount bridal shop in Brooklyn where all the orthodox girls went, according to Caroline. Mrs. Klausner bought the dress for Caroline, scoring one more point for their side.

It was depressing to see my sister, who used to walk down Coventry Road wearing wraparound skirts and gauze blouses, walking down the longest wedding aisle in history, in a fancy, frilly dress, though I'll admit she looked the part. Nevertheless, the fact that she was wearing taffeta instead of cotton was only one example to me of how my sister was selling out.

The truth is, I think my parents were less nonchalant than they were willing to admit. My father's face was breaking out in sweat the entire day, and every so often he'd come up to me at the reception and say, "Is this *Goodbye, Columbus* or what?" My mother, who's usually the star of the show, seemed awkward and uncomfortable, dancing hand-in-hand with a bunch of fancy New York women wearing sequinned dresses and hats covered with feathers and bows.

My sister's biggest concern was my brother William, who was frequently a source of embarrassment to my family, and who might be expected to tell the Klausners' religious relatives and friends some of his outrageous stories. "There's nothing *really* wrong with Willy," I said to Caroline when she confided to me her concern.

We were getting made up for the wedding—that was another thing. Mrs. Klausner had a professional makeup artist do the wedding party's makeup and hair right there in the hotel bathroom, like we were Broadway actresses getting ready to do *Gypsy*. Forget about the hair-waxing expert she'd sent all the in-town bridesmaids to the week before. Not only that; every bridesmaid except me wore a girdle, and I was probably the only one who needed one.

Mrs. Klausner kept looking at Caroline in her makeup and dress and saying "poo-poo-poo!" Then she'd look at me, Caroline's heathen sister, and explain that it was customary to ward off the evil spirit by saying "poo-poo-poo" after you gave someone a compliment.

"Don't worry," I was saying to Caroline about Willy. "He won't queer this." She gave me a hurt look, and I immediately felt sorry for what I had said, but I was getting tired of Caroline's acting ashamed of our family. After all, she used to think we were perfect, and I still did.

I'd never been to a wedding like this one. When I wasn't busy thinking what a ridiculous sham it was, how there was enough food between the smorgasbord and the dinner to feed five thousand people, I was thinking there was something sort of nice about it. Everybody seemed to be having fun, dancing and singing and entertaining the bride and groom. To my father I said, "Talk about conspicuous consumption," while in my head I thought, So what's wrong with a little indulgence once in a while? Believe it or not, the Hebrew wedding music even stirred up some warm feelings in me. I hate to sound schmaltzy, but I actually had to swallow back tears a few times. You really got the feeling of a community in that room. Still, I couldn't help thinking that if they had really been a *religious* community, they would have tried to make my family and our friends feel more a part of it.

Caroline tried to include us, to make us feel comfortable, but Shira and Mrs. Klausner kept taking her away from us, over to their guests. She'd already become more one of them than one of us, and she did the steps to each of the dances like she'd been doing them all her life. Occasionally, she'd look at me and roll her eyes, as if she thought the whole thing were as stupid as she knew I thought it was, but I knew she didn't really think so. For some reason, this was what she wanted.

Mrs. Klausner kissed and hugged her about a thousand times, and Shira, who was eighteen, like me, kept whispering funny things in her ear, probably in Hebrew or something. My mother and I stood together and watched, feeling awkward and left out, but not bad enough to apologize for not doing what didn't come naturally to us. Grandma and Grandpa didn't even watch; they just sat down at a table and told anyone who'd listen how this wasn't their type of affair, they were simple people with simple tastes.

The wedding had started at five o'clock, and the ceremony itself was a lesson in how far a woman will go to keep her man: Caroline the Independent Feminist Thinker walked around Jonathan seven times, to show how the husband is the center of the wife's world!

People didn't start to leave until one in the morning; dinner wasn't even served until ten-thirty. The waiters and waitresses brought out the food: huge portions of rare roast beef, potato balls, greasy cooked carrots. That's the thing about Orthodox food; there's always a lot of it and it's always lousy. Anyway, it all just sat there getting cold, because the men were out on the dance floor having some kind of orgiastic experience, being carried around in chairs, riding around on each other's shoulders, singing at the top of their lungs about how they loved Jerusalem and Torah. Meanwhile, the women were dancing in their own circle, everyone trying to get next to Caroline, Miss New York Modern Orthodox, and Caroline's mother-in-law, Runner-Up Number One.

They were quite a pair, those two: Caroline in her white Carolina Herrera, Mrs. Klausner in her black Mary McFadden. I knew it was a Mary McFadden and a big deal, because everyone kept going over to her and saying, "Is that a Mary McFadden?" She'd nod shyly, as if she didn't want to brag about it or something, as if bragging about it wasn't precisely the reason she'd bought it in the first place. My question is, who wears black to her son's wedding? I bet even Mary McFadden wouldn't! I mean, black is what you wear to funerals, I don't care how chic you think you look. My poor mother, in her pretty print dress, kept moving off to the side, where all the other Clevelanders were standing around. You'd almost have thought she wasn't the bride's mother or something.

Finally, after Jonathan and Caroline had cut the wedding cake, and everybody'd been to the Viennese tables, and people were winding down from all that dancing, the last of the guests stuck a piece of cake in her purse, grabbed one of the extravagant, overdone centerpieces, and left. God only knows why anyone would have wanted one of those awful tiger lily or birds-of-paradise arrangements anyway. They were so tall I had barely been able to see who was sitting across the table from me—maybe just as well—and they smelled so strong they'd given me a headache.

My father came over then and put his arm around me as we were getting our things together to leave. "I can still count on you to get married behind the hemlock trees in our backyard, can't I?" he said. "I mean, *if* you decide to get married at all, which I'm certainly not advising." You could tell he'd had quite a bit to drink, the way he was leaning on me and slurring his words and getting sentimental.

"Of course I'll get married in our backyard, Dad," I said, and then I walked away because I couldn't stand to think about how sad it all seemed. Jonathan and Caroline's limo was waiting to whisk them off through their snowy wedding night to the Plaza (courtesy of my parents, whom I didn't remember Caroline ever thanking); I couldn't imagine actually marrying Eddie; and Mr. Klausner was going around calling my sister *his* daughter.

The wedding itself was only a small part of an entire weekend in which my family was made to feel like guests at our own party. It had started out on the previous Thursday, when Willy took the train in from Connecticut, and Mom and Dad and I met him at the Waldorf, where we'd just arrived by taxi from La Guardia. Grandma and Grandpa didn't come with us, saying it would be too much for them, they'd just fly in Sunday morning for the wedding. My mom and I had missed the bridal shower the Sunday before, and Willy and my dad had missed the bachelor party, but from what Caroline told me, we were better off that way. She said that knowing me, I would have hated the shower, all those girdle-clad girls sitting around comparing the Evan Picone dress they'd seen at Bloomingdale's for $250 to the one at Loehmann's for only $175. She said the bachelor party was worse, and she was crying when she told me that Jonathan's friends had hired a stripper. It was the only time since she'd decided to marry Jonathan that she sounded doubtful about the whole thing, and from the way she described it—a bunch of yarmulke-wearing boys getting drunk and throwing up while they reached for the tassels hanging from a stripper's nipples—I couldn't say I blamed her.

It's not like my family was made out of money or anything, but whenever we went on vacations, we always stayed in the nicest hotels and ate in the nicest restaurants. Caroline had never complained about this custom when we were growing up, but now that she was almost a Klausner, she thought nice hotels and restaurants were a waste of money. She said things like that were overrated and superficial, and that the Klausners spent money on important things, like giving to charities. As if my family didn't give money to charities because we didn't give only to Jewish things. It's not as if the Klausners didn't take vacations, either, by the way, it's just that they probably stayed in the Hilton or someplace ordinary like that, and packed their food if there weren't any kosher restaurants around. But usually, according to Caroline, they went somewhere that had kosher restaurants, like Miami Beach, if you can believe it.

As soon as we got up to our gorgeous two-room Waldorf suite, we spotted the fruit basket sitting on the dresser. Inside was a card from the Klausners, as if we wouldn't have known it was from them by the big kosher label on the cellophane. "They're nice, aren't they?" my father said, reading the card, and I was a little disappointed in him; after all, he was the one who'd told me never to trust the show of love between two people who kept calling each other sweetheart or honey. How could he not be a little more suspicious of my sister's new family?

"I'd be nice too," I said, "if my new daughter-in-law's parents did everything my way." My father looked at me and I knew I'd crossed that old line.

"Jealousy isn't becoming, Jane," he said, and he had a look on his face that made me choke up.

Later, Caroline called to say that Mr. and Mrs. Klausner had plenty of friends willing to put us up in their apartments, and why should we spend money to stay in one of the most expensive hotels in New York. My parents were out at the time, taking a walk down Fifth Avenue to look at the Christmas windows, so I took it upon myself to decline the offer. Willy was parked in front of the television, watching Janet Jackson feel herself up on MTV.

"What, are you kidding?" I said to Caroline.

"I think it's a very nice offer myself," she said.

"Don't get defensive, Caroline, you know Mom and Dad. Do you honestly think they'd want to stay with your in-laws' friends?"

"It was just a question, Jane. Stop acting like I'm some kind of Judas."

"You don't even know us anymore. In the first place, the only thing nice about this trip for Mom and Dad is that they get to stay at the Waldorf."

She didn't say good-bye, and I can't say I blame her, though I think what made her angry was not so much what I'd said, as that what I'd said was the truth.

That night, the four of us had an amazing dinner at the Oyster Bar in Grand Central Terminal, the only nonkosher dinner we would get away with since Caroline wasn't coming with us—she said she was too nervous to eat. Willy and I each had a shrimp cocktail ($9.25 apiece!) followed by oysters Rockefeller. He barely got on my nerves at all, until he started talking about how he'd made the junior varsity basketball team up at school.

"You did not," I said, and I took a big gulp of water to show just how nonchalant I was about contradicting him. After all, it was hardly the first time Willy had made something up. "You can't even do a lay-up, Willy."

"I can too," he said.

"No you can't. And besides, I never heard of a sixth grader being on a junior varsity team."

"God, Jane," he said. "What's your problem?"

"My problem is that my brother lies. Twelve-year-old boys who can barely dribble a basketball don't make the junior varsity basketball team. Knowing you, there probably *is* no basketball team."

"Hey, hey," my father said. "Willy's not a liar."

"Yeah, Jane," Willy said. "You think you know *every*thing. You think you're a psy*chol*ogist. *You're* the liar!"

"Right, Willy, I'm the liar, I'm the one who said I made the basketball team."

Willy just sighed and rolled his eyes, as if to indicate that fighting with me was beneath him. But then he started to cry, which is what he often did when he was backed into a corner.

My mother gave my father a look, and I've got to back her up on this one: telling Willy he wasn't a liar wasn't too helpful, especially when half the time it was my *father* who was berating Willy for his latest flights of fancy, telling him to get his act together, telling him to get control of himself, as if Willy were capable of doing any such thing. The other half of the time my father was mourning the fact that Willy was so miserable with his real life that he had to invent new ones, and trying to protect his son from the likes of me. I didn't mean to be hard on the kid, but I guess that's the way I compensated for how terrible I felt. I was pretty sure I knew what was at the root of Willy's problems: me.

"Hey," I said, poking him in the side. One thing about Willy, he was incredibly ticklish.

"No," he said, and he pushed my hand away. "It's not that easy to make up with me anymore." We all laughed then, even Willy finally, who was *always* a sucker for a little flattery, and he was flattered when people found him funny. It was too easy to win him back—too easy. Didn't he know you weren't supposed to forgive people right away? Then again, he was probably relieved not to have to embellish any further the lie he'd already gotten caught in.

My father paid the check, while my mother lifted a piece of bread off Willy's plate and bit into it. "Do you think you need that?" my father said, a little sharply, and my mother put the bread back onto the plate and glared at him.

"Go ahead," I said, "have the bread, Mom."

"You stay out of this," my father said to me, and my eyes welled up. No matter how grown-up I liked to think I was, I still practically dissolved every time my father became angry with me. I tried not to let him see the effect he was having, though; I wanted him to think about how stupid it was to tell my mother not to eat a lousy piece of bread. Sure, my mom was a little overweight; sure, she could have stood to lose five or ten pounds. Okay, I'll admit she seemed to be getting heavier all the time. But you didn't need to be a psychiatrist to know you couldn't shove a diet down someone else's throat.

After dinner, my mother and I put on our matching red

wool coats and asked the waiter how to get to Broadway and 82nd Street. That's where the mikvah was, and that's where we were going to meet Caroline, Shira, and Mrs. Klausner. The waiter pointed us in the direction of the Times Square subway shuttle, which would take us on the first part of our journey.

While we waited for the train, my mother said, "How about some dessert?" She'd noticed the vendor selling newspapers and candy bars farther down the platform. "Okay," I said, even though I was so full I'd unbuttoned my skirt. She bought a Snickers bar, and we passed it back and forth between us until it was gone. I noticed that she ate it like someone who'd been fasting for a week, chewing and chewing each bite.

"Want another one?" she said after she threw away the wrapper, and then she laughed, though I'm not sure she was joking. She buttoned my top coat button as the train approached, creating a draft, and said, "Oh, let's not ruin your figure too."

All the years my father had been bugging my mother about what she ate, I'd always thought that what aggravated him was not so much my mother's weight—she wasn't *fat*—as how much she seemed to enjoy food. Nothing seemed to give her as much pleasure, including us. But lately I was beginning to think it wasn't so much the food that she enjoyed, after all. Getting fat, the thing my father most wanted my mother not to do, was what I was beginning to think my mother actually enjoyed doing. What more perfect way for her to show my father who was boss?

The subway was terrifying and fast, and my mother and I laughed in excitement and shouted to each other above the noise. We had gotten on the front car, where there were plenty of seats, but my mother wasn't content to just sit, she didn't want to miss anything, so she stood and looked out the front window at the tracks ahead. I realized how often I wished she *could* be content just to sit: it always seemed as if she was loading the dishwasher or ironing my father's shirts or defrosting the refrigerator at the same time she was supposed to be having a conversation with me. As far back as I could remember, I'd never been able to get her undivided attention unless I was running a fever of 102 or something—unless she could get up and *do* something for me.

But I didn't get on her case now, not when my father was doing that so nicely for me, and not on her big night out. Lately, she was like a different person when my father wasn't around—more relaxed, cheerful, fun. If she'd had long hair, I'd say that what she did was let her hair down; but she had short hair, and it was starting to turn from blond to silvery gray, as a matter of fact. It happened to suit her, and I was glad I didn't have the kind of mother who started to dye her hair the minute it turned gray. I liked her the way she was.

Caroline had told us to be at the mikvah at seven o'clock sharp, so that we wouldn't have to wait in line. At Times Square, my mother and I transferred from the shuttle subway to the uptown 1, looking at our watches and laughing about the mikvah, a bunch of women standing in line wrapped in towels, waiting for their turn to be purified in a ritual bath. But when we got there, we stopped laughing. As was to be the pattern for the rest of the weekend, we were the ones who didn't belong, we were the ones who seemed strange.

We shivered as we said hello to Shira and Mrs. Klausner and Caroline, who were waiting outside for us, and then Mrs. Klausner rang the intercom and screamed into it, "We're here for the mikvah?" and the door buzzed open. Other than the sign inside that referred to this place as the "Upper West Side Women's Club," there was nothing here that resembled any of the clubs *I'd* ever want to belong to.

When the five of us walked in, an old lady with a European

accent, wearing a housecoat and slippers, said, "Hello, hello, Mrs. Klausner. You bring the whole *mishpocheh*." There were no women standing around in towels; only a few women fully dressed were milling around the area, their wallets open. They didn't look anything like the religious women I'd seen walking down Taylor Road in Cleveland, with pasty faces and funny-looking wigs and shirt collars that came up to their eyes. These ladies were wearing plenty of makeup and had very chic hairstyles; they looked about as religious as Tammy Faye Bakker.

"How are you?" Mrs. Klausner said, as she kissed the old woman. "This is my future daughter-in-law, Caroline. Caroline, this is Mrs. Blumberg."

"Good to meet you," Mrs. Blumberg said, smiling warmly, and then she looked at the rest of us.

"Would it be all right, Mrs. Blumberg, if we all came in?"

"If it's okay with the *kallah*," she said. "When is the wedding, *bubeleh*?"

"Sunday," Caroline said, and I didn't recognize her voice. All of a sudden it didn't sound like her voice, it sounded like Shira's spoiled little whiny voice, New York accent and all. In fact, I wouldn't have been surprised if the next thing she'd said was, "Daddy's paying for a sit-down dinner for five hundred and seventeen."

"Carmen!" Mrs. Blumberg called out in a stevedore's voice—what had happened to the sweet old European lady who had been there a second before, the one who'd been falling all over Mrs. Klausner and Caroline with her warm Jewish mother act? All of a sudden, she sounded like some kind of taskmaster or something, like she didn't have to be nice to anyone with the name Carmen, an employee, after all, and a goy. And not even a regular goy at that—a Puerto Rican, for God's sake. "We have a bride here," Mrs. Blumberg said, and a minute later, Carmen, a short, dark-haired woman, appeared, carrying a big stack of white terrycloth towels.

"Bath or shower?" she asked Caroline, looking down at the ground as she spoke. What an awful job, I thought, to have to clean up after women who come to purify themselves; to work for a boss who looks down on you so much she can't even look *at* you.

"I already did the bath part," Caroline said, "so I guess I just need a shower."

"That's right," Mrs. Klausner said, real buddy-buddy with Caroline. "After twenty-seven years of going to the mikvah every month, I should know the rules."

Carmen led the five of us to a little room with a bathtub (no curtain), a sink, and a counter lined with emery boards, Noxzema, nail scissors, a toothbrush, a comb, dental floss. There was a set of instructions hanging on the wall that started with the word *Remember,* and then listed all the things you had to remember to do before you could immerse yourself in the ritual bath. Things like taking out your contact lenses, flossing your teeth, cutting your toenails, even cleaning your navel, for heaven's sake! I mean it!

Carmen turned on the water and left the room, and that was the signal for Caroline to start taking off her clothes.

"Shouldn't we wait outside?" my mother asked, but Mrs. Klausner said, "Caroline doesn't mind," and I could have killed her—for putting Caroline on the spot like that, for implying that she knew Caroline better than we did.

"Well, she *used* to," I said, as usual, stepping right into it. "Anyway, it's too crowded in here for all of us. I'm going to wait outside."

"Oh, don't, Jane," Caroline said. "I want you in here with me."

For a second, Caroline sounded like the Caroline I used to

know, and I was so grateful for that, and so grateful that she'd forgiven me for our earlier fight, that I stayed. I didn't even mind that much, watching her treat her mother-in-law as if she were her mother, handing her clothes to Mrs. Klausner instead of to Mom. She took a shower, while my mother and I sort of looked the other way, and then she got out and wrapped herself in the towel, and said, "Did I get off all the eyeliner?"

"You're fine," Mrs. Klausner said, "just fine," and she rang the buzzer above the sink. A minute later, there was a knock on the door: Mrs. Blumberg. I liked the fact that she knocked; not many people seemed to be extending the courtesy of privacy. And my father sure didn't, either; he always barged into our bedrooms without knocking, and screamed his head off if we locked our doors. And then there was my old pediatrician. One time when I was twelve, the year I developed breasts, I went for my annual checkup. The guy was about a hundred years old even then. The nurse told me to take off all my clothes and wait for the doctor to come in; naturally, he just walked right in, he didn't knock, and when he opened the door, I was standing there, completely naked. "Oh my!" he said, and he rushed over to cover me with one of those paper sheets. As if it had been *my* idea to undress, as if *I* were some kind of sex maniac or something.

Anyway, the six of us squeezed into the little room attached to the one where Caroline'd just showered. Mrs. Blumberg looked at my sister's fingernails, then down at her feet, and then she took off my sister's towel, and brushed off her back. "Okay," she said to Caroline. "You can go in."

Caroline—naked—walked down five steps into a little pool below us, while the rest of us stood with Mrs. Blumberg and watched her.

It was Caroline, all right. She had that telltale birthmark smack in the middle of her left buttock, and I wanted to cry, seeing it there, because it reminded me of how modest she used to be, how I'd never even *seen* the birthmark before, I'd only heard about it. She'd never even change her *shirt* in front of me or my mother, when we went shopping at the May Company, and now here she was, parading around naked in front of strangers.

"Every part of you must be under the water," Mrs. Blumberg said.

"Here I go," Caroline said, and she disappeared for a minute, her legs and arms floating about. You could see the bubbles from her nose rising up through the water, like she was in a regular swimming pool or something. Then she came up, wiped her eyes and nose and said, "Was that okay?"

"Fine," Mrs. Blumberg said. "Fine! Now you cover yourself like this and say the prayer." My mother and I looked at Mrs. Blumberg's demonstration, her arms folded above her breasts, and Caroline did the same, though her breasts didn't form the same kind of shelf Mrs. Blumberg's did. Then Caroline said the prayer, and it sounded a lot like the prayer you say over the bread on the Sabbath, with the last few words changed. I couldn't believe my sister—Ms. Barnard Feminist was making a prayer over herself like she was a piece of challah about to be eaten.

"Now what?" Caroline said. "I've completely blanked out on that marriage class I took."

"Go under two more times," Mrs. Blumberg said, and she held up two fingers.

Caroline dunked twice more, then Mrs. Blumberg said, "One more time; last time, your hair didn't go under."

Caroline dunked again, and Mrs. Blumberg declared, "Kosher."

"What's she become, a piece of meat?" I whispered to

Shira, who just stood there in her little denim jumper with the straps hanging down, her shirt sleeves too long and covering her hands, as if that were the fashion. She smiled politely.

"Mazel tov," Mrs. Klausner said, as Caroline got to the top of the stairs, and she embraced her, dripping wet and naked and all. Then Mrs. Klausner wrapped the white terrycloth towel around her. It seemed sort of incestuous, if you ask me, but maybe that was just my dirty mind, out of control again. "May this be the first of many," Caroline's about-to-be-mother-in-law said.

Caroline smiled at me and my mother and winked, as if she were going to take us aside later and give us the real story, tell us this was all a joke. Then she went back into the room where she'd taken the shower and got dressed, while the rest of us just stood around outside, trying to think of something to say.

"Such a pretty girl, Caroline," Mrs. Klausner said to my mother. "She looks like a real shiksa."

"Maybe she is one," I said, making things up as I went along, reminding myself of Willy. "She was adopted, you know."

"And this one's got such a sense of humor," Mrs. Klausner said, but I noticed she wasn't laughing. I didn't really think she'd be too crazy about jokes that called Caroline's Jewishness into question.

My mother nodded and said, "Yes, Jane's got a sense of humor, all right," and I knew she wasn't angry because she smoothed my hair when she said it.

"Would you like to come back to the house for coffee?" Mrs. Klausner asked. "It's still early."

"Daddy can give you a ride back to the hotel later," Shira offered.

"I think we'll take a rain check," my mother said. "With

all the company you're having this weekend, you hardly need us around tonight, and in fact, why don't we take Caroline back to our hotel."

"Oh, that would be so nice of you," Mrs. Klausner said, as if we were doing a favor for *her* daughter. "I'd offer to have her sleep at our apartment tonight, but Yoni—that's what we call Jonathan in the house—Yoni is there, and the two of them aren't to see each other until the wedding."

I couldn't believe my ears, everybody arguing over who would tuck Caroline in that night. The whole thing was ludicrous, considering Jonathan and Caroline's apartment was perfectly available and practically next door. But no; Mrs. Klausner, and even my own mother, wouldn't let the little princess stay there alone. I mean, my God, she'd been living in a tenement house up near Barnard—by herself—and now all of a sudden she needed a babysitter.

"You know," I said, "we have this relative who just came back from a trip to India. He told us that *yoni* means clitoris in Indian. Isn't that a funny coincidence?" The truth is, it was a friend of my mother's who'd come back from a trip, not a relative, and I don't even know if the trip was to India. Not that those little factual errors mattered to me right then; Mrs. Klausner got the gist of it.

"My, what a sense of humor," she said, and she put her arm around me, even though I knew she couldn't stand the sight of me. That made us even, because I couldn't stand the sight of her either, with her braided waist-long hair, as if she were eighteen, her leather-clad anorexic body, her fur coat. "We'll see you tomorrow," she said and then she reached over to kiss me, then my mother good-bye. She fooled both of us, though, 'cause we actually kissed her on the face the way we always had, while she just kissed the air next to us. That's the kind of suckers we were.

After a little while, Caroline came out of the dressing

room, and she looked great, despite the fur-lined leather coat she was wearing, which must have been a hand-me-down from Shira. She was beaming, though, and I thought, either she's very happy or all that dunking in hot water feels great. We stopped while she paid the fifteen-dollar mikvah fee, but Mrs. Blumberg wouldn't take Caroline's money. "Your future mother-in-law already paid," she said. "She's a wonderful woman, that Mrs. Klausner. You're a lucky girl."

"Oh, I know," Caroline said, and then she handed Mrs. Blumberg two dollars and asked if she would give one of the dollars to Carmen.

Outside, Caroline stepped off the curb to hail a cab, and my mother started to say something, but then she stopped herself. To me, she said, "I suppose we *should* take a taxi at this hour."

While we were waiting, I started thinking what a weird city New York was, with a Jewish ritual bath right across the street from a church parish, and next door to a dry cleaner. I didn't have much time for reflection, however; a yellow cab practically ran the curb as it pulled up in front of us. The three of us sat squooshed together in the back seat, my mother in the middle, while the cab raced down Broadway. The driver was listening to classical music, and my mother said, "Is that Brahms?"

"Yes, it is," he said, in a thick accent. His I.D. tag said his name was Spanakopita or something, so I figured he was Greek.

"I'm crazy about Brahms," my mother said. "I know that's not a popular thing to say, but I am."

"You're a musician?"

"No," she said, "but I love classical music, and I happen to have perfect pitch."

"Perfect pitch," the driver repeated approvingly. "My favorite is Mozart."

"Oh, well, Mozart. Who doesn't love Mozart?"

The driver laughed. "It's a pleasure to talk to someone who loves Mozart."

"Thank you," my mother said, and you could tell his comment was about the nicest comment anyone had made to her that day. "It's also a pleasure to hear something other than Christmas carols at this time of year."

Caroline, noticeably silent, apparently didn't find this conversation amusing.

"What's with you?" I said, none too nicely.

"Mom's the only mother I know who's more interested in a taxi driver she'll never see again than she is in the daughter who's getting married in three days," she said.

"Maybe that's because the taxi driver is more interested in *her* than the daughter who's getting married in three days," I said. "Don't be such a selfish bitch." At which Caroline reached over my mother's lap and punched me hard on the right shoulder. I replied by reaching behind my mother and pulling Caroline's hair. All very grown-up behavior.

"Cut it out, kids," my mother said, and that was the end of any conversation in the taxi. When we got out in front of the Waldorf, the driver said, "Enjoy the Brahms, Missus."

The hotel doorman held the door for us, and we walked through the lobby to the elevators. It was a romantic lobby, with lush maroon carpeting and its smell of perfume, and it made me wish I were going upstairs with Dr. Stevens instead of with my mother and sister. I'd only been in a hotel room once with a man, and that was Eddie, and he wasn't even a man yet. It was last May, the same May Caroline graduated from Barnard, and Eddie and I graduated from Randall High School. He and I decided to go to the Sheraton Hotel, instead of to the senior prom. We took two of Eddie's father's *Playboy* magazines with us, and gave each other three orgasms. Even he was having trouble getting turned on after the second one, no matter what I did, so that's when we resorted to the magazines. He read sexy passages aloud to me, but instead of getting aroused, I just got depressed. He mispronounced words, and it sort of changed the whole tenor of the thing, my having to correct him every other minute. "You don't have to get so annoyed," he said. "Math is what I'm good at, not English."

When Caroline, Mom and I got up to our rooms, my mother gave us the key to ours, which adjoined theirs. "Good night, girls," she said.

"It's early, Mom," I said. "Maybe we can all go get coffee or take a walk."

"Or we could go see the Christmas tree at Rockefeller Center," Caroline said. A flimsy way of apologizing, in my opinion.

"I've seen it," my mother said. "Anyway, we have a big weekend ahead of us."

Willy was lying on a cot in our room, watching *Bachelor Party* on TV. "How long is this on?" I asked, but he shrugged, so I looked at Caroline and said, "Let's go for a walk."

"Okay," she said and then she punched my left arm, the one she hadn't punched before, and said, "Got you last."

"Fine," I said, "you win," and we left. I didn't feel like fighting anymore.

We headed over toward Fifth Avenue. It was a great night for ice-skating, but Caroline said she didn't feel like it, she'd just gone the night before with Shira.

"Shira," I said. "What a stupid name. Mom and Dad would never have given us queer Hebrew names. I like plain, simple, unpretentious names."

"So?"

"So, I don't know. So, nothing." As we walked down 50th Street, we were separated by the masses of people walking the same way, and as we rounded the corner to Fifth Avenue, we came together again. We tried to get a glimpse of the Saks windows, but all we could see were the backs of the people in front of us.

"You ought to move out of Mom and Dad's house," Caroline said, as we continued walking. "What are you already, nineteen?"

"Eighteen," I said. "Nineteen in March."

"Well—"

"What does my age have to do with anything?" I said, suddenly feeling a little choked up. I knew it was time to move out, but I didn't want to. Besides, I didn't know where to go.

"You need to start seeing Mom and Dad for what they are. They're not what we grew up thinking they were."

"What you mean is, they're not Mr. and Mrs. Klausner."

"Listen, Jane," Caroline said, "I know you think I've betrayed our family by marrying Jonathan, but it's not true. I could never love anyone else's family the way I love ours."

"Really?" I said, as people jostled us, and we were swept along by the crowd.

"It's just that Jonathan's parents make me feel . . . different, and special, more special than Mom and Dad make me feel. I meant what I said to Mom before—she's so interested in everybody, you hardly feel you're any different to her, even if you're her own daughter."

"Poor Mom," I said. "We go around giving all our attention to Dad, and then when Mom looks to the outside world to make her feel good, we get on her case for not being interested in us. We both do it."

"Yeah," Caroline said, "but the question is, which came first, did Mom bow out because we were giving all our attention to Dad, or did we give all our attention to Dad because Mom was nowhere to be found?"

We sat down on the steps in front of a church where other

people were also sitting around. Caroline took out a cigarette, and I said, "Well, I'm glad to see you still do that once in a while."

She laughed. "That's not a very nice thing to say to some-one you care about."

"You know what I mean."

She offered me a puff, and I took it. "You know what Mom did when I was thirteen?" she said. "She left a pink pamphlet on my bed called 'Becoming a Woman,' and she never even bothered to find out if I'd read it."

"What's wrong with that?" I said. She'd done the same thing to me, and I thought that was what mothers did, that I'd probably carry on the tradition with my own daughter, if I ever had one.

"What's wrong is that it shows how uncomfortable she is with sex, with feelings, even with her own body. I know you all think the Klausners live in this repressed world where women have to be purified before they can have sex with their husbands, but at least they acknowledge that people *have* sex with their husbands."

"Correct me if I'm wrong," I said, "but it seems to me you never had a problem with sex, or being repressed."

"Exactly," she said. "I was so desperate for intimacy that I slept with anyone who asked." She took a puff of the cigarette and laughed, a kind of unpleasant bark.

"What's so funny?" I asked.

"I was just remembering something," she said. "Do you and Eddie ever fool around in Mom and Dad's house?"

"Of course," I said.

"Which room?"

"The basement. Why?"

"I once did it in the kitchen."

"The kitchen? With whom?" I said.

"Monty Thomas."

"Monty Thomas! He was the best-looking guy you ever went out with," I said. "Where were Mom and Dad?"

"Out of town."

"Where was I?"

"Up in your room, doing your homework," and we both laughed. It seemed like anytime anything exciting had ever happened in my house, I'd missed it because I was up in my room doing my homework. Even when I was only six, and my parents brought Willy home from the hospital, I was up in my room doing my homework.

"Aren't you going to miss your old life?" I said. "Do you ever think about that?"

She didn't answer for a long time, but finally she blew out the last of the cigarette smoke and said, "I try not to." Then she stomped out the cigarette and we stood up and walked down the steps. A black man came up to ask us for money, and Caroline dug around in her pocket for change. You had to be grateful for small things; at least she still had a thing for black men.

When we got back to the hotel, we went to the front desk to see if we had any messages. There were two; one from Jonathan and one from Eddie. Caroline said she'd use a pay-phone in the lobby, since hers was local, and I could use the phone in the room.

"Hi, sexpot," Eddie said when he heard my voice. I hated it when he called me sexpot; he'd called me sexpot so long that it was a habit—he didn't even know he was *calling* me sexpot. I also hated hearing about anything related to sex when I was sitting about five feet from my brother William. I had a hard time juxtaposing the two without a lot of discomfort, since I was afraid sex and I had something to do with the way Willy turned out.

"I miss you," Eddie said. "I miss your naked bod, too."

"I miss you too," I said, "but can't we talk about something else?"

"Sure," he said. "What do you want to talk about?"

"Anything," I said.

"Let's see. I'm watching a great flick on TV."

"Yeah? What?"

"I don't know, I just turned it on. I think it's called *Bachelor Party*."

"Yeah, it is," I said. "Willy's watching it too."

"I'm also looking through my Cleveland State catalogue, trying to find the least painful English class I can take next semester."

Of all the preposterous prospects, I thought; Eddie Fiedler, systems-analyst-in-training, was going to be studying Jane Austen and Emily Brontë while I, recipient of the Randall High School special English department award, was going to be studying WordPerfect, along with all the other computer-illiterate secretaries in my office.

"It's these damned liberal arts schools," Eddie went on. "They won't just leave well enough alone, they want to make you into a real Renaissance man."

"Well," I said, "there's nothing wrong with that."

"I guess not, especially when your girlfriend can type all your papers," Eddie said, and he laughed.

"I don't mind," I said, minding.

"It was just a joke, Jane, I'll type my own papers," Eddie said. "Anyway, the real reason I called was to tell you that I'm thinking about moving. I found a great apartment, and I'll only have to take care of the rent. See, my parents figure if I'd gone to an out-of-state college, I wouldn't have been able to live at home, and they would have had to pay room *and* board. This way, they get off pretty easy."

"You're really thinking of moving away from home?"

"Yeah, really. So I think we ought to talk about our future."

"Okay, but when I get back, okay?"

"I mean it, though," he said. "It's been more than a year now. Why shouldn't we get married?"

"When I get back, Eddie," I said. "We'll talk about it when I get back."

Caroline must have been chatting it up with old Jonathan on the payphone downstairs, and Willy was still glued to the TV, so after Eddie finished telling me what he wanted to do to me when I got home, I went into the bathroom to put on my pajamas: an old Camp Ben-Gurion T-shirt and a pair of shorts. Usually I sleep topless, but not when Willy is sleeping in the next bed, or cot, as the case may be. Not only don't I sleep topless then, I even wear a bra.

"The movie's almost over," Willy said when I started pulling back the bedspread on my bed.

"That's okay," I said, really magnanimous, and I buried my head between two fluffy Waldorf pillows. When I'm depressed, I usually can fall asleep in the middle of a battlefield. Now, I lay there thinking about being Eddie's wife, and it was all I could do not to fling myself out the window. Eddie was nice and everything, so why did I feel like my life would be over if I married him? There was something else I wanted, and I'm not talking about Dr. Stevens, although I certainly wouldn't have thrown *him* out of bed.

Friday morning, my father took Willy over to Madison Square Garden, just for the heck of it, and my mother, Caroline and I went shopping—to Saks and Ann Taylor and Bloomingdale's. In the junior department at Saks, I went into the fitting room and tried on a cashmere sweater, while Caroline and my mother browsed. When I came out to ask them how I looked, Caroline just started to laugh.

"It's a little snug, don't you think?" my mother said.

"Snug?" Caroline said. "She's busting out of it!"

"Very funny," I said, but I wasn't really insulted. At least Caroline was being nice to my mother and we were all having fun together. What did I care if they got a laugh at my expense? It's not like I was twelve anymore; it's not like I was going to run home and cry because somebody'd implied I was deformed or something.

"You're a good sport, Jane," my mother said, "better than I'd be. I'm not even brave enough to try anything on, the way I look."

"Oh, Mom, you look fine," I said, and Caroline chimed in too.

"You girls are just trying to be nice," my mother said, "not that I mind."

Naturally, I didn't buy the sweater or anything else, for that matter. I wasn't a good clothes shopper; the truth was, I didn't know what to do when I went into a clothing store. Clothing stores weren't like bookstores, where the right book just jumped out at you, where you could tell right away you were going to fall in love with a book from the very first page. Clothes didn't do that; you had to try them on and then take them off, and try something else, and the things that looked great on the hangers looked awful on you, and the things that you didn't want even to try on ended up looking fine on you, and on and on. I practically salivated when I went inside a bookstore; clothing stores made me sag with fatigue.

Caroline tried on about a thousand outfits at Ann Taylor, all of which looked great on her, but there was this one thing—a navy-blue cotton jumper with a cream-colored blouse—which definitely looked the best.

"Do you like it?" my mother asked Caroline. "I think it looks terrific on you."

"I love it," Caroline said, and all of a sudden she was Miss Good Mood. "What do you think, Jane?"

"You look great," I said.

"Then, let's take it," Mom said. "I'm buying."

"Mom—" Caroline started, but my mother waved her hand.

"It's the least I can do," she said, and I wondered whether she was responding to Caroline's remark in the taxi the night before. It wasn't the first time she'd made reference to the fact that she knew her mothering skills weren't always up to par.

My mother got out her credit card, and I was glad to see that Caroline at least pretended to put up a fight, even though we all knew in the end she would let Mom pay. At least she hadn't been *totally* ruined by her new family yet.

It was just like the old days for a while there, the three of us laughing and joking and swatting each other, until we stepped into Bloomingdale's and started getting sprayed with perfumes and colognes.

"This place has always made me feel crazy," my mother said. "I get a headache as soon as I walk inside. It's so confusing!"

"Once you get past the first floor, it's fine," Caroline said and she pushed forward, my mother and I reluctantly tagging along behind.

As soon as we got off the escalator on the second floor, my mother said, "You know, I really do think I've had enough; maybe we ought to just go get some lunch and go back to the hotel for a while."

"Good idea," I said.

"Okay," Caroline said, and I could tell Miss Bad Mood was taking over.

"What's wrong?" I said. "What are you mad about?"

"The two of you are such sticks in the mud sometimes," Caroline said.

"Compared to who?" I said.

"Compared to nobody," she said.

"We didn't used to be," I said. "We used to be just fine."

"Girls, girls, come on," my mother said. "Stop acting like children."

We walked along in silence then, as Caroline led us back down the escalator and through the perfume sprayers in the lobby. "What about lunch?" I called after her, although she was really beginning to get on my nerves, the way she was walking so fast and acting as if she was embarrassed to be with us, the way she was getting so far ahead.

"I'm not hungry," she said, and without turning back, she stepped into the revolving door.

When we got outside to Lexington Avenue, she said, "I think I'm going to go back to the hotel. Shabbos starts early in the winter, around four-thirty today."

So my mother and I went alone into a Greek coffee shop around the corner on 60th Street and had cheeseburgers and fries. I tried to get my mother to say something bad about Caroline, but all she would say was, "It's just prewedding jitters," as she stuck a handful of fries into her mouth. Why was I the only one who would admit what was happening?

At four-fifteen, my family headed over to the Klausners' apartment for their typical Friday night Sabbath dinner. Before we left, you should have seen the frenzy in our hotel room, starting at about three o'clock. Caroline was running around like a maniac, looking for black pantyhose, running in and out of the shower because she'd left her razor and her conditioner in her overnight bag, blow-drying her hair while she tried to put on lipstick at the same time. Lipstick! The old Caroline wouldn't have even known what to *do* with lipstick.

Willy and I just sat in those comfortable Waldorf armchairs, switching television stations. We were already dressed in our fancy clothes, and we did a little speculating on what would happen if we got to the Klausners' *after* the sun went down. "Think we'd get hit by lightning?" I suggested. "Maybe thunder," Willy said, his sense of humor always off by just enough to make me cringe.

The Klausners lived up near the mikvah, so my mother wanted to take the subway again. "You always pick the wrong things to save money on," my father said.

"Don't yell at her, Dad," Caroline said, but she didn't object to my father's offer of a taxi. In the end, it would have been more comfortable for the five of us to sit on a subway seat than in a cab. Poor Willy, all dressed up in a blue suit, was practically sitting on the driver's lap.

We were running a little late, but Caroline was almost hyperventilating as we drove up West End Avenue and men wearing yarmulkes were hurrying toward the synagogue. "You'll have to get back to Broadway," Caroline said to the cabbie, as if it had been *his* idea to go over to West End, as if Caroline hadn't been the one insisting she knew the fastest way. Finally, we made a jerky right turn onto 86th Street and pulled up in front of one of those modern luxury apartment buildings at the corner of Broadway. It just figured: of all the gorgeous, charming brownstones and prewar buildings in New York City, my sister's in-laws had to live in a glitzy-looking prefab, probably even with a health club inside.

My father hadn't even paid the driver yet when my sister was hopping out of the cab. "The doorman won't be able to call up to their apartment if it's Shabbos already," she called back to us by way of explanation, as if the doorman wouldn't have let us up, as if we looked like a bunch of criminals, just because we weren't Orthodox.

No such luck. When we got up to the apartment, Mrs. Klausner grabbed Caroline and said, "Come on, let's *bentsh licht.* Yoni's in his room, and I told him to stay there until somebody comes to get him. I figured you could eat with us in the dining room, and he can eat in the kitchen."

"Clever," I said under my breath. What was the big deal if they saw each other, a peek or two, before the wedding? All evening long, the two of them would be *hearing* each other's voices, but running the other way if one of them started to approach.

"This is just a little something for all your hospitality," my mother was saying to Mrs. Klausner. Mrs. Klausner thanked her too effusively and opened the little gift-wrapped box.

"Oh, it's just perfect!" she said. "I was saying to Shira only a minute ago how I had run out of my monogrammed stationery." Right, I thought, as if she will ever deign to use stationery from Cleveland. She kissed my mother and then my father, and then she ushered Caroline off to light the Sabbath candles. She didn't even ask my mother if she wanted to come too, or me. You'd have thought we were Roman Catholics.

I looked at my father to see his reaction to Mrs. Klausner's kiss: he hated being kissed by people he didn't love. He looked a little awkward, but I noticed he wasn't sneering all night the way he might have. And I realized that, like Caroline, he was sort of in awe of these people, even though, at home, he made fun of the ritualistic, superstitious life-style that Caroline had started to lead. He even asked Mr. Klausner for a yarmulke before we sat down, and when I told him later he was compromising what he believed in, he said, "You have to respect people in their own homes." Every time Dad was with the Klausners, he talked about his father, "of blessed memory," and how he used to go to shul every Saturday morning. *Shul,* for God's sake. He actually used that word, as if to impress them with how religious he was. But it was only in *this* setting that he bragged about his Jewish roots; everywhere else he pretended he didn't have any.

Willy sat slumped over on the couch, his hands in his pants pockets, his head resting on my mother's shoulder. I'm sure Caroline was praying he just wouldn't talk all night.

"Sweetheart," Mrs. Klausner said to her husband, in the thickest New York accent I'd ever heard—sweetheart sounded like sweethort. "How about 'Shalom Aleichem'?" Mr. Klausner started singing "Shalom Aleichem," and Caroline went into the kitchen so that Jonathan could come out into the living room with the rest of us. Mr. and Mrs. Klausner held hands, and Shira had both arms around her mother's stomach, like they were lovers or something. My parents weren't even sitting near each other.

"When can I come out?" Caroline called from the kitchen after Mr. Klausner stopped singing. My father had joined in the singing, at first, but he didn't know the second song—a song, Mr. Klausner explained to us, that proclaimed that a wife was a woman of valor because of the way she took care of the home-making and the child-raising. Like those things were unique! Like it took all of a woman's brains to make a good chicken or change a dirty diaper.

"You go into our bedroom," Mrs. Klausner said to Caroline, "while we get Jonathan into the kitchen. Then we'll get you and take you into the dining room." There was a lot of laughing and gaiety surrounding all these logistics and maneuvers, particularly on Shira's part. She kept saying, "This is so exciting! I can't wait till it's me!" Frankly, I didn't see what was so exciting, the whole thing seemed to me like a farce. I just sat there sucking on a piece of kosher licorice and comparing their living room with ours.

In fact, there was practically no comparison, since theirs looked as if they'd walked into a department store and bought a whole nouveau-riche floor-model living room—black and red chrome and leather, like a goddam checkerboard—while ours was the product of years of Sunday afternoons spent in antique galleries searching for the perfect thing to go here and the perfect thing to go there, or the closest thing to perfect that we could afford. Clearly, I thought we had much more interesting and original taste.

"How's school, Willy?" Mrs. Klausner asked, as she and Shira stood up, their arms around each other. I was getting pretty tired of their lovey-dovey act; I mean, no mother and daughter were that attached to each other, were they?

"School? What school?" Willy joked.

"It's that bad, is it?"

Willy laughed and nodded. "Worse," he said. "The food there is like from a concentration camp." Oh, God, there he went again, trying to be funny and clever, and ending up being embarrassing; between Mr. and Mrs. Klausner, Caroline once told us, they'd lost four uncles and five aunts to the Holocaust. Why couldn't Willy have been like every other unimaginative twelve-year-old and compared his school's food to a jail's? No, he had to go and dig up the most offensive metaphor around, the whole time probably congratulating himself for thinking up something so Jewish. Poor Willy, he wanted so desperately to fit in, but every time he opened his mouth, he alienated himself even further.

As soon as Mrs. Klausner recovered from Willy's faux pas, she directed everyone to the table and then gave us seat assignments, as if this were some kind of fancy dinner party. Mr.

Klausner sat at the head of the table, and it was strange to see another man at the head of a table around which my family was sitting. How was it that my father, who always seemed so important in our house, seemed so diminished here? At our family get-togethers, it was always my father who was the center of attention, my father whose profession stimulated the topics of discussion. But it didn't take a rocket scientist to see that, in the Klausners' opinion, being president of Cleveland General Hospital was not particularly impressive; not as impressive, for instance, as if my father had been a rabbi from some poor section of Brooklyn.

Mr. Klausner said the blessing over the wine, then passed around little cups for us to sip. Then he said we could wash. Willy and I looked at each other and laughed, I guess we were thinking the same thing: wash? But Caroline must have seen our faces, and religious expert that she now was, she led us over to the kitchen sink, where everybody moved their lips and then poured water from a cup over their hands. I moved my lips too, just like when I was in the seventh grade and had to sing "O, Come All Ye Faithful" at the Christmas concert. Back then, I thought Jews got punished even for saying the name "Jesus," so I just mouthed it. Funny, I thought, how I had to do the same thing to fit in with Orthodox Jews that I'd had to do with Christians.

After Caroline cleared out of the area and went back into the dining room, Jonathan came and splashed water over his hands, and then we sat down for dinner.

"Does anybody feel like joining me in here?" Jonathan called from the kitchen, after his father had said the blessing over the bread, and everybody except me laughed about how the groom was sitting there all by himself in the kitchen. I didn't feel like laughing at anything.

"I'll go," Willy said, and I caught the look of panic on Caroline's face.

"Great," Mrs. Klausner said. "Willy's the best company in the house, Jonathan's got the best date of all." Willy smiled; he was so insecure and hungry for compliments he'd take them from anyone, but I gave a long disbelieving sigh. I knew as soon as we left tonight she'd have some choice words to say about him. I could just hear her discussing with Shira the way Willy was hanging all over my mother or the way he said such inappropriate things or the way he just sat around looking distracted.

The challah was soft and chewy, and I couldn't help filling up on it while we were waiting for Shira and Mrs. Klausner to bring out the rest of the food. I mean, what was it, a biological imperative that women had to be the ones who served the food? The most depressing part was that Shira and Mrs. Klausner didn't even seem to notice, let alone mind.

"And what do you do, Jane?" Mr. Klausner asked.

This might sound paranoid, but I knew that what he was really asking me was, why wasn't I going to college like every other eighteen-year-old he knew?

"I'm a secretary. For a psychiatrist."

"I can't stand psychiatrists," Mrs. Klausner said as she reached over my shoulder with a bowl of mushroom barley soup. "I think psychiatrists are nuts. That Freud was the biggest nut of all."

"Some people think *The Pleasure Principle* has more wisdom in it than the Talmud," Caroline said, and I had to stop myself from crawling under the table and kissing her feet. At least part of Caroline's brain was still functioning!

"But the Talmud is *based* on something," Mrs. Klausner said. "It's a way of *life!* It's *God-given!*"

"How do you know?" I said, but then my father jumped

in, saying, "You'll have to forgive Jane, she's a real believer, and I don't mean in God."

"I believe in God," I said, giving my a father a really dirty look. There he went again, my very own dad, pretending he was Joe Jew. *He* was the one who used to go around quoting Freud.

Dinner, I'll admit, was delicious, but not nearly as superior to my mother's cooking as Caroline always managed to make it out to be—mushroom barley soup, chicken with peppers and onions, kasha and bow ties, cucumber salad, and some kind of rich chocolate cake for dessert.

Before we could dig into the cake, though, Mr. Klausner made an announcement. "My beautiful daughter Shira has asked to give a *d'var Torah* on this wonderful occasion, the forthcoming marriage of our little Yoni and my new daughter Caroline." I looked at Caroline, who was looking at my father, as if to say: This is why I'm marrying Jonathan, because I'll finally have a father who introduces his daughter in public as beautiful. Didn't she know that no matter what Mr. Klausner said, nobody would ever love her as much as my father? Didn't she know talk was cheap?

Shira, wearing a dress whose shoulder pads practically reached her ears, stood up and started talking about the *chassen* and the *kallah,* about the *parshas hashavuah,* about the *sheva brachos* and the *chuppah* and the *mishkon,* until I finally just tuned out and started thinking about the way Dr. Stevens's beard would feel against my chest. Between the overheated apartment (*our* house was always kept slightly on the cool side) and the heat my fantasy was producing, I was sweating when at last my fantasy was interrupted by the sound of Shira's singsong voice being replaced by Mr. Klausner's jubilant one.

"Yasher koach," he was saying.

"Yasher koach," my father joined in, clapping his hands for extra effect. "Where'd you learn all that?"

"At Stern College for Women. You know, Yeshiva University," Shira said proudly. Clearly, she'd fallen for my dad's admiring act. Of course, you couldn't expect Shira to know what I knew, which was that my father didn't like people, particularly women, who held illusions about themselves. I mean, several times he'd practically come right out and said to me that unless a woman was as attractive or intelligent as, say, Diane Sawyer, she shouldn't draw attention to herself. That's why my father liked me so much. I didn't have Diane Sawyer's looks and I didn't have Diane Sawyer's smarts and I knew it.

After the cake, we sang the grace after meals, and then everybody raved for five minutes about how delicious everything was, and we left.

"That dessert was inedible," my father said in the cab, and when we got back to the hotel, he asked if any of us wanted to go with him to Oscar's, the Waldorf coffee shop, for an ice cream sundae. We'd left Caroline at the Klausners' neighbors', since she wouldn't travel on the Sabbath, and Willy said he wanted to go back to the room and watch a movie. You couldn't blame him, I guess; he probably didn't get HBO or Cinemax up at that loony bin in Connecticut.

My mother, in what was becoming a pattern, said she was tired and wanted to go to bed. That left me, and even though I thought Mrs. Klausner's chocolate cake was all right, I would have eaten twelve sundaes in order to keep my father company. As we walked through the lobby, he wrapped his arm around my neck the way he always did before he was about to say something nice, and he said to me, "You're the best." I didn't care what Caroline said; that beat a public announcement any day.

"Thanks, Dad."

"No, really," he said. "You're an independent thinker. How'd you get to be so smart?"

"From you," I said.

"No," he said. "From Mom."

Why did he always say such nice things about my mother behind her back, but never to her face, I thought. I didn't say that, though, for fear he'd tell me to mind my own business. Instead I said, "Mom's an independent thinker?"

"Just don't be stupid and throw it all in the toilet," he said, ignoring my question. "Don't go marry some idiot who'll tell you how to think or make you have babies so you're too tired to."

"You mean, like Mom did?" I said.

My father laughed and squeezed my neck—he loved it when I insulted him. He liked to think I was tough, different from other girls, not soft and stupid. We both ordered sundaes, and he didn't even tell me I should be watching my calories, that's how nice he was being.

Saturday morning, after a great Oscar's breakfast of eggs and sausage, my father suggested we take the subway up to the synagogue where Jonathan was having his *aufruf,* the prewedding ceremony where he'd be called up to the Torah and then pelted with candy, courtesy of the congregation. "Oh, now you don't mind taking the subway?" my mother said, mimicking his tone of voice from the day before. "You always save money on the wrong things."

"It makes sense to take the subway now," he said, enunciating every word, like my mother was either a moron or hearing-impaired. "It's broad daylight. It's safe."

"It would have been perfectly safe last night too," my mother said. "Jane and I took it the other night, if you'll recall." Sometimes I wished she would just give in, even when he was wrong; I couldn't stand it when they argued. Neither could Willy, who always just stood apart and looked at the ground.

"Fine," my father said. "You want to take a taxi? We'll

take a taxi," and he left us standing there in the lobby and walked over in a huff to the Waldorf doorman. I looked at my mother, expecting her to laugh and say in her cheery voice what a lunatic he was, but she didn't. She didn't say anything.

So, once again we were heading back to the Upper West Side. It was beginning to feel like home already. Of course, the one thing that none of us had thought of was how it was going to *look* for Caroline's family to drive up to the Klausners' synagogue on a Sabbath morning. There were about twelve thousand people standing around in front, women in hats and fur coats rocking their baby carriages, little girls and boys in their good clothes running around, and it seemed like they all stopped moving when our taxi pulled up. Maybe I'm paranoid, but I could have sworn I heard them whispering as we walked up to the synagogue door, "That's not Jonathan Klausner's . . . ?"

Mrs. Klausner saw us walking in, and she stepped out of the women's section to come over to us. The women's section! She was wearing a big black hat, and she pointed my mother in the direction of the little white doilies they provided for married women who came to the synagogue without knowing enough to cover their heads. My mother plopped the doily on her head, stuck two bobby pins through it, and started chatting it up with old Mrs. Klausner. Shira came rushing out then and embraced us. "Hi!" she said. "Isn't this exciting?" Even though she and I were exactly the same age, something about her made me feel old and jaded. I wished that I could have felt excitement, but all I felt was dread.

I was clearly not dressed correctly, but instead of getting depressed about it, I decided to feel superior, as if I were the only really religious one, the one who didn't care about the material world. I was wearing a wraparound cotton skirt with a big cableknit cotton sweater, and a pair of short leather boots. Shira was wearing a black silk dress with gold buttons down the front, gold hoop earrings and a gold bracelet, and black suede heels. I don't care about the way I look in clothes, I thought, I have Eddie at home waiting to see me naked. Shira probably hasn't been seen naked since the day she was born.

My mother and I sat down in the row next to Shira and her mother, and we opened our prayer books. Considering we were in an Orthodox synagogue, I wasn't exactly being over-whelmed by spirituality over there in the women's section; most of the time, the women were talking to each other as if they were in a restaurant or store or something, they certainly weren't praying. And when they did pray, it was like some kind of ritual dance, the way they stood up and bowed and bent over and stepped forward and back and to the side. I thought of my temple at home, how quiet it was, how people never talked above a whisper during the service, and how we were only Reform Jews, we weren't even supposed to be the religious ones. Mrs. Klausner introduced my mother and me to her friends, and my mother acted like her usual friendly, charming self, asking them to repeat their names, she wasn't quite sure she'd heard right. They answered, but you could tell they were more interested in the way we looked than in my mother's charming and friendly personality, and suddenly I wanted to protect her from them.

"Don't be so friendly," I hissed. "They're not interested in us."

"What do I care?" my mother said, and I realized she was right. Why should she stop being herself, just because this partic-ular audience didn't appreciate her? Everybody was saying mazel tov to each other, even Mrs. Klausner and Shira were saying it, as if this were everybody's celebration, not just theirs. My mother, though, said congratulations, not mazel tov, and you could tell she didn't care whether they thought she was a genu-ine Jew or not.

Willy opened the ark, and my father was called up to say a blessing over the Torah. Mrs. Klausner pointed out my father and brother to all her friends.

"Could you die from the little one's hair?" she said about Willy. Like Caroline, Willy had blond hair, but his was even more blond, practically white, and silky-looking; his hair was one of his best assets. All the women chimed in, agreeing that William had beautiful hair, and that my father had a beautiful voice. But I'm sure all they actually noticed was that the men in our family wore black silk yarmulkes, the telltale sign of men who only wore them in the synagogue. Jonathan and his father wore knit yarmulkes, handmade by Shira; they probably even wore theirs to bed.

A little girl in a red velvet dress came around handing out plastic Baggies full of candy, and with much rigmarole, everyone threw the candies at Jonathan after he'd completed reciting the final and most important Torah blessing. I noticed later that I was still holding on to my Baggie, so mesmerized was I by the way Jonathan then went on to chant the Haftarah, as if he'd been chanting biblical Hebrew all his life, which I realized he had. He didn't articulate the words, and his voice was not nearly as sonorous as my father's, but you got the feeling he knew what it was all about, so he didn't have to worry about the way he sounded. Come to think of it, saying that my father had a good voice was probably a put-down, in Mrs. Klausner's opinion, since you only complimented superficial things like voices when there was nothing more substantial to point to.

My father patted Jonathan on the back and shook his hand, and I could see he really approved of him. All my father ever said to Eddie was, "How's your computer?" It wasn't fair, I thought, none of this was fair! What was the point of being loyal to your father if he still preferred your sister despite her defection?

Caroline, meanwhile, wasn't even there. She was sleeping

late at the Klausners' neighbors' apartment since she couldn't see Jonathan until the wedding the next day. Some religious observance, I thought, sleeping instead of praying.

After they'd sung the closing hymn "Adon Olam," which I knew and sang loudly in order to prove that even Reform Jews know something, we followed Mrs. Klausner and Shira into the party room, where there was a luncheon for the out-of-town guests and relatives.

"Wait till Dad sees what they're serving for lunch," Caroline had said, and she was right. After the blessings over the wine and the bread, and after another three-ring circus of ritual hand-washing, we got into line for the buffet-style lunch, the main dish of which was a vat of mushed-up meat, potatoes and beans. "Cholent," Mrs. Klausner said as she put some on my dish, and my father practically turned green.

"I think I'll just take some salad," he said.

"A little too ethnic for you, Alex, huh?" she said, as if she shared his feeling, which she clearly didn't. I swear, we must have seemed as strange to her as if we'd been, heaven forbid, non-Jews. I could only imagine what she would have thought of my mother's second cousin Thomas, who married a Catholic woman and then left her for a Protestant man.

The four of us sat at a little table by ourselves, away from the other, religious relatives. Jonathan's aunts and uncles from Queens and his grandparents from Israel were also at the luncheon, and my mother suggested to my father that perhaps we ought to spread ourselves out instead of sticking so close together. "I'd like to get to know some of Jonathan's family," she said. My mother was always very interested in people, especially if they were somehow exotic or different from her, the same way she was interested in those long, abstruse articles in *The New Yorker*. Ordinarily, I admired my mother's curious nature, but not when so much was at stake. Didn't she understand, these people were our competition now, they weren't just some strange tribe or endangered species she could study from afar, they were the ones trying to take Caroline away from us.

"You should feel free to do whatever you want," my father said. "I'm not moving."

My mother hesitated a moment, sitting there in her chair, but then she finally started eating, in a defeated, purse-lipped way, and though everyone else in the room may have felt the atmosphere was festive, we didn't. Soon Willy was picking the beans out of the cholent and pulling on my mother's sleeve, saying, "When can we leave?"

As the meal was drawing to a close, Mr. Klausner stood up. "I want to make a toast to our new *machetunim*, who've graciously given us their lovely daughter Caroline—"

"She's all yours," my father interrupted, and everybody laughed.

"Who is all ours," Mr. Klausner confirmed, chuckling amiably, "and who has made our Jonathan happier than we could ever make him ourselves."

Everybody shouted "l'chaim" and then someone started singing Hebrew songs, and a few people started dancing. Soon, everyone was dancing except Willy and my parents and me. Then Shira came and grabbed my mother and me for the women's circle, and Mr. Klausner grabbed my father and Willy. I smiled as I stumbled over my feet, trying to do Israeli dances I'd never learned at Camp Ben-Gurion, but I felt like a fraud. Occasionally, I'd glance over at my father and make eye contact with him, and he'd give me a smile which meant, what are we doing here anyway? Then I felt better, because I knew I wasn't the only one who felt like a fraud. Willy was holding my father's hand and clumsily following along as best he could; my mother was holding my hand and bumping into me, which got us both laughing hard enough to let us forget about our awkwardness for a second.

People danced and sang until about three o'clock in the afternoon, and then, as it started to get dark outside, everyone sort of pulled their chairs into a circle and collapsed, singing more Hebrew songs, but ones with a sad sound to them. My mother whispered to me that the reason they sounded sad was that the melodies were in minor keys; such was the kind of maddening trivia you could always depend on my mother to supply, particularly at the times when all you wanted was for her to put her arm around you and tell you that everything was going to be okay.

I wondered whether Caroline wasn't feeling lonely by then, being without us all day in a stranger's apartment, even though she'd often told me how much she liked the Klausners' neighbors and friends, how they felt like "family" to her. I imagined her sitting in their living room, reading *People,* feeling more at home with them than she did now with her real family. Her real family, who sat in a party room feeling silly and out of place.

Saturday night, after the sun had been down for several hours, Caroline came back to the Waldorf. My parents had taken Willy to see *Cats,* and I was in bed reading *The Catcher in the Rye* for about the eightieth time.

"You're reading that again?" she said, by way of openers.

"It makes me feel like I'm not so alone in the world," I said, hoping she might ask me what I meant, but she didn't.

"Did you have a nice time today?" she asked.

"Yeah, I guess."

"Did Mom and Dad get along?"

"I suppose so. Why?"

"They just seem to be fighting a lot lately."

"They've always fought a lot," I said. "You've just been away for so long, you don't remember. I don't even notice it anymore."

"You would if you spent time with other married people."

"Like your perfect in-laws, I suppose."

"Right," she said, rolling her eyes, as if I cared that she thought I was acting paranoid. "I'm taking a shower."

"What'd you do all day?" I called after her.

"Read," she called back, and I couldn't help noticing the way she flung her shoes off and buried her toes in the soft carpeting, as if she didn't mind being in the Waldorf-Astoria even though she had objected to this display of my family's superficiality and materialism. When she was done with her shower, she came out with one fluffy towel around her body and one around her head, leaving either Willy or me with a hand towel.

She sat down on the edge of the bed and combed out her hair. It was beautiful hair. "Are you ever going to go to college, Jane?" she said.

"Why?" I asked, suspicious. "You know, you've really become a snob, Caroline. Who says every Jewish girl in America has to go to college? I should go to college so you're not embarrassed in front of your new family?"

"Jesus Christ," she said. "I just think you're probably the first valedictorian in the history of Randall High School to graduate and become a secretary."

"Mom and Dad don't have the money for college."

"What?" she said, incredulous. "They stay in the most expensive hotel in the country and they don't have the money to send you to college?"

The reason they didn't have the money was because they

had sent *her* to the most expensive *college* in the country! I didn't say that to Caroline, though. Instead I said, "What's happened to you anyway? You used to be so unspoiled."

"I'm not spoiled," she said. "I just don't see what's wrong with giving your children a lot, if you have a lot to give. Mom and Dad always had this 'suffering is good for you' theory. Jonathan's parents didn't, and he's not spoiled."

"Yes he is," I said. "I like the way Mom and Dad raised us."

"I'm *not spoiled*," Caroline said again, only this time she really seemed to want me to believe her. She went into the bathroom and when she came out, she was wearing pajamas. I was glad she didn't get undressed in front of me; maybe she was back to being herself again.

"Tell me about your job," she said.

"It's a mindless typing job," I said. "There's nothing to say about it."

"Tell me about Eddie, then."

"Well, let's see. How can I describe him? I guess it would be safe to say he's no Holden Caulfield." I pointed to the book.

"What?"

"Forget it."

Caroline looked at me and laughed. "You'll meet your Holden Caulfield someday."

"What if I don't?"

"You will," she said. "Look at Jonathan. Who would ever have thought it? After all those losers."

As if Jonathan were Holden Caulfield.

"So what you're telling me is, if you're totally willing to compromise what you believe in, if you're totally willing to observe rituals that make you feel silly, then you can find somebody like Jonathan to marry you."

"I haven't compromised what I believe in," she said. "I'm just a good actress. And I worry, sometimes . . ."

"About what?"

"About . . . whether Jonathan's the right person. About whether I can really fit into his world. About what I'll do if I've made the wrong decision."

"Don't worry," I said. "You and Jonathan love each other; that's all that matters."

Frankly, I thought I was being pretty mature and selfless, considering how much I didn't want her to go through with this whole wedding in the first place. We both lay down on our beds and stared up at the ceiling. Then I closed my eyes and thought about Willy, sitting at a Broadway play, his mind on God-only-knew-what.

What *did* Willy think about anyway? Was he always busy concocting stories, like the one about how he was once on *Good Morning America* as a spelling-bee finalist, or was he beginning to see that no one ever believed him? Maybe he even had some friends up there in Connecticut he didn't *need* to impress, kids who, like him, were intelligent enough but for some reason could barely make passing grades.

Willy hadn't had many friends in Cleveland; once they'd caught him in a few lies, they'd pretty much disappeared. He'd had one good friend, though, Paul Caplan, who stuck around longer than the others. I think they may still keep in touch, though you never know what you can believe from Willy. Paul lived up the street from us, and he and Willy had played together every day from the time they were about six until they were about nine, when Willy went off to the Winthrop School. Paul never seemed to mind Willy's empty promises, promises of free Cavaliers tickets, or free T-shirts from the Coventry clothing store where Caroline was working part-time during high school. It was as if, even at such a young age, Paul knew that Willy didn't mean any harm, that his only goal was to get people to admire him, and so he didn't mind humoring him.

"I hope Mom and Dad will feel comfortable enough tomorrow," Caroline said all of a sudden. "After all, it *is* their daughter's wedding. They *are* paying for it."

I was so glad to hear her finally say something that showed she knew the Klausners weren't her natural parents, that I got up and hugged her. She sort of hugged me back, but then she pulled away. "Since when does anyone in our family hug anyone else?" she said. "Let's save our hugging for the Klausners."

We both laughed, and I felt better than I had for a while. At least Caroline hadn't totally rejected us, at least she recognized that our family had its own set of rituals which, in my opinion, were far more original than those of the Klausners.

2

Believe it or not, my family survived the wedding—the bridesmaids, the band, even the video camera lights—and soon enough my parents and I were back in Cleveland, Willy was back in Connecticut, and Caroline was settling into her role as Mrs. Klausner the Second of New York City's West 82nd Street. I trudged along through the coldest Cleveland months, much as I had every January and February before—shoveling the driveway, bringing in the logs from the garage for our wood-burning fireplace, going sledding on Saturday afternoons. My father dropped me off at work every weekday morning on his way to the hospital, and some mornings the roads out near our house were so treacherous we'd have to leave at seven so my father could get downtown by eight. When spring finally arrived, I was more than ready to trade in my down vest for a cotton sweater, and Eddie liked spring too, for that was when my father had all his out-of-town conferences, and when my parents were away, I always slept over at Eddie's.

One Monday morning in mid-April, I woke up to the feel of Eddie's fingers lazily tracing the circumferences of my breasts. "Harder," I said finally, hoping that if he hurt me a little, maybe I'd feel *something*.

Afterward, when I looked in his bathroom mirror as I was getting dressed for work, I imagined that my breasts were turning black and blue, and I thought, a little bruising seems a small price to pay for feeling.

Eddie was sitting at his new butcher-block breakfast table when I came out of the bathroom, drinking a glass of orange juice while he read the front page of the *Plain Dealer*. That was the thing about Eddie; he drank orange juice because that's what you're supposed to drink at breakfast.

After I had come back from the December wedding weekend, I had started noticing such things, and I didn't seem to have an answer to his questions about our future. He'd decided to move into his own apartment anyway. Perhaps something had told him he'd be living with his parents forever if he waited for me. His apartment was in the same complex of buildings in which my grandparents lived, right across the street from Beachwood Place, one of Cleveland's more genteel shopping malls, but unlike the halls on my grandparents' floor, the halls on Eddie's floor didn't smell like mothballs and chicken soup. As a resident, he was entitled to free use of the pool all summer long and his rent was only six hundred dollars a month ("Six hundred dollars a month?" Caroline had whined when I told her. "In New York that wouldn't buy you a closet," as if she'd even consider leaving New York to come back to little old Cleveland). There were always plenty of parking spaces around, and now that the evenings were warm, we often sat on his terrace, which overlooked the half-empty parking lot and the swimming pool.

"I'm going to miss you tonight," I said to Eddie, as he finished his juice. I was standing behind his chair, rubbing his shoulders. "I get spoiled when my parents are away."

"They're coming back today?"

"Tonight. Caroline says it wasn't a good time for a visit because her mother-in-law was cleaning house for Passover. Like the main reason my parents went to New York was to see the holier-than-thou Klausners. Like my father didn't have a ton of business meetings there anyway."

"So you're not sleeping over tonight."

"Of course not," I said.

"I don't get it."

"You know I can't be out overnight. What would I tell my parents?"

"If we were married, they'd probably understand. This apartment was supposed to be ours, not just mine."

"I'm going to be late for work," I said, taking my windbreaker from the back of the other butcher-block chair.

"My mother invited you to come to our seder this year," he said. "You could come if you wanted to."

"No I couldn't. My parents would be really hurt if I weren't at home for ours. Caroline won't be there this year, as you know."

"It's always about Caroline, isn't it," he said.

I loved the drive to my office, as far as I was concerned it wasn't long enough. I played the radio real loud and opened my window all the way. A great R.E.M. song came on, and I sang along with it, enjoying the way I sounded. I thought I looked pretty cool in my new car, a used Oldsmobile my parents had bought me in March, on the occasion of my nineteenth birthday. A used Olds may not be everybody's idea of cool, but at least I didn't have to get up at the crack of dawn so that my father could drop me off at my office and still have time to get to his by eight. Nobody, not even Rena the Omnipresent Receptionist, was in my office before eight.

The whole commute, from Eddie's apartment in Beachwood to the Family Institute in Shaker Heights, took no more than thirteen minutes. I pulled into my usual spot in the parking lot, but I didn't get out of the car until the radio d.j. announced the next song. It turned out to be something by Foreigner or some other equally insipid group that depressed me, because it reminded me of my high school. I turned off the engine and looked at my hair in the rearview mirror, before I went inside.

I went to my boss's office, the way I did every Monday morning, to water his plants and get the tape out of his dictating machine. There was a pink message slip on top of my typewriter saying that my father had called but would call back, so I sat down at my desk and put on my earphones. Why would my father be calling from New York, I wondered, but then I got distracted by what I heard on the tape. It was a memo to Dr. Stevens, asking him to take my boss's place at an all-day conference on "Treatment Modalities in a Community Practice Setting" on May 1. May 1 was in two weeks, and already I felt lethargic and depressed about the fact that Dr. Stevens would be away. After all, he was the only reason I worked at the Family Institute; when he wasn't there, I wondered why I was; I was his boss's secretary, typing up papers about "Psychotherapy for the Homosexual Patient" or "Clinical Evaluation of the Preschooler." I loved my boss and everything, it wasn't that; it's just that the only reason I'd taken the job in the first place was so I could be near Dr. Stevens without having to be his patient. I'd been working there ever since graduation, almost a year before, ever since I'd told Dr. Stevens I didn't need to see him anymore.

When I came back a few weeks later to interview for the job as his boss's secretary, I passed him in the corridor and explained, "We probably never discussed this, but I can type ninety words a minute." He didn't tell me I couldn't work there, and at least one thing about me improved—I could type almost a hundred.

Every morning, he passed by my office in order to get to the communal refrigerator, where he'd put his paper bag lunch. Some mornings he'd say "good morning"; those were good mornings. Some mornings he'd close the refrigerator door, looking distracted, and walk away without saying anything to me; those were bad mornings. But not necessarily bad days, because later on we'd often pass each other as he went into the men's room and I came out of the women's room, and then he'd say "How are you?" The worst days were the ones when he didn't come in at all, when he was sick or out of town or on vacation. Those were the days I felt despondent; I didn't know what the point of living was.

The way my typewriter was situated on my desk forced me to sit so that a person passing by my office would see me in profile. I didn't like my profile, so whenever I felt that someone was coming, I turned around, just in case it was Dr. Stevens. Back when I was his patient, the first time I lay on his couch, I drew up my knees and dragged my hair over my face so he couldn't see my profile. It was in that way that I related to him what I'd done to my brother Willy, when he was six and I was twelve. I had never told anybody about it during the four years after it happened, and the relief of giving voice to it was so great that I cried and cried. Dr. Stevens tried to make me feel better by telling me that at least half the women in his Analytic Theory class had had similar experiences with their brothers, but I didn't believe him. Otherwise, I'd thought, why didn't anyone else I know have brothers who had to go to special schools in Connecticut? Anyway, for two years I had confessed to him all the terrible things about me, and for two years he had absolved me of the guilt. But instead of growing to love myself, I grew to love him.

I had just finished typing the memo to Dr. Stevens and had started on the next one—something about a new service for AIDS-Affected Clients—when Rena buzzed me: my father was calling.

"Grandpa died in his sleep last night," he said. "We tried to call you at home this morning but there was no answer."

"Oh," I said. "Oh God." I started to cry, not so much because I'd been so close to my grandfather, but because someone who'd been alive the day before wasn't alive anymore.

"Mom and I are at La Guardia now, we're supposed to land in Cleveland around noon," he said. "I'm sorry to tell you this over the phone, Jane, but I didn't want you to come home tonight and see all the cars and think something even worse had happened."

"Cars? At our house?"

"Mom thought it would be better to have people at our house than to have them at Grandma's."

"Oh," I said again. "Okay. How is Mom?"

"She's okay. She's not falling apart, if that's what you mean. But I think we should all try to be as sensitive to her as we can. It's not the people who fall apart that you need to worry about. If you know what I mean."

I couldn't help thinking that if only my mother knew the way my father spoke about her, if only she knew how much he really cared about her, maybe she would feel better about herself and wouldn't need to eat so much. "Can I talk to Mom please?" I said.

"She's getting our boarding passes."

"Is Caroline coming too?"

"She can't come with us," my father said. "Pesach is in two days, and I don't even know whether she can fly."

"I've seen plenty of pregnant women fly," I said. Five minutes with the Klausners and everybody starts calling Passover Pesach.

"Jane, there's Mom, we're boarding now."

"Should I call Grandma? What should I do? When's the funeral?"

"Grandpa didn't want a funeral," he said. "He wanted to be cremated."

When I hung up the phone, I tried to pick up where I'd left off typing, but my eyes kept watering as I replayed my father's voice saying "Grandpa died last night" and then "He wanted to be cremated." I was so distracted I didn't even notice Dr. Stevens; by the time I looked up and to the side, all I caught was the back of his coat trailing behind him and the sound of his voice saying good morning to Dr. Rimer, my boss and his.

"Good morning, Jane," Dr. Rimer said. He was holding a bouquet of flowers in his hand and smiling. He was always cheerful, even when he was putting a handful of Tums in his mouth to settle his anxious stomach.

"Good morning," I said, and sniffed.

"Nice weekend?" he said.

"Yes, thanks."

"Good," he said. "Could you come into my office please?"

I picked up my yellow pad, a pen, and followed him into his office. Out of his window you could see only trees and a small pond. "So bucolic," Caroline would say, as if she'd been born in New York. I sat down in the swivel chair across from his desk and crossed my legs. Sometimes when I did that, I forgot what I looked like and saw instead of me the other secretaries, who were all much older—widows, divorcées, never-married—who wore blue eye shadow and nude panty-hose. It seemed as if everyone who worked there, even the mailroom clerk, had a sad story, and I often wondered whether an agency whose purpose it was to help emotionally fragile people made it a policy to hire them as well.

"Oh, you won't need that," Dr. Rimer said as I headed up my yellow pad with the date. "I really just wanted to give you these tulips. It's National Secretary's Day today, and this is the first year I've wanted to acknowledge it. I hope you've been as happy these last ten months as I have."

"I've been happy," I said, and then I burst into tears.

"What's this, Jane!" he said, and he came hurrying around to the other side of his desk, clutching the tulips.

"My grandfather died last night," I managed to say.

"Oh dear. Oh dear. I'm so sorry—"

"And I'm not even a real secretary! I mean, I was the valedictorian of my high school class, for God's sake! I'm just here because of Dr. Stevens."

"What does Dr. Stevens have to do with anything?"

"When I was in high school, I used to be his patient," I said. "And then I thought I was cured, but I guess I wasn't, and when I saw this job in the *Plain Dealer* I thought it was the perfect solution."

"Well, Jane," he said, "I suppose none of us is ever really cured."

"I don't want to get Dr. Stevens into trouble—"

"It wasn't his place to tell me," he said. "And frankly, I don't see why this has to change anything. It may have been an accident that this worked out so well, but it *has* worked out well."

"Yes," I said, but I felt confused. Here I'd given him the perfect excuse to fire me, and he wasn't taking it. It was like Eddie all over again.

"Now don't you think you ought to get home to your family?" Dr. Rimer said. "Take as much time as you need; I believe the role of a grandparent in a child's life has always been underestimated."

It was only ten o'clock in the morning, and my parents wouldn't be home until after noon, so I decided to stay and finish transcribing the tape I had started earlier. Dr. Rimer ducked out of his office every so often, and seeing that I was still there, asked me to place a few phone calls. He usually made his own calls, so I couldn't get too mad when he occasionally asked me to do it for him; nevertheless, there was nothing in my job that made me feel more anonymous or more depressed than dialing some number that meant nothing to me and then asking if so-and-so was available for Dr. Rimer. It made me feel as if I were only a voice or something. It made me feel like the invisible woman.

The letters on Dr. Rimer's tape were boring, all about funding and quality assurance and the difference between RTFs (residential treatment facilities) and RTCs (residential treatment centers), a difference I still didn't understand after typing about them for almost a year. I had to rewind the tape about a million times to make sure I'd put C and not F, and vice versa. I was practically falling asleep after two hours of mostly uninterrupted typing, when I heard the sound of Dr. Stevens's change rattling around in his pockets.

"Morning," he said, like it would have cost him to say "*Good* morning," like he couldn't be bothered with one extra syllable on my behalf. I hated this mood of his, where he started referring to me as Dr. Rimer's secretary, where he started acting like he'd forgotten my name. I'll admit I wasn't as important as he was, I was only a lowly secretary after all, and I hardly expected him to remember *every* secretary's name, but I *had* been his patient. I mean, I didn't make a big deal that the nine other psychiatrists (all male, of course, except one) didn't refer to the nine of us secretaries (all female, of course) by name, but the guy *had* been my goddam psychiatrist for two years!

"Morning," I said, like *I* couldn't afford the extra syllable. As he breezed into Dr. Rimer's office, I put the cover on my typewriter. I'd show him, I thought; I'd be gone before he even came out, and he'd just have to wonder what had happened to me.

When I got home, the cars were overflowing from our driveway onto the street, and inside people were milling around, holding cups of coffee and talking. What was the point of being cremated and not having a funeral if people still came over and bothered your surviving loved ones?

Now that the weather was warm, my parents left the sliding glass doors open, and the house smelled like spring. Rabbi Wax was standing at the dining room table, loading up his paper plate with lox and cream cheese from Corky & Lenny's, while Grandma was saying in her soft-spoken but pointed way, "Sam never believed in religion; he was an atheist all his life and, frankly, so am I." Rabbi Wax didn't get the point and if you'd told Grandma she was trying to make one, she wouldn't have believed it. She thought of herself as shy and self-effacing, but she could speak her mind with the best of them.

"Grandma," I said. "I'm so sorry." She was very short and I had to stoop to hug her.

"Did you hear?" she said. "Even Caroline's coming in. Now isn't that something? From New York. And pregnant."

"She's something else," I said, although why Caroline should've gotten extra credit for basic human decency was beyond me. Nevertheless, I couldn't deny I was happy the Fertility Goddess was coming.

My mother was running in and out of the kitchen, replenishing trays and paper goods until my father said, "What are you doing?" Only he could make concern sound like an accusation, and my mother made it clear she didn't appreciate it.

"Somebody's got to do it."

My father clenched his teeth and turned to walk out of the room, but before he did so, he said, "Stop trying to be the perfect hostess. Your father just died."

"Oh, is that so?"

"Yes, that's so," he said. "And don't you think you ought to put some lipstick on?"

"My father just died," she said. "I think people will understand my lack of lipstick."

Nevertheless, Mom took off her apron, put on some lipstick, and went into the living room. She and my grandmother sat on the couch and talked to Rabbi Wax while he and the others ate. My father went to sit in his chair in the study and sulk, and I went to get him. He always needed to be coaxed out of a funk after he insulted or scolded someone else. In some complex mental maneuver, he always managed to turn everything around so that it was *he* who'd been insulted.

"Come on, Dad. Mom needs you."

"How would you know?"

"Don't be mean," I said. "Don't start your persecuted act."

"Being a secretary for a psychiatrist makes you a psychiatrist?"

I started to walk out, but he grabbed my wrist and said "Wait. Don't give up so easily; you were on the right track. I'm coming." It was always that way with my father; mean, mean, mean, nice, and all I ever remembered was that last nice. Caroline would probably say that that was a problem, a problem she used to share before she entered the perfect family, but I clung to my original theory: nobody in the world would ever love me, Caroline, Willy or my mother as much as my father did. Not even perfect Mr. Klausner.

"Does Willy know about Grandpa?" I asked.

"We decided not to tell him over the phone," my father said. "He's coming in tomorrow for his spring break anyway. It's not as if there's a funeral to attend."

People came and went all day, paying their condolences and reminiscing about the charming man my grandfather was. Grandma got teary every once in a while, usually when someone reminded her of the wonderful trips they'd taken together, to Japan and India and France. "How am I going to live without him?" she said more than once, and my mother, who didn't get teary at all, put her arm around her and said, "You're going to be just fine."

Eddie came over after work, when the house really began to fill up, and I barely had a chance to say hello I was so busy refilling the coffee pot and throwing away paper plates stained with herring juice. His parents, Bob and Nancy, came too, and I thought with a certain bitterness how I'd still never score the points that Caroline had, just by having married into the Klausner family. I didn't notice Jonathan the perfect son-in-law paying his condolences, nor did I hear Mrs. Klausner's loud New York voice when I was picking up the phone all day long. I thought of my mother's date book, how she had started to keep track of the birthdays of every single one of Jonathan's relatives, so she could send a birthday card a week in advance. Goddammit, I thought, the least they could do was call when my mother's father died, even if we weren't Orthodox, even if we weren't from New York, even if we weren't sitting shiva the way they would.

Caroline walked in around seven o'clock, much to everyone's surprise, since we were all waiting for her to call and say what time she'd need to be picked up from the airport. "I took a cab," she said, and she put her bag down in the middle of the kitchen floor. It was a nice bag, a real piece of luggage with her initials on it and everything, not like the plastic grocery store bags she used to pack her clothes in; nevertheless, it occurred to me that that didn't give her the right to block everyone's way.

"A cab?" I said. "People don't take cabs in Cleveland."

"Well, I did."

She went and sat down next to my grandmother on the living-room couch and started to cry. "I'm going to miss him so much," she said. "I can't believe he died before his first great-grandchild was born." Leave it to Caroline to make herself the center of attention at my grandfather's party.

"Well," my grandmother said, and you could tell by the tone of her voice that she was about to make one of her points. "He wasn't like Jonathan's grandfather. He didn't live only for his grandchildren and great-grandchildren."

"I know," Caroline said. "But he would have wanted to see my baby, I'm sure."

"Of course he would," Grandma said.

Caroline was wearing a pair of white flats and a tailored spring suit made out of a floral print. She looked great, and you could hardly tell she was pregnant, except for her chest, which actually stuck out, for once. Her engagement ring was turned around so that you couldn't see the diamond, something she did in New York to avoid being mugged, but here in our house it looked odd. Actually, I realized, Caroline looked great; suddenly, it was our house that looked odd, with Caroline in it.

"Jonathan wanted to be here," she said to me, as we went to get a cup of coffee, "but with his schedule, he just couldn't."

"You don't have to apologize," I said.

"I'm not apologizing."

"Doesn't he ever get a day off?" I said.

"He does, but he switched his days off with the other interns so that he would be off on Pesach."

"Oh, I see," I said. "So you decided to come in since he's working tonight anyway."

"Give me a little credit, Jane," she said. "Grandpa was my grandfather too."

"Does your mother-in-law know that?"

"What's that supposed to mean?"

"Mom hasn't exactly gotten a call from her."

"She's very busy now; she has to turn her entire apartment upside down before Pesach. You know, she invites about twenty people to each seder."

"That's nice," I said. "I'm sure she would have found the time to call if we were Orthodox."

Caroline didn't answer, but her silence was not a defensive one. Instead, I got the feeling that somehow she agreed with me, that she felt bad about it, and that there was nothing she could do about her mother-in-law's xenophobia. I decided to lay off.

"When do you have to be back in New York?" I said.

"Tomorrow, before sundown."

"Passover is going to be so lonely this year. With Grandpa gone, and you in New York."

"I'm sorry, Jane," she said.

That night, Grandma slept over, in Willy's room. She said she couldn't stand sleeping in her own apartment without Grandpa; she said she didn't know how she'd ever be able to go back there. Meanwhile, Caroline and my father and I sat outside on the patio, talking about the time Willy had gotten bitten by a snake in the woods behind our house.

"Do you think that might account for everything?" Caroline asked, smiling.

"I think it was the time Dad almost ran him over in the driveway," my mother said. She was standing in the kitchen, looking out at us through the screen door, holding a glass of iced coffee. Caroline and my dad laughed, whether because my mother had said something funny or because they were grateful she didn't seem as distant as she had seemed all day, I wasn't sure. I didn't laugh. It wasn't the first time the three of them had sat around trying to figure out what could have traumatized Willy so much that he went around telling people he was related to Michael Jackson, or some other equally unbelievable tale, while I sat there knowing the whole time that it was I. I was the one who was responsible.

"Why don't you come out here, Mom?" Caroline said.

"I'm awfully tired."

"Come on, Lip," my dad said. My mother's name was Flip, short for Philippa, and when my father was feeling affectionate, he shortened it even more, to Lip. As in, Don't give me any of your lip. Only my father would consider Lip a term of endearment.

My mother opened the screen, came out, and sat down next to my father on the half-broken patio chair. When he thought we weren't looking, Dad took her hand and held it. Caroline and I obliged by pretending not to notice, because we knew that to draw attention to his gesture would embarrass him and make him stop. It was hard for him to show his feelings.

My family lived on a quiet street in a suburb called Pepper Pike, a ridiculous name which just about said it all. I'd always been miserable there, and apart from my high school English classes, which were excellent, I didn't think there was much to recommend the move we'd made from Cleveland Heights, the less affluent but more wholesome suburb we'd left when I was twelve. Nevertheless, sitting on our patio that warm spring night amid the sounds of an occasional motorcycle or car radio, my father holding my mother's hand, my sister Caroline sitting next to me, my grandmother sleeping safely upstairs, I only wanted for everything to remain just the way it was. I didn't even mind that Caroline had given up her one remaining post-Klausner vice: smoking. After all, she *did* have to think of the baby.

I didn't go to work the next day, and in the morning Caroline and I got up early and made coffee for my mother and grandmother before people started arriving. The night before, I'd heard Caroline on the phone in her old room after everyone else had gone to sleep. Our house was modern, its walls and ceilings thin, not like the prewar buildings in New York or the old houses over in Shaker Heights. I could hear almost every word she said, except when her crying muffled her words, and so I knew she was talking to Jonathan. She was yelling at him for not being with her, saying that if he were truly religious he would have come to Cleveland out of respect for her mother instead of reserving his days off for Passover. She accused him of looking down on her family because we didn't "sit shiva" cor- rectly and because my grandfather had been cremated instead of buried in a wooden box. She said that if they gave birth to a boy, she wasn't sure she wanted him to wear a yarmulke all the time because it just ended up making divisions between people in- stead of uniting them. She sounded like the old Caroline again, the one who'd starved herself in an antiapartheid march when she was a Barnard freshman. I was so thankful I could barely stand it.

I don't know what Jonathan was saying on the other end, but by the time she hung up the phone, Caroline was telling him how much she loved him and how he was the most understand- ing, sensitive husband in the world. I was glad to see they'd made up and everything, but I guessed that meant she'd be going back to New York before sundown the next day.

Grandma felt worse after a good night's sleep. "I thought it was all a bad dream," she said, and she looked shorter than ever. People sort of trickled in during the morning, but it was raining outside, and it probably seemed a good excuse to the people who were looking for one not to leave their houses. My father, on the other hand, was looking for an excuse to leave *ours,* rain or not, and so he decided he'd pick up Willy from the airport and make himself useful. When he got there, he called to say that Willy wasn't there, and that it was my mother's fault for not raising the rotten kid to know his left hand from his right. My mother, seemingly unruffled by my father's assessment, made a few calls, first to Willy, who was still in his dorm room, and then to the airline, who happily booked him onto the next flight. Naturally, my father wasn't too pleased about sitting in an airport for another three hours, but I think my mother secretly was. These days, she seemed to prefer it when my father wasn't around.

"Can I do anything for you, Ma?" I asked. My mother was bent over the ficus tree in the living room with a watering can in her hand.

"No thanks, sweetie," she said. "Not unless you can get some sleep for me. But I think I have to do that for myself."

"Why don't you go lie down? Grandma is. Caroline and I will let you know if more people come."

"I couldn't sleep now," she said. "I can't even sleep at night when I'm supposed to."

"Because of Grandpa," I said. She looked at me sort of strangely for a second, and then she nodded, as if *she'd* never thought of that or something. "You're going to miss him," I added.

"He was a dear, sweet man," she said, wiping off one of the leaves on the tree with her sleeve, and while I certainly loved my grandfather and his sense of humor, wit and open-mindedness, I wouldn't exactly have called him a dear, sweet man. That would have been like calling *my* father a dear, sweet man. He may have *been* one (I certainly thought he was!), but those weren't the first adjectives that came to mind when you thought of him.

"I hope Dad won't be too hard on Willy," my mother said.

"Willy will be fine," I said, more for my own benefit than for my mother's. "He'll just dig up his why-I-missed-the-plane excuse from his excuse repertoire. You don't need to worry about Willy."

"Right," my mother said. "Why worry now? It's a little late in the game for that sort of indulgence."

I suspect if I hadn't been so obsessed with my own guilt about Willy, I might have heard my mother expressing *her* regret about something she did or didn't do, should or shouldn't have done. As it was, I thought she was alluding to what I'd done to Willy, even though she wasn't supposed to have known about that.

"I love that outfit on you," my mother said, looking up from her plants. "You look so pretty in blue."

"Thanks, Mom," I said. "You look nice, too. I especially like those jade earrings on you, with your green eyes and everything."

"Oh, well," she said, "better to look above my neck than below. I'm getting fatter every minute."

"You are not," I said, and I guess she appreciated my little white lie, because she came over and actually kissed me on the cheek. Then she went on, watering the plants and wiping up the water that spilled over onto the floor.

By the time Willy and my father arrived home from the airport, the rain had cleared up, but the three of us didn't go outside to sit on the patio until later in the afternoon, after the two of them made up. My father used most of the early afternoon to bawl Willy out for neglecting to look at his plane ticket, and Willy countered with something about how the airline had changed the flight schedule at the last second, so it wasn't his fault. Then for the next little while, my father gave Willy the silent treatment, accompanied by some of the meanest looks known to mankind. Finally, and for no discernible reason, they became friends again, my father saying it could have happened to anyone, Willy still clinging to his argument that it hadn't been his fault.

So there we were, the three of us sitting on the patio, playing Three Thirds of a Ghost, when a blue VW Rabbit pulled up the driveway. My heart started beating so fast, I thought I was going to have a heart attack. That was Dr. Stevens's car! That was Dr. Stevens! Dr. Stevens was in my driveway! Dr. Stevens was seeing my house! Dr. Stevens was practically in my bedroom!

"Who's that?" my father said, and I didn't know whether to say my old shrink or my current colleague. Even though my father was the one who'd gotten Dr. Stevens's name and the name of his agency when I was sixteen and renewing library books about suicide, he'd never made the connection between that and the job I took at the same agency. He could be fairly dense sometimes.

"Someone I work with," I said, and I ran out to the driveway to prevent their meeting.

"I heard about your grandfather," Dr. Stevens said, as he stepped out of his car, "and since I had to pass your house on my way home from work, I thought I'd stop and say how sorry I am."

"You live out here?" I said. If you went much past our house, you ended up having to watch out for deer crossing the road.

"In the area," he said, and I tried not to get upset about the vagueness of his answer. He knew how I felt about him; when I was his patient, I was always telling him I loved him and wanted to have sex with him, and so now I wondered whether he thought I was like another Fatal Attraction, that if I knew where he lived, I'd come and destroy his family.

"I guess Dr. Rimer told you what I blurted out to him yesterday. I hope you're not angry with me."

"To tell you the truth, I'm glad you finally said something. I think we'll both be a lot more comfortable now."

"Oh. Okay." I guess I should have been happy about what he said, but I wasn't. Comfortable? What would happen to all that sexual tension, the only thing I enjoyed these days, if we turned into two regular people who happened to work in the same office?

"Anyway, I don't want to keep you from your family," he said. "And besides, my job is to make the horseradish in time for the seder."

"You're Jewish?"

"Well," he said, smiling slightly, "I wouldn't want to destroy any of your fantasies." Then he touched me on my back and said again how sorry he was. He backed up out of the driveway and drove slowly down the street, as if he were accustomed to driving on a street where little kids were playing, as if he were accustomed to little kids, period. I wanted to run after him and ask him if I could be a part of his family, tell him all the bad things that were happening to mine. I knew I couldn't do that anymore, and I cursed myself for having taken that stupid job and ruining my chances for ever being close to him again.

Nothing physical had ever happened in my sessions with him, but just talking to him had been sexier than fooling around with Eddie. Sometimes, I'd even be talking about something that was painful or embarrassing, like how it felt when I was twelve and all of a sudden I looked like Jane Russell, and just by referring to my body—which was right there in front of him, right there in broad daylight, right there in the flesh (so to speak), not just a distant memory unrelated to the present—I'd get so turned on I could feel myself blushing. Dr. Stevens didn't blush, but I think he was also turned on; his voice got quieter, his body got still, he even stopped stroking his beard. He was always a good listener, but when I told him about a fight I'd had with Caroline or a conversation I'd had with Eddie, he didn't seem quite as involved as when I talked about my breasts and all the feelings they gave me. Sometimes I even talked about them when I didn't particularly *need* to talk about them, just to please Dr. Stevens, just to keep him interested and aroused. I didn't want him to die of boredom, after all.

Willy and my father had gone inside, and I was glad, because it took me a minute to compose myself and to get over the disappointment that Dr. Stevens wasn't my father instead. Caroline was in her room packing her bag to go back to New York, and you could almost feel her sense of relief to be leaving this depressing place. My grandfather was dead, my grandmother wanted to be, my mother was in no mood to prepare for a seder, my father was harassing everyone the way he always did when he was away from his office for too long, and Willy was flipping baseball cards with himself, lonely and alienated as usual.

I went up to Caroline's room and sat on her bed while she pretended to be sad about leaving, but kept on throwing things into her bag as fast as she could.

"I wish I were going with you," I said.

"Why? I wish I were staying here."

"No you don't. Don't even say that."

"Okay, I won't say it."

"You hate it here. You think Cleveland's a big bore, and you think Mom and Dad aren't even Jewish because they don't feel like having a seder tonight."

"I hate it when you tell me what I think," she said.

"But I'm right, aren't I?"

"I'm looking forward to seeing Jonathan, but other than that I don't have any reason to run back to New York."

"It'll sure be less depressing at the Klausners', though, won't it?"

"Maybe, a little," she said and smiled. "I'm sorry, Janey. I wish you could come with me."

"Don't feel sorry for me," I said. "We'll be just fine here without you."

"Okay," she said. "I'm sorry for saying I'm sorry. Are you satisfied?"

I started to cry then. I'll admit I was due for my period, and maybe that was part of my weepiness, but it was more than that, I swear. I hate it when people blame everything on PMS. Caroline patted my hair and then tried to cheer me up by saying funny things about her mother-in-law, like how she taped her soap operas when she wasn't home and how she kept buying hats for Shira so that Shira would get married already. I laughed a little bit, but I didn't really feel any better. I let her think I did, though.

My father took her to the airport, after announcing to everyone that he didn't have to if he didn't want to(!), and when he got home, we sat down at the kitchen table, not even the dining-room table, and had leftovers from all the trays that nobody'd eaten from all day. The phone rang, and I picked it up to hear Mrs. Klausner saying, "I'm so sorry I haven't called before now, it's just been so busy." Then she went on to recite her guest list for the seder, which was starting in a few hours.

If she was waiting for me to get down on my hands and knees and thank her for deigning to call us in the midst of her very busy and important life, she was going to have a long wait. She was always acting like we were some kind of charity case or something, like we were just sitting around waiting for her to notice us. "I'm so sorry about your grandfather," she went on. "When Caroline told us, I practically cried even though I hardly knew him." I thanked her then and asked her if she wanted to speak to my mother, but she said she was sure my mother was busy and she didn't want to be a bother (oh, right!), so could I just send my mother her love? She was always sending her love to everyone; in my opinion, when your love is sent around and spread that thin, it's not worth all that much.

It was four-thirty in the afternoon, and there my family was, eating dinner because we had nothing else to do. Forget about the four sons or the four questions or the *afikomen;* we weren't even getting matzah or *charoset* on Passover this year. Willy's eyes kept welling up with tears, as if he were hearing the words *Grandpa died* again and again, the words my father had finally said when he'd finished punishing Willy for missing his plane. "I don't understand why a person has to die anyway," Willy said. Nobody could really give him an answer for that, and my father, who was usually quite sensitive to Willy's fears, must have felt he'd exceeded his sensitivity quotient for the day, because he said, "That's life; you'd better get used to it." Grandma excused herself after eating a tiny piece of white fish, and then my mother left to check on Grandma.

"Some seder," my father said.

"It's your own fault," I said.

"What'd you say?"

"I said it's your own fault. I'm sure Caroline's in-laws never skip their seder, even if someone dies."

My father pushed back his chair with a loud squeak, wiped his mouth, threw his napkin down on the table, and walked out of the room. He came back a second later and said, "You can just fuck off, Jane, with all your criticisms of me. Go find

Eve Horowitz

yourself a new person to hate." Then he opened the screen door
to the patio, and slammed it shut so that it almost came off its
tracks, and walked back into the woods behind our house.

"Good job, Jane," Willy said, and if he hadn't been crying
when he said it, I might have started a fight with him too. As
it was, I said, "Let's clean up the kitchen," and he was so
relieved that someone was including him in something that he
didn't even protest what it was. He cleared the table and then
asked if he could be excused, like I was his mother or something.
The next thing I knew, the house was being bombarded by the
sound of the basketball missing the net and hitting the gutters on
the roof instead.

I called Eddie from the kitchen, while I put detergent in
the dishwasher. He said his family hadn't even started their seder
yet, but that if I was so upset, he'd just go back to his apartment
and meet me there. First I'd had to get through saying hello to
his father, who picked up the phone, and that had been no easy
task since all I could think of when I spoke to his father was
Eddie saying to me the first time I'd met Mr. Fiedler, "My father
thinks you could use your boobs as life rafts if you were ever
drowning." It wasn't entirely unarousing to think of his father
talking about my boobs, but I couldn't exactly imagine Mr.
Klausner talking about Caroline's.

"I don't want to ruin your family's seder," I said. "We
could meet after you're done."

"Why don't you come here, to my parents', and then we'll
go back to my place? My mother really wants you to come. She
wants to introduce you to her friends."

I knew I'd just be leading Eddie on by going there and
being introduced to his mother's friends, like we were an official
couple or something, but I decided I didn't care. I was tired of
thinking about how everybody felt all the time, tired of trying
to protect my mother from Caroline's mother-in-law, tired of

trying to protect my father's feelings from getting hurt by Caroline. I wanted to be selfish, and so I went to Eddie's parents' house, and met his mother's friends.

The Fiedlers didn't have much of a seder either, but somehow it wasn't as sad not to have a seder in their house as it was in mine. It wasn't as if they used to be one kind of family and now they were another. They'd always had nothing much of a seder.

Mrs. Fiedler, or Nancy, as she liked me to call her, was wearing this funky pantsuit (I'd guess a size 2) and a little hat that was right out of the 1920s. It was strange that a woman like her, who was a weaver and made art projects out of other people's garbage, gave birth to Eddie, a computer wiz who thought there wasn't much point to art. She was flat as a board, and her voice sounded spacy.

"I don't have matzah this year," she announced when we sat down to eat. "But I think crackers will do." Let's just ask Mrs. Klausner about that, I thought, but the truth was I was feeling a little better, a little less depressed.

Eddie helped to serve the rest of the food, which consisted of this very green cream of broccoli soup, a mushroom soufflé in this flaky filo dough crust, endive and avocado salad, and rice pilaf. For dessert, there were baked apples and chocolate ice cream. It wasn't the most traditional Passover dinner I'd ever eaten, but at least there were people around who were talking to each other and to me. And, just so it would have the feel of Passover, Nancy served Manischewitz Concord grape wine, even though another wine would have gone better with the meal. I had four small cups of it, out of deference to the holiday.

"How about if we just say there were four different kinds of sons—a smart one, a stupid one, a smart-ass one, and one who doesn't know how to talk yet—and call it a night?" Everyone laughed at Mr. Fiedler's—Bob's—joke, but no one laughed harder than Mr. Fiedler. He was a crude guy, but at least he was unpretentious, I thought, trying to imagine him as my father-in-law.

Nancy's friends were two single women in their forties, one with a blond afro and the other with long red hair, and they kept saying how adorable Eddie was, and how adorable Eddie and I were together. I didn't know the first thing about these women, but I was beginning to think, well, if they think he's so adorable, maybe he is, maybe I *should* marry him.

"Are you two also artists?" I asked them, practically choking on the word "artist," since I still didn't think garbage qualified as art, even if the entire city of Cleveland did.

"I'm a secretary," the afro-headed woman said.

"So am I," the redhead said.

"Me too," I said, although no one had asked.

Eddie was smiling all this time, like he was *proud* of me, like it was a *good* thing that I had something in common with his mother's friends, even if it turned out that they were legal secretaries and I was only the secretary of a shrink. I mean, if he had really loved me, wouldn't he have wanted me to do something I enjoyed, something that challenged me and mattered to me, something that required more than the nimbleness of my fingers and the anonymity of my telephone voice? But then, that was the problem with Eddie; he didn't know that things mattered to me.

After dinner, we all helped clear the table, except for Bob, who stretched out his long legs and lit up his pipe. I got the last plate, a pretty hand-crafted platter with one baked apple left on it, and as I came around the table with it, Bob leered at me in such a way that I almost expected him to reach out and grab my ass.

The thing about me was that I was neither insulted nor infuriated by the way he checked me out. I was sort of flattered and nauseated at the same time, and I gave him a look which was so ambivalent it must have confused him, because he didn't say another thing to me for the rest of the night. When Eddie and I left for his apartment, Bob had all but disappeared without saying good-bye.

My head ached from the wine, but I wasn't drunk and so I followed Eddie in my Olds. He was a very careful driver, and very slow; I was practically on his tail the entire way. Fortunately, what with my tipsy condition and all, I was forced to concentrate only on the road and the other cars (all three of them!) and not on the fact that I lived in such a hick town. I never used to think of it as a hick town, of course, not until Caroline married Jonathan.

We parked in Eddie's lot and then waited for the elevator in his building. When it finally came, it was full of kids and parents, obviously coming from their grandparents' seder. The whole building smelled of chicken soup tonight, and I couldn't wait to get inside Eddie's apartment, which only smelled of aftershave. We were barely inside the door when I was taking off my clothes, everything but my underpants since I'd worn a sanitary napkin in case my period started. Eddie picked up after me and folded my skirt and sweater neatly on the chair in his bedroom, then lay down next to me on his bed. I was feeling very passionate, full of the images of Dr. Stevens in my driveway, of my father saying "fuck off," of Eddie's father ogling me.

As usual, we did everything short of screwing, using our hands and mouths to substitute for the real things, and after we'd satisfied each other, I leaned back on the soft pillows and threw my arms around Eddie's head. Then I thought, aha! here's something I have that Caroline doesn't. Not only are she and Jonathan prohibited from having sexual relations *during* her period, Caroline told me they're also supposed to abstain right before, to avoid the potential sin of bringing on the menstrual flow. It wasn't the greatest consolation in the world, but it wasn't bad.

"What are you thinking about?" I said to Eddie, after we'd been lying there awhile.

"I wish we could have sex," he said. "I mean real sex."

"Why," I said, "that wasn't good?"

"It was great, but . . . I want more."

"Okay," I said. What the hell. "When we're married."

"Really?" he said. I didn't hear that much enthusiasm in his voice, but on the other hand he hadn't even looked at his watch once, the way he usually did when we were done fooling around. "Are we going to get married, Jane?"

"Of course," I said. "Didn't you ask me?"

"Yes, but I didn't think you were going to say yes."

"Remember the first time we went out?" I said. "I was trying so hard to act like I didn't like you. My father had told me before I left the house that night that that's how you got people to like you, by acting like you didn't like them. He said oil was expensive because it was scarce, or something like that. It *was* during an energy crisis, so he probably said exactly that."

"I did think you liked me, though," Eddie said.

"I know. I'm a bad actress; always have been. It's a good thing, too, or I might have gotten the lead in *Gypsy* instead of just a chorus part, and then I would have been too important to notice the lighting manager."

God only knows why I took my clothes into the bathroom to get dressed then; it's not like I'd been Miss Modest a few seconds before or anything. The mini-pad I'd worn was still clean and white, so I peeled it off my underpants and wrapped it up in about twelve feet of toilet paper. I suppose I could have thrown it into Eddie's wastebasket, but I didn't, I stuck it into my purse. The truth is, I'd once thrown a used one in a waste-basket at a friend's house the morning after a slumber party. The next thing I knew, my friend's dog Pokey was walking around the house with the entire contents of the wastebasket hanging out of his mouth, and everyone at the party was denying that they were the ones who had their period, saying they only used tampons anyway, you could ask anyone.

When I got home, it was only ten o'clock, and my father was watching the Channel 3 local news. "Where were you?" he asked. His voice sounded mean, but it was the kind of mean I knew he wanted to be coaxed out of.

"At Eddie's parents' seder."

"Did you have fun?"

"Yeah."

"Good," he said. "Sit down here and watch the news with me."

I sat down, and we watched the sunny weather forecast for the next day. He took my hand and locked his fingers between mine. It hurt, but it meant that I could forget about having insulted him because he'd forgiven me. He was wearing this old bathrobe that Willy and Caroline and I had given him for his birthday several years ago, and he looked terribly vulnerable to me. He was just sitting there, watching the weather forecast and holding my hand, and not even knowing that I was planning to be the next daughter to leave him. I didn't enjoy his explosions, but in a way I preferred them to moments like this, when I felt sorry for him. He'd never gotten as much attention from my mother as he'd gotten from Caroline and me, and now neither one of us would be around to give it to him. In fact, sometimes it had even seemed as if my mother used us kids to get my father off her back, he was so needy. What was going to happen to my parents when Willy went back to school and I got married to Eddie?

As soon as a commercial came on, I turned to my dad and said, "Eddie and I are going to get married."

My father put his arm around my neck and kissed the top of my head.

"You're not going to try to talk me out of it?"

"You're the Freud expert," he said. "There are two things in life that you have to decide by your gut: love and work."

"Oh yeah," I said.

"Did you tell Mom?"

"Not yet."

"Don't you think you should? She's very sensitive these days."

"She's not like you, Dad. She doesn't care about me the way you do."

"Are you kidding?" he said. "You're wrong about that."

"Well, don't say anything," I said. "I'll tell her pretty soon."

"Wait. Where are you going?" he said, grabbing my arm as I stood up to leave.

"The kitchen, why?"

"First tell me what I said at dinner before. I need a good laugh."

"Come on, Dad. Let me go."

"Just tell me what I said," my father pleaded, and he tightened his grip on my arm.

"Okay, okay. Do the words 'fuck off' ring a bell?"

"Ha! Did I really say that? Boy, I'm more eloquent than I thought."

"You're crazy, Dad."

"But to the point, right? You gotta give me that." Then he laughed; it was almost enough to make me wonder if the reason he had his tantrums in the first place was so that I could amuse him with a rendition afterward. He let go of my arm, and that was how I knew I'd been excused.

Willy and Grandma were playing gin rummy on the kitchen table, and my mother was sorting laundry in the laundry room. "Gin!" Willy shouted.

"Not so loud," my mother called.

"What's the difference?" I called back, and poured myself a glass of ginger ale.

My mother didn't say anything right away, and then she said, "I guess there isn't any." Earlier in the day, after Willy had finished defending his airplane mishap to my dad, my mother came up with a few questions of her own. *She* wanted to know why Willy had brought home only half the winter clothes he'd taken to school in the fall, and why his English teacher thought he couldn't afford to buy the books he needed for class. When she questioned his explanations, Willy became furious, stomping out of the kitchen saying, "Fine, *don't* believe me, don't believe that I lost the suitcase that had my sweaters in it, don't believe that my money fell out of the hole in my pocket!" It seemed as if it had now gotten to the point where Willy couldn't even say "gin" without raising my mother's suspicion.

I drank my ginger ale and decided I'd tell my mother about Eddie the next day, when Grandma and Willy weren't sitting in the same room. She didn't seem to be in the mood to hear anything anyway; she seemed like she wanted to fold laundry for the rest of her life and not be bothered by any of us.

The next day, things started getting back to normal. My father and I both went back to work, Grandma and my mother stayed home to receive visitors, and Willy sat in his room, watching the black-and-white television he'd lugged upstairs from the kitchen.

"How was the horseradish?" I said to Dr. Stevens when he passed my desk on the way to the refrigerator.

"Very strong," he said. "How about yours?"

"I didn't have any," I said, "but I am getting married."

"Oh?" He closed the refrigerator door, and came into my office.

"To Eddie. I don't know if you remember—"

"Of course I remember."

"Oh. Sometimes it seems as if I'd imagined all those sessions I had with you."

"Well," he said, with a smile whose meaning I couldn't fathom, "congratulations."

"Thanks."

He was being pretty nice, and I had to resist the urge to ask him whether I was doing the right thing, did he think I was making a mistake. I kept trying to read something into his "congratulations," but he'd honed his neutrality to such perfection that I couldn't read anything at all.

Dr. Rimer's door was closed, which meant that he was already here, probably having an early-morning session with one of his private patients who couldn't come in at night. I felt a pang of sadness, remembering how I used to see Dr. Stevens in the mornings before school, if I couldn't make it to my regular evening session because of *Gypsy* practice or S.A.T. study-group sessions. Here I'd thought I would be even closer to him now than I was before; when I'd taken the job I'd imagined the two of us becoming friendly, having lunch together, having an affair on the couch in his office. Instead, it was much worse than before; rather than becoming closer in our new, more equal roles, we'd never been further apart, and I longed to be sitting in his office again, telling him intimate things.

I tried to concentrate on my work and, fortunately, during my absence, plenty of typing had accumulated so I barely had time to feel anything. Dr. Rimer was as friendly as ever, but my confession to him about Dr. Stevens made it uncomfortable to be near him. It wasn't that I was embarrassed about seeing a shrink; after all, Dr. Rimer was a shrink himself. It was that, being a shrink, Dr. Rimer must have known what kinds of things people talked about in their sessions, which meant that he knew I was perverted in some way. It's hard to be someone's secretary if you think they think you're perverted.

Willy was lying on the living-room couch when I got home from work, watching Phil Donahue on the color TV. I guess he'd had enough of black and white. I tried to keep the annoyance out of my voice when I said hello to him; rationally speaking, why should I have cared if all he did was watch television all day and all night?

"You should see this episode, Jane," Willy said. "It's really funny."

Willy moved over so I could sit down next to him on the couch. The topic of the program was "When Your Man Cheats On You" or something.

"Don't you have anything better to do than watch this crap, Willy?"

"No," he laughed, "I really don't."

"You don't have any homework?"

"I'm on vacation, Jane. And besides, I'm all caught up, I'm doing really well in my classes this term."

"Really? What about that English teacher of yours who says you haven't even bought the books yet?"

"Oh, her. I hate that lady. She fails everyone."

"Willy—"

"I'm serious, Jane. Everyone hates her."

"But what does that have to do with you?"

"I'm just saying, it won't be my fault if I fail. She should learn how to teach."

"But Willy, why is it that every time you fail a class, it's the teacher's fault?"

"I don't know, it just is."

"Fine, Willy." I couldn't do it, I just couldn't talk to the kid. I guess I was sounding like my mother or something and maybe that was annoying to him, but it was just so frustrating; you never got the straight goods from him about anything, you never really knew what was going on with him. I got up and went upstairs to change my clothes. Fortunately, I was going out to dinner, so I wouldn't have to stick around and look at that depressing lump of a brother of mine.

Eddie picked me up at around six and took me to Houli-han's. He said he had a coupon for a free entrée.

"This is for you," he said after we had ordered, and he handed me a little velvet box. Inside was a diamond engagement ring. "It was my grandmother's."

"It's beautiful," I said, and I meant it. It was an antique ring, and I didn't care what Caroline's mother-in-law would have said about it. She preferred everything modern and had prevailed upon Jonathan to get Caroline a ring that was so new and shiny and contemporary that it went perfectly with the decor of the Klausners' apartment.

"I've had this ring sitting in my dresser drawer for three months," Eddie said. He said it sort of cocky, like he knew all along I was going to say yes, like he thought I'd been playing hard to get.

"I love it," I said, and the waiter arrived with our food.

The two of us were happily eating our T-bone steaks when all of a sudden Eddie said, "We won't be able to eat like this every night, you know." I couldn't believe my ears! I certainly didn't need to eat like that every night, I could have eaten a bowl of Cap'n Crunch for dinner and been satisfied. Neverthe-less, I didn't say anything to Eddie. Instead, I tried to quiet the voice in me that was saying, Nip it in the bud, You can still get out, You don't love him, He gets on your nerves.

I looked at my engagement ring and admired again how much nicer it was than Caroline's. Caroline, who was probably eating bitter herbs and matzah for the second night in a row, while I was sitting in a *treif* restaurant with Eddie. *Treif!* Even *I* was beginning to sound Orthodox, thinking *treif* instead of nonkosher.

After dinner, we drove over to one of those outdoor malls, where everything was closed by five except for the movie theatre. Even Corky & Lenny's, the deli which had sent over trays when Grandpa had died, was closed tonight, because of the second seder. I noticed they had matzah in the windows instead of fresh rye bread, and I could almost imagine Mrs. Klausner's response: "I don't understand these Jews who eat lobster all year round but don't eat bread on Pesach," as if she had the monopoly on religious observance.

It was a beautiful warm spring night, and Eddie and I walked back and forth on the sidewalk in front of the shops until it was time for the movie. I hadn't seen a movie in this theatre since the time I went with Caroline, before she got married. "I can't believe it," she'd said. "In New York, the line would be around the corner for a movie ticket on a Saturday night." She said it as if it were a compliment to Cleveland, but I saw right through it. She was so glad to be out of this town she could hardly stand it.

"Let's see, do I want a Kit Kat or a Hershey's bar?" I said when we got inside the theatre. You definitely needed something sweet after a steak and baked potato, and I loved candy bars.

"Are you sure you want something?" Eddie said.

"What do you mean?" I said, knowing exactly what he meant.

"We just had a huge dinner," he said.

"So are you worried about the money or the calories?"

"I'm just so full, I can't imagine eating candy now."

"You don't have to," I said, and I took out my wallet and bought a Kit Kat *and* a Hershey's bar. That'll show him not to talk to me about food the way my father talks to my mother, I thought.

We watched the movie, and afterward I cried, not because it moved me in any way, but because I didn't like it and Eddie did, so it was one more thing that we didn't have in common.

"She's not bad, is she?" Eddie said.

"Who?" I said, though I knew perfectly well who.

"Julia Roberts."

I rolled my eyes to myself. It was so *unoriginal* to think Julia Roberts was pretty. Why couldn't he at least have thought Grace Kelly was pretty, if he was going to start lusting after someone?

"I have a great idea," he said as we walked through the parking lot. It wasn't hard to find his car; it was the one with the sticker on the back windshield that said WMMS Home of the Buzzard. Like he really listened to WMMS or something, like he wasn't just trying to seem cool, like he didn't prefer soft rock. *Nobody* really listened to WMMS, all that Led Zeppelin and so-called classic rock; it was just the kind of thing you said you did. "Let's tell my parents now."

"No, let's not tell them yet."

"You're still not sure, are you?" Eddie said.

"Why do you say that?"

"Then let's tell my parents."

We drove out of the parking lot and then down a boulevard lined by a Dairy Queen, a bowling alley, another small shopping center where no one ever shopped, and a few gas stations. Eddie was being his usual, careful self, and so when we reached the rotary which branched off into six roads, he came to a complete stop, even though there wasn't another car in sight for about ten miles. Finally, he made a slow right turn and drove halfway around the circle, where he turned right again and continued down the boulevard. The further we drove, the less commercial the boulevard became, and after we passed our old Randall High School on the right, the road became narrower and empty, huge trees to each side of us. We were still in Pepper Pike, but in a part that spooked me, a part I'd always felt was inhabited by members of the Ku Klux Klan. We turned onto Eddie's street and parked in his driveway. There was a spotlight on, but even so, it never got this dark in New York.

Bob was sitting in "his" chair in the living room, and Nancy was in the kitchen getting him a bowl of ice cream. A rerun of *Taxi* was playing on the television. The living room was a combination of weird and typical suburban. The weird part was the stuff hanging on the walls, things Nancy had made on her loom, and the typical suburban were the walls themselves, fake wood that was supposed to look like tree bark or something. The fireplace was also fake, but the objects on the mantelpiece were real—things Nancy had made out of plastic containers, orange juice bottles, whatever. She'd even gotten a grant from the city of Cleveland for her "trash art," which enabled her to interview garbage men and go through other people's rubbish in the first place.

"What a treat!" she said when we came in.

"Hi, Mom," Eddie said.

"Hello," Bob said, and he gave me the old once-over.

Nancy sat down next to Eddie and me on the leopard-skin sofa. She hardly made a dent, though, she was so petite. I felt like a horse next to her. "Jane and I are engaged," Eddie said. "We're getting married."

"Oh, hooray!" Nancy said, and she threw herself at me, kissing me with her bright red lips. "I was *hoping* this would happen."

Bob shook Eddie's hand and nodded at me. "Very nice, Edward," he said, like calling him Edward was supposed to impress me, make me think he was a respectable guy when I knew exactly what he was.

"I hope you're not planning to elope," Nancy said. Elope! Only Nancy would assume we were going to do the unconventional thing before assuming we'd do the conventional. At first it bothered me that such an idea would never even have *occurred* to Caroline's mother-in-law; I mean, why couldn't someone spoil *me* the way Mrs. Klausner spoiled Caroline? And then I remembered there was a price to pay for having a typical Jewish mother-in-law; Caroline had to call Mrs. Klausner Ema. Nancy, on the other hand, probably didn't even know that *ema* was the Hebrew word for mother.

"No," I said. "We're not going to elope."

"Good," she said. "Are you going to be a June bride? I love June brides." It was already late April, and even though I didn't need eight months to prepare, the way Caroline did, I thought June was pushing it.

"I think we'll probably wait until my sister has her baby in the fall," I said. Eddie looked at me; we hadn't exactly discussed a date.

"What kind of a wedding are we talking about here?" Bob asked.

"Nothing fancy," I said.

"I hope not. These things cost money," he said. Then he looked at Eddie and said, "Doesn't the bride's family pay for the wedding? I think so, come to think of it. Hey, the sky's the limit." He and Eddie laughed, and Nancy smiled. "Lighten up, Janey," Bob said, putting his arm around me. I guess I was looking pretty serious, so I smiled while old Bob gave my waist a little squeeze.

Then Eddie started talking about our finances, and how it

was perfect, I could just move into his apartment, we wouldn't even have to find a new place. And we both had cars already, so we wouldn't need to worry about that. He was very practical. I was surprised he didn't say that we'd practically almost had sex, so we wouldn't need to worry about that either.

After a while, Eddie drove me home and turned off the engine when he'd pulled up to our garage. He reached over to kiss me, and I kissed him back with a ferociousness he must have mistaken for love. "Should I come inside?" he said, his denseness only intensifying my fury.

"I'm pretty tired," I said. "It's that time of the month." It really was, as of that morning.

I went inside and found my mother cleaning up the kitchen, her glass of iced coffee on top of the microwave. She was wiping off the counter and listening to some classical music on the radio.

"It's late, Ma," I said. "Why are you up cleaning the kitchen so late?"

"It's the only time nobody's bothering me," she said, but I saw the pretzels hanging out of the cupboard. It was the only time nobody was bothering her, all right. "Look at this," she said, and she slid a little white envelope over the counter to me. I opened it up to find this frilly little stationery with "Shira" on the front. On the inside was her babyish handwriting; at the top, three Hebrew letters, which Caroline had once told me was something Orthodox Jews included on every piece of paper they wrote on. Talk about superstitious! I mean, even *I,* Miss Intimidated by God, stopped putting the little dash between *G* and *d* when I was about ten.

"Dear Mrs. Singer," the note said, "I was *so* sorry to hear that your father passed away. My mother and I have been crying ever since we heard, as if he had been our father and grandfather as well as yours. Please accept my deepest sympathies." She signed it "with love," of course, because you couldn't get any more insincere than that.

"Oh brother!" I said. "Now you're supposed to go around telling everyone how Mrs. Klausner raised such perfect children, they even write condolence notes to people they barely know." I couldn't stand parents who made their kids do things so that other people would say what great kids they had.

"Perhaps," my mother said, though her fingers lingered on the frilly paper as if she wanted to savor anything nice that came her way, calculated or not.

"So, anyway, Mom," I said, opening the fridge and then closing it, "I'm getting married."

I had been looking down when I said it, and when I didn't hear anything from her, I looked up. My mother was holding her finger up and listening intently to the soft voice of the radio announcer.

"Ah, I knew it was Vivaldi," she said. Then she looked at me and said, "What? You're getting married?"

"I am."

"Well, that's news."

"Boy, Mom, don't go crazy with enthusiasm. Don't let my news stop you from scouring the kitchen sink. I mean, don't wear yourself out with joy."

My mother put down the sponge. "I'm sorry," she said, "I guess I just didn't realize you were serious about Eddie."

"I guess you don't like him."

"Oh, Jane, that's not true."

"Well, you don't seem very happy for me."

"Give me a chance," she said. "Why are you getting so upset?"

"Because you're always so damned objective and unemotional, Mom! I swear, it's as if I were just any old person to you, as if I weren't even your very own flesh and blood!"

"Take it easy, Jane," she said. "I'm happy for you if this is what you want." She turned off the radio and said, "Are you coming upstairs?"

"Oh, you just don't get it!" I yelled, and I stormed out of the kitchen. I was in my room when I heard her finally coming up the stairs; her footsteps sounded slow and tired. Her father had died two days before, and there I was, sitting on my bed and crying that my mother wasn't happy for me. I knew I was being an asshole, and that my timing couldn't have been worse, but I wanted something so desperately from her, and no matter what I did, even becoming engaged, I couldn't seem to get it.

Grandma was sleeping in Caroline's old room, the room next to mine. Her door was open, and she had a nightlight on. She'd been having a hard time falling asleep and staying that way, so now she was taking sleeping pills. In the mornings before work, I'd find her sitting up in bed, looking around, as if she could no longer remember what a person was supposed to do when they got up in the morning. I helped her get dressed a few times, and unlike my own mother, she didn't mind being naked in front of me. She had large, pendulous breasts, and looking at her, I saw what I would look like in fifty years. "He was a passionate man, Grandpa," she said to me once. It was obvious that she couldn't imagine that part of her life being over. I felt sad, but not for her—for me. Here she was, seventy-one years old, and she still wanted passion. I was only nineteen, and I was relinquishing passion for someone who'd save me. I wondered what it felt like to love someone so passionately that you needed to take sleeping pills when they died. And then I thought, does Dr. Stevens count?

The next evening, my father was wearing a handsome sports jacket, a turtleneck underneath, and he didn't look at all diminished in the company of Eddie's father, even though Bob Fiedler was several inches taller than my father. My mother had called Eddie's mother that morning, the morning after the night I'd yelled at her for not being happy for me, to invite them all for a drink to celebrate Eddie's and my engagement. The six of us stood around our living room, holding glasses and talking about irrelevant things, like the price of the vacant house next door.

"Two hundred thousand for that?" Bob was saying, while he jiggled a bunch of toasted almonds in his hand.

"That's a bargain," my father said, yawning, as if he'd thought it a thousand times before but was too bored to say it out loud.

I'd all but forgotten Willy even existed when at around eight o'clock, about an hour after the Fiedlers had arrived, he came bounding down the stairs to join us. He didn't have much to say, as usual, but at least I could one day tell my children that I'd had a sibling in attendance for my moment of glory. I mean, Caroline hadn't exactly come flying in to celebrate my engagement the way I'd flown to New York with my parents for hers. It was pretty clear all the way around that our engagements weren't in the same league, and when Nancy agreed that a wedding in our backyard would be beautiful, you could tell that my father lost whatever respect he'd had for her. Like, anybody who was so agreeable didn't deserve his respect.

There was no Shira walking around offering champagne, and no Mrs. Klausner insisting on a New York wedding. Instead, there was Bob. Bob, who always seemed about to make a pass at me, and Nancy, who was too into garbage to know it. And of course, Eddie was no Jonathan. He didn't aspire to move to Israel to help the Jewish people; he aspired to analyze computers, and to make money so that we could live in a house like our parents'. There were no "mazel tovs," and only Nancy seemed interested in discussing when the wedding would be. My mother was walking around overcompensating for the fact that she didn't like Eddie or his parents by talking in this condescending way she probably thought was friendly. As if people didn't know when they were being talked to like idiots.

Eddie kept calling my father Mr. Singer, and I couldn't help remembering how Jonathan called my father by his first name before Caroline and he were even engaged. Eddie always seemed stupid next to my father, whereas Jonathan could answer any question my father posed, no matter how perfectly it was designed to stump him. To tell the truth, Jonathan was probably even more well read than my father. Could Eddie help it that his father read *Playboy* while Jonathan's father read the *Yiddishe Velt* or something?

Bob suggested making a toast to the young couple, so everyone held up their glasses, even Willy, who was proudly drinking a Virgin Mary. "Here's looking up your old address," Bob said. Then my father said, "L'chaim," as if I needed to be reminded of the Klausners at that very moment.

We were celebrating my impending marriage, and I had never been more miserable in my life.

3

Caroline was already seven months pregnant in July when she and Jonathan finally came for a visit. It was Jonathan's first trip to Cleveland, so naturally everybody was bending over backward to make sure he would be comfortable. There was something about him, despite the fact that he was born and raised in New York City, that made you want to shelter him from the real world. After all, in certain ways, he was more naïve than Willy, who, as always, was home for the summer. For instance, I honestly believe that ours was the first Jewish home Jonathan had ever been in where you could more easily locate a book about India than you could a book about Israel.

It was a Thursday morning, and Jonathan was walking

around the living room when I came downstairs for breakfast. He was wearing a square box on his forehead, leather straps around his left arm and a blue and white tallis over his shoulders. The fringes of his tzitzit—the garment he wore under his shirt that was supposed to remind him of God's omnipresence—were hanging out over the top of his pants. It was early, but it was already eighty degrees, and so I stepped into the living room to turn up the air conditioner before going to the kitchen to eat breakfast.

"Oops, sorry!" I said when I saw him. I couldn't help staring at him; I'd never before seen anyone actually wearing phylacteries, especially in my parents' Hazelnut Lane living room. Nor had I ever personally known, let alone been related to, a man who wore tzitzit. The night before, when I'd gone to the bathroom to brush my teeth before bed, I'd noticed them hanging over the shower rod, water dripping off the fringes into the bathtub below; it had seemed strange to see such a piece of holy clothing just drip-drying there like any old undershirt. They were sort of gray and shapeless from wear; I wondered how many pairs Jonathan had, and if they came in any color but white, the way my underpants did. It was hard to believe that he would put them on the next morning as casually as I put on my bra, or that he could possibly feel their holiness anymore after so many years of habit.

"I'm almost done," Jonathan said and laughed his nervous, funny laugh. He was holding a little brown prayer book in his hand, and moving his lips. It was pretty obvious that he didn't want anyone watching him, since he chose the room least likely to be frequented by any of us on a summer morning before work. I turned up the air conditioner and walked out through our slate-tiled foyer to the kitchen. Caroline was sitting at the kitchen table, massaging her stomach and moaning about the heat. She looked enormous in her maternity nightgown. My mother was reading the obituaries in the *Plain Dealer,* and Grandma was nursing her cup of coffee.

"Jonathan's mother thinks it's going to be a boy," Caroline said.

My mother looked up from the paper. "Based on what?"

"The way I'm carrying," Caroline said. "See the way it's all in the front?" She stood up and showed us how from the back you could hardly tell she was pregnant.

"That's an old wives' tale," my mother said.

"What do you think it's going to be?"

"How would I know?" my mother said.

"Obviously, you wouldn't know, but maybe you'd venture a guess, just for the fun of it."

"What's the point?"

"Forget it," Caroline said. "There doesn't always have to be a point to everything. Some things can just be fun." Caroline was always getting angry with my mother for the wrong reasons. She got up from the table, put her breakfast dishes in the sink, and hesitated a minute before saying, "I need a paper plate and plastic silverware for Jonathan."

"I'll get it," my mother said. "I have a special cupboard for all of Jonathan's equipment." There was a certain kind of energy in my mother's voice all of a sudden, as if she were finally being called upon to do something she *could* do, accommodating other people's needs instead of having to guess the sex of Caroline's baby and trying to be someone she most certainly wasn't. She took out of the cupboard twelve little boxes of cereal. "This way Jonathan can have a selection," she said, "and he doesn't even have to use a bowl. He can just pour the milk right into the cereal box." My mother never did things like buy twelve-packs of cereal in order to give a person a selection, but I guess she wanted Jonathan to feel at home. I suppose his mother was always buying twelve of everything.

"Oh, okay," Caroline said.

"How about, thank you?" I said.

"Why don't you mind your own business, Jane?"

"Mom goes to the trouble of getting twelve boxes of cereal for Jonathan to choose from, and you say 'oh, okay'? I mean, what do you want her to do? Go out and get new pots and pans so she can make him French toast?"

"Bug off," Caroline said. "Stop acting like you have the exclusive on sensitivity."

I poured a cup of coffee for myself, and sat down at the table next to Grandma. She was just watching all of us do our thing, as if she were there in body but not in mind. Compared to your soul mate dying, I suppose our little arguments didn't amount to much.

"Good morning," my mother said when Jonathan walked in, getting up to show him his cereal selection. He was so innocent-looking, his little yarmulke perched on his head with two bobby pins, his blue and white Columbia College T-shirt, it was hard to imagine him going down on Caroline. Maybe he didn't go down on her, though, if he was as religious as he appeared to be. When they were engaged, he and Caroline had to take this marital relations class, and Caroline told me that one of the things the rabbis taught was that the husband wasn't allowed even to look at the vagina, because the vagina was the most sacred part of the human body. Leave it to the rabbis to give that kind of backhanded compliment. All of a sudden, the vagina's the most sacred part of the body. How convenient. Maybe the rabbis and Sigmund Freud should have gotten together to get their stories straight. I mean, if the vagina was so damned sacred, why would women want a penis? Caroline, by the way, also mentioned that she didn't know of any laws against blow jobs, though the teacher mumbled something about not wasting the man's seed.

"I think I'll go with the Frosted Flakes," Jonathan said, and my mother opened the box for him and even poured his milk. Then she gave him a plastic tablespoon and said, "How's that? It's not scrambled eggs, but it's the best we can do under the circumstances."

"It's better than scrambled eggs," Jonathan said. Where did he learn to be so goddammed charming, I thought, but then I looked at his hair and noticed he had a little dandruff problem. Eddie's got great hair, I thought.

"What do you have planned for today?" my mother said. "We're so flattered that you're using your vacation time to come to Cleveland; we have to make sure you get to see the sights."

"Why are we so flattered?" I said. "What's wrong with Cleveland?"

"Some people might have chosen Hawaii or Paris for vacation," Caroline said. "That's what's wrong with Cleveland."

"Then go to Hawaii or Paris. Who asked you to come to Cleveland?" I said.

"Not this again," she said and she looked at Jonathan as though my immaturity were a frequent subject of conversation between them. I started getting that old ache in my throat, the kind that comes when you're about to cry, so I just listened as they discussed all the things they were going to do. They'd walk around University Circle and look around the Case campus, they'd get tickets for the Cleveland Orchestra, they'd go to the art museum. Then tomorrow they'd drive in the other direction, out to Chagrin Falls and maybe as far as Amish country.

"They have this great soft ice cream in Chagrin Falls," Caroline said. "We'll have to stop there."

"It's not kosher," I said, as the ache in my throat began to subside.

"It doesn't matter," Caroline said. "It's just ice cream."

I looked at Jonathan for his confirmation of this strange new fact. "It's not cooked," he said. "I eat things that aren't cooked, you know, cold things, like salads or ice cream, even in nonkosher places."

"How come you're allowed to do that?" I said.

He shrugged. "You got me." He laughed. "I've done it for so long I don't remember how I decided to do it."

Caroline looked at him eating his cereal and rubbed the back of his slightly dandruffy head in this kind of loving way I'd never seen in her before. She didn't even seem to notice his dandruff problem. "Isn't he adorable?" she said.

He wasn't bad, I had to admit, but even Caroline's mouth dropped open a little when my father walked in. I mean, *he* was handsome.

He had on a freshly polished pair of black wing tips, a pinstripe suit that was perfectly tailored to his slim body, and a bowtie with his initials on it. He had a close shave, unlike Jonathan, who always looked as if he'd sort of shaved but not really.

"Good morning, everybody," he said. Then he sort of turned and posed, as if he were making fun of a model for men's clothes. "How do I look?"

"Fantastic," Caroline and I both said. Caroline, Miss Non-materialistic, Religious Zionist, wasn't exactly repulsed by the way my father dressed. In fact, you might say she wouldn't have minded if Jonathan looked a little more dapper.

"Fantastic," my father repeated, and chuckled as if we were just his silly admiring daughters, people with no objectivity. Not that he minded.

"Lip?" he said to my mother.

"I think you know how you look," she said, and she went back to the paper. She was always angry with him these days, even when he didn't do anything to make her angry. It was as if she'd decided to be angry for all the things he'd ever done, things she didn't used to let herself be bothered by but for some reason had decided now was the time to catch up. He knew she was angry, and he tried to charm her in all the ways he used to be able to, but she wasn't budging. She was serious about this, and it didn't help that he looked so good while she sat there in her old bathrobe, her lower lip almost raw from the way she gnawed at it, her fingernails even worse.

"I wish Mom wouldn't be so mean to Dad," I'd said to Caroline the night before, after Jonathan had gone to bed.

"Mom mean to Dad? That's a good one."

"You know what I mean. She's trying to prove something, but pretty soon, he's going to blow up."

"So, let him. It's about time she stood up for herself."

"Oh, so now you're against him too?"

"I'm not against him. I just think we've all been tiptoeing around him for too many years, hoping to stop him from ex-ploding, and for some reason Mom got tired of doing that. Maybe he'll see that he has to change."

"He's not going to change," I said. "He's got too much pride."

"Then that's just too bad. She's been living under his thumb for too long. I knew there was a feminist lurking around in her somewhere."

Whatever happened to the feminist lurking around in you, I wanted to ask my big pregnant Barnard graduate sister who used to talk about becoming a lawyer but now sat around instead waiting for her baby? This is a new one, I thought: Caroline living vicariously through my mother.

Willy ran through the kitchen and practically through the

screen door in his hurry to make the bus to soccer day camp. He was wearing his green and white soccer outfit. Everybody called out after him to have a good day, and he turned around and smiled, so happy was he to be acknowledged. We, of course, were equally happy to have him out of our hair, so we could get on with the business of forgetting he existed.

It's true; we were always forgetting about Willy. On Mother's Day, Caroline or I would pick out a gift from all of us, and forget to sign Willy's name. Or we'd forget to save a place for him, like at Caroline's wedding reception; my father had to go and take a place setting and a chair from another table before Willy noticed that we'd forgotten to include him as a member of our family. Naturally, I suspected that forgetting about Willy the way we did had something to do with wanting to forget the roles we played in shaping him—at least that was true in my case. And it didn't hurt that for the last three years, he'd only been around to remind us of his existence during the summer.

The thing is, whenever Willy was at school, six hundred miles away, I would think of how I wanted to make things up to him, how I wanted to talk to him and let him know I thought about him. After all, in my opinion, to know someone is thinking about you makes all the difference in the world when you're feeling lonely. But then when he was right there under the same roof with me, I could barely even have a conversation with him, let alone make things up to him. This may not sound very profound, but talking to Willy irritated the hell out of me, the way he lied, the way he blamed everyone but himself for the things that happened to him, whether the thing was getting a lower grade than he *should* have gotten, or missing a flight that was *supposed* to have left an hour later. "The teacher never told us" was the most frequent way he started a sentence, and "I knew you wouldn't believe me" his most frequent refrain.

Sometimes, it just didn't matter that I knew Willy was a

soul so lost and in pain he could barely hold his head up; sometimes it didn't even matter that I thought I was the *reason* he was lost. Sometimes, all that mattered was that Paul Caplan, who had come to Willy's thirteenth birthday party in June, was everything Willy was not: articulate, honest, and most of all, undamaged by me. Could I help it that sometimes I even thought we would all have been better off had Willy never been born?

When I got to work Thursday morning, there was a note taped to my typewriter from Dr. Stevens. "See me," it said. See me, I thought. What could that mean?

At first I was worried, trying to remember whether I'd done something wrong. Had I said something to his secretary Barbara that had gotten back to him? She didn't know I was his former patient, but she'd once caught me staring at him in the Xerox room, and I guess it was rather obvious how I felt about him because after that, she started coming to me with little pieces of information about him, like what he ate for lunch (salami on whole wheat) or what his wife's name was (Susan). She didn't know that every time she told me something about him my heart would skip a beat, or maybe she did. She was the kind of person who liked to stir up trouble, I guess because her own life was so dismal; she was about a hundred years old, never married, no children, and still living with her mother.

One time, she told me about how Dr. Stevens had been flirting with Dr. Lanz, the one female psychiatrist in the office, the one woman in the whole joint who wasn't there to babysit the male psychiatrists (and a real witch, I might add; why was it that the *one* woman in the office who was in a top position was even more patronizing to the rest of us women than the men were?). Barbara told me she could just *feel* the sexual tension between them. Frankly, it was hard to imagine Barbara, Miss

Stiff Hairspray, feeling anything sexual; nevertheless, that night I'd gone home so depressed I could barely come to the phone when Eddie called. The next night, I practically attacked Eddie, and we performed sixty-nine on my basement floor while I pretended he was Dr. Stevens and I was Dr. Lanz.

I took Dr. Stevens's note and stuck it into my purse, then walked to the bathroom to put on some lip gloss and blush. I brushed my hair in front of the mirror and then casually walked around the corner to his office. He was sitting behind his desk looking down at some papers, so I knocked on his open door.

"Hi, Jane," he said. "Come in."

"Should I close the door?"

"What? No."

I hadn't been inside his office since the last time I'd been on his couch making some kind of confession or other. He still had the same old plants sitting on his phone table, and a funny little statue on the shelf above his chair. I remembered how he used to sit in that chair, his legs crossed in that sexy, adult way that important men have. His wood-stained bookshelves were lined by Freud's books, so substantial-looking they'd always made me want to throw myself at Dr. Freud's or Dr. Stevens's feet and say, "Save me! Take care of me! Let me follow you around! Let me climb into your briefcase!" There was an over-sized box of tissues sitting on the table behind the couch, and when I was his patient, Dr. Stevens always covered the pillow with a fresh one before I put my head down. His air-conditioner was blowing freezing cold air the way it always did in the summers; I'd never seen him sweat.

"Have a seat," he said, but he pointed to the chair next to his desk, not to the couch.

"I got your note," I said. I was shivering and sweating at the same time I was so nervous. Was he going to ask me out to dinner? To a movie? Was he going to beg me not to get married? Was he going to tell me he would leave his wife if I'd marry him?

"I wanted to ask a favor of you," he said. "My secretary is going to be away next week; her mother has to have gall bladder surgery or some such, and Dr. Rimer said you might be able to take over some of the typing so we don't have to hire a temp."

"Oh, I see," I said, though the only thing I saw was what a fool I was. I felt as if I'd had the wind knocked out of me, as if I'd been punched in the stomach. I felt the same way I'd felt when I'd gotten a chorus part in *Gypsy* and then found out you didn't even have to *audition* to get a part in the chorus.

"He says you're a great typist," Dr. Stevens continued, oblivious to my mental state. "Really fast." He smiled at me, as if he could butter me up by complimenting my typing. I was cursing that damned typing class I took in high school; it just might have been the root of all my problems. If I hadn't taken that, maybe I would have gone to college.

"Well, I'm pretty busy these days," I said. "Dr. Rimer dictates a lot of letters, you know. And he's got this research paper I'm putting on the word processor."

"Okay," he said. He looked sort of crestfallen, like it had never even occurred to him that I might say no to any request he made of me. "I just thought I'd ask."

Naturally, I couldn't stand even a second of his being unhappy with me. I mean, God forbid he should be mad at me even if I was mad at him. "I might have a little more time next week," I said.

"That'd be great," he said. "I'll try to keep it to a minimum."

After my meeting with Dr. Stevens, I went to the bathroom again, even though Rena the receptionist stopped me in the hall to say Dr. Rimer was asking for me. I went into a stall and sat on the toilet seat.

How could he have led me on like that? I cried to myself. How could he have humiliated me that way? I waited for my eyes to stop boiling over, and when they did, I got myself together and walked back to my desk. After all, I couldn't type if I couldn't see.

When I got back to my desk, I put on my headphones, stepped on the pedal and typed so fast I was transposing characters. I didn't think about Dr. Stevens, I didn't think about all the things Jonathan and Caroline were doing, I didn't even take a lunch break. I only stopped long enough to answer the phone and file my carbons. As fast as Dr. Rimer could dictate was as fast as I typed, and occasionally we collided in the doorway, me bringing him letters to sign, him bringing me cassette tapes to transcribe.

I left the office at five o'clock promptly, my fingers still typing in the air. Clearly, working overtime didn't get me any closer to Dr. Stevens, so I went home. I had a life away from him, I wanted him to know. Two could play his game, I thought, and I grabbed my sunglasses and keys and ran down to the parking lot.

My father was sitting in the study with Jonathan when I got home, giving him the entire history of the temple we belonged to, as if Jonathan were interested just because he was Orthodox. It was depressing to see how my father tried to impress my sister's little pip-squeak husband, how his whole personality changed. He didn't have one temper tantrum the entire time Jonathan was there, as if only Jonathan were worth behaving for, as if he—my good-looking, brilliant, charismatic father—were looking for *Jonathan's* approval. Meanwhile, Jonathan always looked like he was trying to ward off a yawn, and I couldn't stand to see how unimpressed he was by my father. I mean, he wasn't disrespectful or anything. It was just that you could tell he wasn't going to go around quoting his wisdom or anything, the way I did, the way Caroline used to. Everybody had always thought my father's job was the most important job around; he ran a hospital, and he was in charge of doctors and nurses, and most important, money. But then Jonathan came into the family, and he *was* a doctor, and suddenly it seemed that all my father knew how to do was pay the bills, while Jonathan went around saving lives.

We all wanted to go over and have dinner at the kosher pizza place, even my father, but my mother was still in a bad mood, and without her, Dad wouldn't go. Even Grandma, who was just getting settled in her new apartment, called to say she'd meet us there. But when she heard that my parents weren't coming, she changed her mind.

Jonathan drove, and Caroline sat next to him, while Willy and I sat in the back seat. Eddie said he had to study for one of his systems exams, and I wasn't sorry he couldn't come. He paled next to Jonathan and made it harder for me to go on being engaged to him.

I always started feeling better about life the further away we got from our house and our neighborhood. I knew that my parents had only been trying to improve our life-style by moving out to Pepper Pike, but I'd never felt right there. The pizza place was in our old Cleveland Heights neighborhood, a neighborhood that was now a combination of religious Jews and middle-class blacks. I'm not sure which group my family had been trying to move away from.

"See that?" Caroline was saying to Jonathan as we drove down Taylor Road. "That's an old Orthodox synagogue, and there's the kosher butcher, and there's the Hebrew Academy." I couldn't believe it; Caroline used to turn up her nose at this street in the old days. Now she was proud of it, bragging about Cleveland as if it were the Jewish center of the universe. Don't get me wrong; I was glad. I started thinking that maybe Caroline missed us so much she wanted to move back here, and so she was trying to convince Jonathan of its attractiveness.

We got a table in the pizza place, though it wasn't easy. There were little kids running around the place, holding pizza or falafel, their yarmulkes flying off their heads, their mothers calling after them. "Yankele! Shmulik! Yakovele!" Jonathan, who was ordinarily about as assertive as a lamb, went right up to the counter to order a pizza, as if he'd been in this restaurant a thousand times before. The four of us shared a pizza, and it was the first time during their visit that Jonathan actually seemed to eat with gusto, taking big bites and gobbling them up as if he hadn't eaten in a week. Every time he ate something in our house, even the cereal, he seemed to be trying, but failing, to convince himself that it was the right thing to do, that it was better to eat in a nonkosher home than to offend his wife's parents.

"I wanted pepperoni," Willy said as he bit into his second plain piece. He wasn't interested in peppers or onions or mushrooms; he was only thirteen, after all.

"They don't make pepperoni here," Caroline said.

"That's too bad," he said. "What about sausage?"

"No, they don't make sausage either."

"Poor Willy," I said. "He just wants a regular pizza."

At this, Willy put his head down on my shoulder and started playing with my hair. That was the problem with Willy; you couldn't be nice to him without running the risk he'd start molesting you. At least *I* couldn't.

"What are you going to name your baby?" Willy said.

"We can't really talk about it," Caroline said. "It brings bad luck."

"Why does it bring bad luck?" I said.

"It's presumptuous to assume that we're going to have a healthy, living baby before we actually have one. Right, Jonathan?"

Jonathan's mouth was full, but he nodded. How come *I* knew their baby would be just fine? Caroline had married into a family where bad things never happened, babies were always born healthy and full term and at least fifty percent of the time, male, since it seemed males were really the only ones who counted to Orthodox Jews.

When we were done, we walked over to Cain Park to see if anything was going on. Jonathan and Caroline walked arm in arm, and I could hear Caroline apologizing for the fact that Cain Park was no Central Park. Willy stuck his arm in mine and instead of immediately yanking my arm away from his the way I usually did, I tried to be reasonable and think about whether I'd think it was weird if any other brother and sister were walking like that, or whether it was only weird because it was Willy and me. I tried to give Willy the benefit of the doubt, and once or twice I even patted his head affectionately with my other hand.

I felt nostalgic, walking through the park, lit up by the old-fashioned street lamps, though for what I didn't know. It was a warm, balmy night, and I suppose I was nostalgic for the feeling of being in love, not that I ever had been, except with Dr. Stevens. Eddie and I rarely took walks through the park; it wasn't purposeful enough for Eddie, who liked to have a destination in mind.

We hadn't even gotten to the Cain Park amphitheatre when Caroline stopped and said she had to head back. "It's these shooting pains in my legs," she said, stooping over.

"Are you all right?" Jonathan put his arm around her

hunched back and she sort of shook him off and straightened out. I think he was getting on her nerves.

"It's hard to be pregnant in July," she said. "I want this baby out of me already. Can you understand that?"

Jonathan nodded, looking down, and in that split second I thought I understood that she hadn't wanted to be pregnant now in the first place, and that he would be apologizing in some way for the rest of his life.

The next day was Friday, and as usual, I was longing for five o'clock, for the weekend, and at the same time depressed at the thought of being away from Dr. Stevens for two days. It's not like I even *saw* him a lot at the office; sometimes I only caught a glimpse of him as he was walking out the door, but I felt safe just knowing he was *there*.

Usually my father and I arrived home from work at around the same time, and my mother'd have dinner ready. But when I got home that Friday night, I was informed that dinner wouldn't be served until after sundown, when Jonathan and Caroline returned from Sabbath services at our temple. I could hardly believe that Jonathan had agreed to go to a place where the women congregants were just as likely to wear yarmulkes as the men.

"Dinner at nine o'clock?" Willy said, as if it were the most outlandish thing he'd ever heard. "But I'm hungry now." Caroline sort of rolled her eyes and said that all food tasted better when it was sanctified. Jonathan made fun of her and said he'd turned her into a religious monster, and then told Willy he was pretty hungry too. Jonathan had a way of making even Willy feel good.

My mother and I watched Caroline light the candles and waited for her to start singing the blessing so we could sing along. In the old days, before Rosh Hashanah or Yom Kippur, my mother and Caroline and I used to light the candles and sing the blessing in three-part harmonies. But now Caroline didn't start singing; instead, she made some funny hand motions over the flames, then covered her eyes and whispered what must have been the prayer. My mother, who was trying so hard to do everything right, went back into the kitchen, checking again to see that the wine had the right label for kosherness on it, and that the two loaves of challah hadn't been sliced at the bakery. Caroline had given her tons of instructions on how to make Friday night dinner the way her mother-in-law did, and my mother had already had to go back to the store once to exchange the cake she'd bought for one that contained no butter or milk.

"I think Mom wanted to sing the prayer with you," I said to Caroline when she stepped away from the candles.

"You're not supposed to sing it out loud with other people," Caroline said. "We were doing it wrong all those years."

"Who told you that? God?"

Caroline ignored my question. "Why don't you come to shul with Jonathan and me?" she said.

"What's in it for you?"

"I just think it would be fun," she said, and that was reason enough for me. Not even *I* was paranoid enough to think she was just proselytizing. Besides, what else was I going to do? I took off my work clothes and changed into a cotton sundress and a pair of sandals. Caroline put on a white net beret, and as the three of us started walking out the door, my father said, "Maybe I'll join you."

"That'd be great, Dad," I said, trying without success to ignore the fact that he was looking me up and down with disapproval. "I'll even change my clothes," I said.

"Well, I don't know," he said.

"Come on, Dad," Caroline said.

"Should I?"

"Yes!"

"Or maybe I should stay here and watch the news."

"Come on, Dad," Caroline said again. She had her impatient tone on, and I could tell she was busily making a mental comparison of her father and her father-in-law, and her father-in-law was winning.

I ran up to my room to change my clothes, and before I knew it, standing there in my closet, frantically flipping through all my clothes, I felt tears streaming down my face. I didn't *own* anything my father would like, he *always* hated the way I looked, I couldn't have done anything to improve my situation if I had tried! All of a sudden, I felt the same way I'd felt when I was in the second grade, when my teacher had hit me on the back for being unable to cut out a valentine from a folded piece of red construction paper.

"Jane, come on!" Caroline called from downstairs.

"I'm not coming!" I called back, trying to disguise the upset in my voice.

The next thing I heard were Caroline's heavy footsteps trudging up the stairs. "Come on, would you?" she said, breathless, as she reached the top of the landing.

"Look at me," I said. "I have nothing else to wear, and Dad hates the way I look."

"Still trying to make Daddy happy?" she said, grabbing my arm and dragging me downstairs with her. "Haven't you grown out of that yet?"

"I guess not," I said, but Caroline just kept pulling me, and we practically had to run to catch up with Jonathan and my father, who had already started walking.

Our temple was only about half a mile away. It was the suburban branch for Jews like us who rarely frequented the neighborhood where the original branch was located, unless we happened to be going to the art museum or the symphony or something cultural like that; we'd never go that far just to pray. But even though the suburban branch was so close, we'd never even considered walking there before, not even on Yom Kippur. It wasn't like New York, where there were sidewalks for walking. The four of us had to walk single file along the skinny streets, occasionally having to step up onto the curb when there were cars coming in both directions. I could only imagine how strange we looked in our neighborhood, Jonathan in his yarmulke and his tzitzit hanging outside of his pants, Caroline seven months pregnant, the four of us actually *walking* somewhere. Nobody ever walked anywhere where we lived; the nearest drugstore was three miles away.

"Your strap is showing," my father said from behind me. I tucked my bra strap under my sundress and continued walking. "It's showing again," he said about two seconds later. "You look like a common washerwoman."

I tucked it in again, though I don't know why I bothered; it would just keep coming out. Besides, why couldn't my father just be like other fathers for once in his life and pretend he didn't notice what wasn't his business to notice, let alone comment on? I didn't even like the idea of his knowing I *wore* a bra, let alone have him talk about it.

"It's showing again," he said. "Why can't you do something about it? You should never wear a dress like that!"

"What's the big deal?" I said, finally turning around to look at him, pretending I was just as unflappable as I could be, pretending I wasn't the person who'd been crying ten minutes before over how awful I looked.

"Do you see *my* underwear sticking out?" he said.

"To my knowledge, you don't wear a bra," I said.

Even he had to laugh. "My underpants don't show."

"Neither do mine," I said. "And I don't see you telling Jonathan up ahead there that his undershirt is sticking out."

"That's different," he said. "But you do have a point, Jane. Except it's not an undershirt; he leaves his tzitzit out for religious reasons." Like it was okay for your underwear to stick out as long as it did so for religious reasons! There he went again, making allowances for Jonathan that he'd never make for anyone else. I tucked in my strap again and held my fingers there for a while so it wouldn't slip out, but finally I gave up.

When we arrived, my father held the heavy door open for us. Rabbi Wax seemed so glad to see people, he came rushing over to us saying "Shabbat Shalom!" My father proudly introduced Jonathan, and then led us into the sanctuary, where there were about twelve people. First he took us to a row of seats in the back, but then he changed his mind several times, like we were going to the movies or something, and we finally ended up in the second row. He kept pointing out the window at the trees, as if Jonathan preferred one house of worship over another depending on what you could see through the windows. Caroline was busy adjusting her hat, and she looked just like one of those women she and I used to make fun of when we had to sit through those interminable High Holiday services. You could tell she didn't remember ever having done something like that.

"Did you smuggle in your tic-tac-toe pad?" I whispered to her, joking.

"Oh, yeah," Caroline said, "remember how we used to play on Yom Kippur? I was always x's."

"I actually always liked Yom Kippur," I said. "Sometimes it felt good to repent."

"Repent? All I remember about Yom Kippur was the ride home from shul, Mom and Dad both in the worst moods. Neither of them was at their best on an empty stomach. I remember before we were old enough to fast, Mom always hated having to serve us lunch."

Like Yom Kippur at the Klausners was just one big spiritual

ecstasy. Like Orthodox people didn't get hungry when they fasted.

We stood up for the opening hymn "L'cha Dodi," which the cantor sang into the microphone so he wouldn't be entirely drowned out by the choir and the organ. I hated that stupid organ, it was so embarrassing; the music always sounded like it belonged in an amusement park, on a merry-go-round.

My father sang along loudly, getting some of the words wrong and shifting back and forth a little as if he were having a religious experience. Jonathan was sort of moving around, singing occasionally, but mostly he seemed bored. Here we were doing this for him, and he was bored.

Rabbi Wax announced the page number for responsive reading, but only my father and I joined in. Jonathan and Caroline just sat there quietly, as if they were too good for the common herd.

"You don't know English anymore?" I whispered to Caroline.

"It's all a show here," she said. "Rabbi Wax is more like a performer than a rabbi."

"Geez, Caroline." It was really annoying to hear Caroline's new take on things; the changes in her seemed too sudden to be genuine. Nevertheless, I had to admit I agreed with her about Rabbi Wax, though probably for different reasons. She probably objected to his "performance" on a religious basis; I objected because I couldn't stand the cloying and ingratiating way he conducted the service, the way he so pointedly replaced the word "mankind" with the word "humankind" when he was reading from the prayer book, the way he replaced the word "man" with the word "person." I mean, I would have appreciated his efforts at egalitarianism if they hadn't seemed so contrived for his audience; I just couldn't shake the feeling that at home, his wife was still the "person" who did all the shit work.

I looked out the sanctuary windows, and I could see why my father would be more moved by the view here than by the service. There had to be a God if nature could be so beautiful. The trees were sort of swaying in the summer breeze, and the sun was setting behind them.

When it came time for the silent prayer, I closed my prayer book and made up my own prayers. I prayed that Caroline's baby would be born healthy, that my parents would get along better, that Willy would be okay one day, that Eddie would break our engagement, that nothing bad would ever happen to Dr. Stevens, that Grandpa wasn't being punished for having been cremated, that Grandma would be cheerful again, that I would be happy. Then I opened up my prayer book again and read the last paragraph of the silent prayer, begging God to guard my tongue from evil. Talking about people behind their backs was one of my biggest faults, as you can probably tell, so I always made sure to include the part about guarding my tongue, even if I started backstabbing again about five minutes later.

At the end of the service, Rabbi Wax announced that Saturday morning services would begin at ten-thirty, and then the choir broke out into a new "Adon Olam" I'd never heard. They were always coming up with new melodies, as if that were the way to attract young people. I had to admit it was a pretty stupid tactic.

"Shabbat Shalom," my father said and kissed me and Caroline, then shook Jonathan's hand. As we were walking out of the sanctuary, I felt a tap on my shoulder and instinctively reached up to see if it was my father alerting me to that damned strap showing again. But it wasn't, it was Lenny Levitsky, though he didn't look anything like he had at Camp Ben-Gurion three summers before. We were C.I.T.'s there and that's where he introduced me to my first orgasm. Back then, Lenny had long hair which he tied up with a bandana, and a scraggly beard. "I have a treat for you," he'd said to me one night when we were lying on his bed in the boys' cabin. The campers were at free swim, and he slithered down my body, kissing me all the way from my face down my stomach and not stopping there.

"Lenny?" I said. His hair was short and cut close to his head, and he didn't have a beard anymore. He was wearing a knit yarmulke like the one Jonathan wore.

"Shabbat Shalom," he said.

"What are you doing here?" I said. "You don't believe in God."

"Actually, I always believed in God," he said. "I just didn't believe in religion."

"You believed in Kahlil Gibran," I said, remembering all the hours we spent reading *The Prophet* together.

"My father died last year," he said. "After that, I had to come here to say kaddish for him. Now I just come because I like it."

"I'm sorry about your father," I said, but I was beginning to think the whole damned world was going crazy, becoming religious fanatics. If Lenny Levitsky was wearing a knit yarmulke, anything was possible.

"Maybe we could get together sometime," he said. "I see your sister has become religious—"

"She's not religious," I said. "She just married someone who is."

"Whatever," he said. "But I guess you're no stranger to it. There are so few people our age who can appreciate what ritual does for your life."

"Why do you come to this synagogue if you're so religious?" I said. "This is a Reform temple, you know."

"Of course I know, but this is where my father always davened, and I've become very close with Rabbi Wax. Pretty soon I'm sure I'll graduate to an Orthodox shul."

As we walked out Lenny put his fingers to his mouth and then to the mezuzah on the door. "I'll give you a call *Motzei Shabbat*," he said, and then as if I were an idiot or something, he said, "Saturday night, that is." He walked off in the opposite direction, and I realized he was going to walk all the way to his house, which wasn't exactly in the neighborhood.

Our walk back wasn't bad, though it was still about a thousand degrees, even without the sun. There were practically no cars at this hour, so instead of walking single file, my father said we could walk in pairs. It didn't matter that I was nineteen, Caroline was twenty-three, and Jonathan was twenty-six; we would have walked single-file if my father had told us to. My father and Caroline walked in front, Jonathan and I behind them.

"Are you hoping for a boy or a girl?" I said, just for the sake of conversation. Jonathan wasn't exactly Mr. Conversationalist.

"A girl," he said.

"I thought girls don't count to Orthodox people."

"That's why I don't tell too many people I want a girl." He smiled, like this was just between me and him. He looked a little like Dr. Stevens when he smiled, around the eyes. Then again, anyone I'd ever had a crush on in the last three years had looked a little like Dr. Stevens. And the thing is, none of the people who looked a little like Dr. Stevens looked anything like each other. Take the actors Jimmy Smits and Raul Julia—no resemblance whatsoever, and yet each on separate occasions has looked like Dr. Stevens. Of course, each one of them was probably taken—Jonathan and Dr. Stevens for sure, and Raul Julia too, according to a feature article I read once in the Sunday *Plain Dealer*.

By the time we got home, Caroline looked like she'd never walk again, no matter how religious she was. Grandma and my mother and Willy were all sitting in the dining room, waiting for us. My mother had put the white holiday tablecloth on the table, which would have been beautiful if it hadn't been for the paper plates and plastic foam cups sitting on top of it.

"What's this?" my father said.

"What does it look like?" my mother said. I was beginning to long for the old days when my mother cared enough about pleasing my father that she'd try to convince him that he actually liked paper plates better than china.

"This is how we eat on Friday night?"

"All of a sudden Friday night is so special?" my mother said. "Don't start acting like you're someone you're not."

"She had to use paper plates, Dad," Caroline said. "For Jonathan."

Jonathan was examining the wine, meanwhile, as if he were really intrigued by it or something and had never seen a bottle of Carmel Chenin Blanc before. Willy was slouched over in his chair, and Grandma was fingering the long beads that she wore around her neck. Finally, my father looked at Jonathan and said, "Why don't you do the honors?" I wondered whether it was as obvious to everyone else as it was to me that my father hadn't said the blessing over the wine in so long he wouldn't have remembered the words.

"Are you sure?" Jonathan said.

"Absolutely."

Jonathan said the prayer, and then passed around the foam cup he'd filled with wine for all of us to taste. When everyone was done, Jonathan looked at my father and almost as if apologizing, he said, "We're just going to wash." He and Caroline got up from the table and went into the kitchen. When they came back, Caroline held the two loaves of challah together and said the blessing. Then she sliced one of them up, while my mother and I looked at one another and smiled. After she salted it, she passed a piece of challah to everyone, and Grandma said what the rest of us were thinking. "Did you really need to cut up the whole thing? Such good bread. It'll just get stale now."

"Part of the spirit of Shabbat," Caroline said, as she was chewing, "is to overdo it. So there'll be a little left over. No big deal."

Clearly, Caroline didn't know my family anymore. It *was* a big deal to waste food, and just because her mother-in-law served vats of food that never got eaten, our mother didn't. The truth was, it didn't matter; my mother would just use the leftover bread to feed the birds outside the kitchen window, or to make bread crumbs the next day when the bread was dry enough.

"What'd you think of the services, Jonathan?" my mother asked.

"Very nice," he said. "I liked being able to sit with my wife. I've never done that before."

"That's what you *liked*?" my father said. "That's the only good thing about being Orthodox, you don't have to sit with your wife." Everybody laughed at my father's stupid joke, except for my mother, who didn't seem to think it was a stupid joke.

"Guess who I saw?" I said. "My old boyfriend Lenny Levitsky."

"That's who that was?" my father said. "Nice-looking boy. He used to look awful."

"Does he still have that terrible chin?" my mother said.

"No," I said. "He's got a great chin now."

Willy giggled. "What a stupid question, Mom," he said, and I looked over at him in surprise. It *was* a stupid question, and though it may not sound like much to anybody else, to me

Willy's comment was incredibly significant. To me it meant that I wasn't alone in the way I saw my mother, as always focusing on the detail that had the least to do with anything. I mean, if she hadn't been so busy noticing Lenny Levitsky's chin when I was sixteen, perhaps she would have noticed that I was having oral sex with him on her basement floor because it was the only thing that made me forget about how miserable I felt.

"What was Lenny Levitsky doing in a synagogue?" Caroline said. "Didn't he used to be a Buddhist or something?"

"You should talk," I said, and everybody cracked up, even Grandma. "It seems like everybody who used to be something else is an Orthodox Jew now," I said.

"I've always been an Orthodox Jew," Jonathan said, and you could tell that that was true. He didn't have to kiss every door he walked through or put tape over the lights on the Sabbath in order to prove it either.

After dessert—a dry, tasteless honeycake from the kosher bakery, which we complimented as if my mother'd made it herself—Caroline brought out the little booklets from her wedding which contained all the blessings, and we began to sing the grace after meals. Everyone knew the first paragraph, and we harmonized and sang loudly. Even my mother joined in, though she was becoming more of an atheist every day. When we finished the paragraph, only Jonathan and Caroline continued, and you could tell they were trying to hurry up so that the rest of us wouldn't feel so left out.

After dinner, everybody congregated in the kitchen. Willy was rummaging through the freezer for a "real" dessert, my father was standing at the sink, waiting for the water to get cold. Caroline and Jonathan were smooching in front of the dishwasher. Grandma and I just stood in the doorway, watching.

"Maybe you all could go into another room," my mother finally said to no one in particular, as she made her way around us, clearing the table, throwing the paper plates in the trash, transferring the leftover food into plastic containers.

My father smooshed the Dixie cup in his hand and said he didn't like the tone in her voice, then he stormed off into the living room, and I followed him.

"Go help Mom in the kitchen," he said, as if *I* was the one who'd just acted like an infant, as if *he* couldn't sweep the floor as well as I could. "You kids are spoiled rotten."

"You're the one—" I started, but the look in his eyes stopped me. It wasn't that I was afraid he was going to hit me, but sometimes the things he said made me feel worse than being hit. Oh well, I thought, so much for standing up to him, and I went to help my mother in the kitchen.

Dad was still in a foul mood later when Eddie came over and I brought him in to say hello, but once his perfect son-in-law Jonathan joined us all in the living room, Dad managed to keep it under wraps.

Eddie and Jonathan shook hands as I introduced them. Eddie smelled like he'd just poured a whole bottle of cologne over his head, while Jonathan smelled like he needed a shower; nevertheless, I couldn't help wishing Jonathan were the one who was my fiancé.

"How's your computer?" my father asked Eddie.

"I'm using it religiously," Eddie said and laughed. Why was it that non-Orthodox Jews said such stupid things in front of Orthodox ones? Jonathan just smiled, but you could tell he'd heard "religious" puns like that about a million times before.

"Mazel tov on your engagement," Jonathan said. Caroline was standing with her back to his stomach, her head against his shoulder. Jonathan's arms came around her stomach and rested there. "Being married is great."

"All the sex you want, right?" Eddie said, and sort of winked at Jonathan. Like making a sex joke was going to earn him some points with Jonathan, Mr. Pure, or my father, Mr. Pretending to Be Pure in Front of Jonathan.

My father gave me a dirty look, but Willy laughed, as if he appreciated Eddie's sense of humor, as if he even knew what sex was, the mere idea of which made me squirm. I didn't *want* him to know what sex was, I didn't *want* him to have sexual feelings, because once he did, he might understand what drove me to do what I did to him all those years ago, when I was even younger than he was now. I didn't want him even to *remember* what happened back then, let alone understand *why* it happened.

"Let's go," I said to Eddie. Willy reached up and cupped his hand around my ear, whispering a request to come with us. Oh why not, I thought, it's a perfect way to get out of having to be alone with Eddie. So I said sure, and Eddie just looked at me, and then he said why didn't we go play miniature golf. Jonathan went to sit on the couch and read the *Plain Dealer;* Caroline gave me a disapproving look which she would probably deny was disapproving, would say was noncommittal. I mean, just because she didn't go out on Friday nights anymore didn't mean the rest of the world had to stay home.

Grandma asked us to drop her off at her new apartment, up the street from the old one, and I went inside with her to make sure her keys worked. The week before, she hadn't been able to get the bottom lock open, and she'd stood in front of her apartment jiggling the key and crying for an hour before the old man next door heard her and came out and opened it.

"Don't marry that Eddie if you don't love him," she said to me after we'd gotten her door open. "If you do, you'll miss an awful lot. Both of you will." She reached up and kissed me.

"I love you, Grandma," I said. I don't usually say things like that, but for some reason, I was feeling like I desperately needed to be close to someone right then. One time, when I was in the eighth grade, I had this English teacher, Mrs. Graham, whom I really loved. In fact, I loved her so much, I was worried I was a lesbian. One day she told my class she'd lost her son in a car accident many years before. When I got home from school that day, I felt so sad, like *I'd* been the one whose son had died, that I called my father in his office, something I usually did only in emergencies, and told him I loved him. I don't know why I did it, I just felt so lost.

The miniature golf course was located between a gas station and a parking lot, and across the street from the deserted Mayfield Heights shopping center. We got stuck behind a group of four, two girls wearing halter tops and shorts, and two guys from my high school who were nicknamed the Gearheads because they were always fixing things under their cars. They had skimpy mustaches and greasy blond hair and sharp fingernails. "Hey," they called over to us, and we waved. One of the guys was practically having sex with one of the girls right there on the putt-putt green. The other guy was Wayne Vecchio, and he sort of looked the other way when he saw who it was he was saying "hey" to. In high school, he'd been the stage manager for *Gypsy,* and when I didn't get the part of Gypsy Rose Lee, I was so depressed I went back into the green room with him and gave him a blow job. After that, I hung around sometimes, sitting in the auditorium, listening to the girl who had gotten the part, telling myself her voice wasn't even that great, but I never went to the green room again.

A few weeks later I met Eddie. He was the lighting manager for the play, and sometimes he took me up to his little lighting room. It was much more private than that old green room.

"Your body is just as good as hers," Willy said to me about Wayne Vecchio's girlfriend. "Why don't you ever wear a shirt like the one she's wearing?"

"Yeah," Eddie said, looking over at Willy.

"Willy," I said, "do me a favor, don't look at my body." I couldn't believe this kid, this baby brother of mine, this boy whose dirty diapers I'd helped change! I couldn't believe he was making comments about the type of clothing I should wear to enhance my sexiness! Christ, since when did he notice the way girls looked, and who ever heard of a thirteen-year-old boy talking so knowingly about what made a girl sexually attractive?

"What about me?" Eddie said. "Can I look at your body?"

"No," I said, annoyed at him too. It was a little depressing to see that my nineteen-year-old fiancé and my thirteen-year-old brother shared the same concerns. But even more distressing was the fact that Eddie didn't seem to know how inappropriate it was to make his comment in front of Willy; I mean, did I have to remind him that Willy was just a little boy, that he wasn't one of our peers?

I kept score of the game with the little eraserless pencil, but after a while I stopped trying to be too accurate. Willy was taking about six swings to get the ball in the hole, but every time I told him "six," he'd start a fight with me. "It was only two," he'd say, and finally I decided I didn't give a damn about keeping score if it was going to make him so happy to win for a change. Eddie was actually competing with him, as if this game took any kind of real skill, as if parting with a buck was going to break his bank account or something. I played a half-assed game, and on the last green I just picked up the ball and dropped it into the little hole. This kind of obstacle course just didn't seem worth negotiating, I thought, not compared to the obstacle course of my life.

After the game, as Eddie and I were paying the golf course attendant, I turned around to see that Willy was having a conversation with Wayne Vecchio's girlfriend, who was standing alone on the last green. Willy was laughing and running his fingers through his hair, the girl was smiling.

"Eddie," I said. "Look at Willy."

Eddie put his wallet in his back pocket and turned around to look, then said, "It's not going to be too cute when Wayne Vecchio comes out of the john, or wherever he is, and sees your little brother flirting with his girlfriend."

"My God, Eddie, Willy's a baby, he probably never even heard of the word *flirting*."

"Willy may seem like a baby to you, Jane, but he doesn't look like one, and you don't know how 'grown up' his hormones are either. But Wayne Vecchio knows. In fact, I think I'd better go get Willy right now, before the Gearhead comes back and beats the crap out of him."

I didn't even have a chance to tell Eddie how ridiculous he was being, how we weren't in some kind of John Wayne Western where guys really punched each other out over a girl, how even if we were, nobody would be threatened by Willy, when he was already on his way over to save them. He stood there with the two of them, innocent little Willy and the halter-clad whore, and I couldn't help noticing that Eddie was behaving a little flirtatiously himself. After a few minutes, he and Willy were walking back in my direction, laughing.

"What's so funny?" I asked, as the three of us headed over to the parking lot and got into the car.

"Funny isn't the word," Eddie said, though he and Willy were still cracking up. As we pulled out of the parking lot, Eddie said, "The word for Willy is impressive. Little Willy here has got his method down to a science. He knows how to score."

"Well, I wouldn't say score," Willy said, "I just got her phone number, that's all."

"Her phone number?" I said. "You did not."

"He did," Eddie said, "I saw it. Show her, Willy."

Willy dug a ragged-edged piece of scrap paper out of his

pocket and handed it to me. It had a phone number on it, all right. I laughed.

"Eddie, don't believe everything you see," I said. "Willy is a consummate storyteller; he probably scribbled this meaning-less phone number down himself as soon as he saw the girl and started fantasizing about her."

I reached over my seat to give Willy back his phone num-ber, but he was busy shaking his head and looking out the window. "Damn you, Jane!" he cried to the window. "I'm so sick of the way you treat me, I'm so sick of the way you never believe me. I've been trying so hard not to do those things I used to do, but nobody in our whole stupid family will let me change. Stop the car, Eddie, I'm getting out. Stop the car already!"

"He can't stop the car, Willy," I said, reaching back to grab his arm before he flung the car door open, "he's in the middle of a four-lane boulevard. Calm down now, just calm down." Even as I was saying "calm down," I knew I sounded the way my mother sounded when she was talking to me, more and more rational as I became more and more emotional, more attentive to the way I spoke than to what I was saying; it was strange how you sometimes ended up doing the very same things to others that you most hated having done to you.

Willy shook my hand off his arm, and nobody said any-thing more as Eddie moved into the right-hand lane and then pulled into a Dairy Queen parking lot.

"As long as we're here," Eddie said, "why don't we go inside and have some ice cream?" Poor Eddie, I thought, he just wanted to have a good Friday-night time, and here he was in the middle of something that was no fun at all. To make it up to him, I agreed that ice cream was a good idea, and Willy eventu-ally came in too.

Inside, the three of us sat at a table, eating our Buster Bars in silence. Finally, when I was down to the last nut on mine, I said, "I'm sorry, Willy, if I upset you. But it upsets *me* when I hear you saying things that couldn't possibly be true. Why would a girl my age give her phone number to a little boy?"

"First of all," Willy said, "she's not your age, she's sixteen. Second of all, I'm *not* a little boy, I'm only three years younger than she is."

"You *are* a little boy, Willy, no matter how many hormones you've got."

"God, Jane, you sound just like Mom and Dad, with their whore-moans, or whatever they're called, prostitutes, I guess, I don't even know what they're talking about, I've never even seen a real prostitute—"

"Oh my God, Eddie, he thinks hormones are prostitutes—"

"Go ahead, Jane, make fun of me if you want, but pretty soon this family's not going to have me to use as their guinea pig anymore." Willy hesitated. "Not guinea pig—I mean skate goat—"

"Scapegoat," I said, though I still thought he had the wrong animal.

"Scapegoat, yeah," he said. "Everybody's so used to me doing things wrong that they blame me for everything. But I'm not taking it anymore."

"Okay," I said, "so the girl's sixteen, not nineteen. I still think—"

"Jane," Eddie finally interrupted. "Jane, I saw the girl write down her telephone number for him. I saw her do it. She really did. I was there."

I looked at Willy. He wasn't even gloating, he was just looking down at the table, like he felt sorry for *me*, like he didn't want to embarrass *me*. All of a sudden, I felt so depressed and so lonely, so completely forlorn, I didn't know what to do with myself. I didn't even feel like crying, that's how numb and empty I felt. I stood up from the table to throw my ice cream stick and wrapper into the garbage can. "Are you ready to go?" I said to Eddie.

In the car, Eddie and Willy pretended to discuss the World Series or something, but I knew they were really just trying to smooth things over for me. Imagine, Willy trying to protect me; just what was going on?

When we got home, everybody in the house had already gone to sleep, so Willy plopped himself down in the living room in front of some mind-numbing MTV, and Eddie and I went down to the basement. I didn't want to fool around, but I felt like I owed it to him; we hadn't fooled around much since we had become engaged three months before. I got the blankets from underneath the staircase and dragged them over to the floor behind the furnace. We lay down, and I unzipped his jeans. I could tell you what I did to him, but how many ways are there to describe a regular old hand job? I mean, the truth is, it's probably not that exciting unless you're the recipient.

Then it was my turn, and I have to say this for Eddie; he sure was fair when it came to sexual favors. The only thing was, I realized I didn't really *want* a sexual favor, that there was nothing too sexy about doing something because you felt you had to.

Then, when Eddie started reaching for my breasts, I felt such a surge of rage rise up in me that I thought I was going to choke. What was wrong with me anyway, why did I feel like screaming all of a sudden? I didn't want to hurt Eddie's feelings by removing his hands or telling him to stop, so what I did was I made my rage disappear, something I realized I'd done plenty of times before; what you do is you just turn it into desire. So there I was again, moaning like a maniac, and I guess Eddie— literal-minded guy that he was—took that as the usual sign of pleasure, and increased the pace of his hands.

I didn't even fantasize about Dr. Stevens; it was too painful to fantasize about him or most other things in my life. And then I decided to fantasize about Lenny Levitsky, about the time he said he had a treat for me, and just thinking about it got me so angry all over again, like he'd been doing me some kind of gigantic favor or something, that I started positively gyrating. That's it, I thought, it's easy to turn rage into desire. It occurred to me then that I didn't even remember anymore what real sexual desire felt like—all I'd felt for so long was rage.

I took my time, and when I finally reached that old peak, I wasn't sorry I'd gotten involved in the whole thing after all. That's the thing about an orgasm; unless you're having one, it's hard to remember why anybody bothers, what's so great about it that you'd want to go to all the effort of trying to have another one.

After we'd held each other for a sufficient amount of time, Eddie looked at his watch and went home. I stood in the kitchen eating old graham crackers and peanut butter. They didn't help much; I still felt empty.

Jonathan and my father walked to temple again the next morning, and I was wondering whether my father was going to start making a habit of it or something. Willy was playing basketball by himself in the driveway, and my mother was on the patio in her nightgown putting stale challah in the bird feeder. Caroline was sitting at the kitchen table with a glass of milk, watching Mom. "Isn't that typical?" she said. "Mom is such a good person."

"You make it sound sad being a good person."

"It's not sad," she said. "It's just awfully hard to be close to someone who's so busy being good all the time. She's always getting up in the middle of a conversation to feed the birds or take a snack out to the gardeners. She never just sits."

Of course I agreed with Caroline, I felt the exact same way

about my mother. I wished I could have said so, I wished I could have been as close to Caroline as I was before she got married, but now that she had another mother to compare mine unfavorably to, the last thing I wanted to do was give her more ammunition to take back to New York with her.

Willy came in from outside, took his glass of juice from the refrigerator, sweat rolling down from his hair. He didn't even stop drinking to breathe. When he finished, he refilled the cup and put it back in the refrigerator. "Anyone want to play tetherball?" he said.

"No," Caroline and I said simultaneously.

Willy took a paper towel and wiped off his face and sat down at the table with us. After a minute, Caroline said, "Don't you have any friends your own age?"

"Leave him alone," I said, a little surprised at myself, because I too wished he were like other kids, I too wished he had friends to play with. Nevertheless, after hearing the things he'd said about my family the night before, things that hinted of real insight, about how *we* were the ones who wouldn't let him change, about how he was the family scapegoat, I was beginning to think that Willy might one day turn into the like-minded sibling I'd lost in Caroline. I guess that's why I leapt to his defense, and Willy looked at me gratefully.

Caroline didn't say anything more, but I couldn't help it, I was furious with her. She sat around all day making quiet judgments on our dysfunctional family and then took refuge in the knowledge that she'd be returning to her functional family in New York, where everybody had tons of friends and nobody fought and there was always more than enough food. Not that we were starving or anything, but I do have to admit that the lunch my mother served that Saturday was a little sparse. Of course, everything's relative, but you could see that to Caroline the lunch wasn't sparse, it was nonexistent.

Jonathan and my father came home at around noon, and after all the blessings, my mother brought out about eight thin slices of salami on a paper plate, a handful of potato chips in a bowl, a lettuce salad with about a thimbleful of Italian dressing, and a pitcher of water. We weren't used to eating a big Sabbath lunch, but even I couldn't find a way to explain this.

Everybody filled up on the sliced challah; some of us were even eyeing that stale stuff my mother had put out for the birds that morning. My father, who criticized Mom even when there was nothing to criticize, said nothing to my mother about the meal, and instead seemed to be examining her for a nervous breakdown or something. Only Willy could get away with saying, "What's for lunch?" when everything on the table had disappeared. After all the blessings, Caroline and Jonathan excused themselves for their weekly Saturday afternoon nap, and my father and I went for a walk, leaving my mother in the kitchen as usual. The sad part was, I realized, she preferred it that way.

We walked slowly up our street and every so often we waved or said hello to one of our neighbors, who stood in their driveways with their Walkmans on their heads and their gold chains around their necks, examining their Corvettes or motorcycles. Some people were in their backyards sitting by their pools and smearing suntan oil on themselves, or playing tennis, their radios blaring, like they might die of boredom if they only had their thoughts or a single game to entertain them. Everybody used the same landscape architects and the same alarm systems, and in the winter they hung their Christmas lights in the same boring way as their next-door neighbor. There were lots of Jewish families on our street, but everybody except my family hung out Christmas lights, so eager were they to think they weren't Jewish anymore now that they lived on Hazelnut Lane. My father absolutely put his foot down when it came to

Christmas decorations. Until I met Jonathan's family I thought that made us pretty religious. I kept thinking of Caroline's wedding, when my father had said "Is this *Goodbye, Columbus* or what?" The truth was, at least the people at the wedding had something behind all the gaucheness—at least they knew what was in the Torah. But the people on our street were just plain morons. Why didn't my father know that?

"I'm worried about Mom," he said when we were halfway up the street, as if that were some kind of casual comment not important enough to merit a whole walk. He didn't look at me; instead, he pulled me closer to the curb so I wouldn't get hit by a car coming over the incline. He was holding my hand and twisting my fingers, and by the time we reached the cul-de-sac my hand felt cramped, but I didn't say anything for fear he'd let go altogether.

"Did you ever tell *her* that?" I said.

He shook his head. "It's not good for people to know you're worried about them."

"Where'd you ever pick up that piece of wisdom?" I said. "People like to know they're cared about."

"No," he said. "Never let a person know you care too much about them, or it's all over."

"Or what's all over?"

"I think I've said about enough, Jane," he said, and then he pointed to the Caplans' flower bed. "What do you think of those begonias? Think we ought to plant some?"

"I don't care about begonias, Dad. I'm worried about you. I'm worried about Mom."

"Don't worry," he said, kissing the top of my head and then pulling my hair as if he meant to straighten it out. "You just worry about the begonias, and how they'll look for your wedding."

When we got back to the house, I went up to my room and

took out a manila folder from my desk drawer. In the folder were all my old elementary school report cards, a journal I'd kept for my fourth grade English class, and a picture of my Hebrew school consecration class. I liked to sit on my bed and look through the folder when I was depressed; my teachers had the nicest things to say about me, the Hebrew school picture was taken when I was in the first grade and still flat-chested, and the journal reminded me of a time when I was overflowing with self-confidence. All the entries had something to do with my three-year-old baby brother Willy, and at the end Mrs. Prince commented on what a wonderful sister I was. I felt sort of guilty when I read that, remembering how I used to babysit for Willy all the time, how I'd push him in his stroller and play with him on our old living-room floor, and how I hardly even said two words to him now except for when I was accusing him of something. I got up and went over to his room. Naturally, he was sitting on his bed, watching TV.

"Want to play tetherball?" I asked, and he practically jumped off his bed, he was so eager. We went downstairs and out through the sliding doors in the kitchen, being careful to close them behind us to keep the air-conditioning inside. Out in the backyard our little tetherball set stood alone. It was a little embarrassing to live on a street where everybody else had at least a swimming pool in their backyards, and all we had was a tetherball set. Nevertheless, we made the best of it; we actually had fun hitting the ball around the pole for a while.

Every so often, I'd let Willy wrap the ball around the pole unimpeded by me, and I'd go off into one of my silly dances. Willy loved it when I got into a nutty mood, and I loved getting into one in front of him; who was a better audience than someone who looked up to you even after you'd made a complete fool of yourself? He particularly liked the jig I called the potato scrubber, where you held out an imaginary potato in your left hand and scrubbed each side of it with the imaginary brush in your right hand. It's pretty queer and stupid, but Willy actually fell on the ground, he was laughing so hard. "Janey, stop," he said, "my stomach is killing me!"

Willy was the only one in the whole world whom I didn't mind calling me Janey, I suppose because, believe it or not, *Janey* was his first word. Well, maybe it was *Yaney,* but still, you get the idea. I even remember my mother's response when she heard him say it, since we were all waiting for him to say mama or dada. "I suppose it's only fair," she said, "what with all the time you spend babysitting for him." At least she recognized that much.

My parents seemed so tired of raising kids by the time Willy came along, I hardly blamed them for using me as an extra parent, but my friends were not quite as forgiving. They used to call to invite me to go roller skating or bowling on Saturday afternoons, but before I could even answer, they'd always say, "I know, I know, you have to babysit." I don't even know where Caroline was back then, maybe at her dulcimer lessons, or in the back seat of some guy's car smoking pot and getting laid to the music of Bob Marley. I didn't really mind babysitting for Willy, actually, it was just that then, when I did that awful thing to him, I ended up feeling like a child abuser rather than just the twelve-year-old child I was. At least that was Dr. Stevens's theory.

When even Willy had had enough tetherball, we went inside, back upstairs, and into our separate bedrooms, closing the doors behind us. Then I came out of my room and knocked on his door again. When he opened it, I said, "I was just wondering, Willy, what did you mean last night when you said you were the scapegoat in our family?"

"Oh, that," he said, "I don't know, I don't even know why I said it."

"Yes, you do, and if I understood you correctly, I'd say you were probably right."

"I don't know, maybe scapegoat is the wrong word, you know how I sometimes get the wrong word. I guess it just seems like everybody's always feeling sorry for *me*, when I'm not even the one with the biggest problems. I mean, look at you, you don't even act like you *like* Eddie, so why are you going to marry him?"

"I like him," I said, a little worried. Was I that obvious?

Willy wasn't deterred. "You have to admit that Caroline's messed up," he said. "She always looks like she's going to cry."

"She's just uncomfortable because of the baby and the heat."

He shrugged. "What about Mom? Yesterday there was a whole container of vanilla fudge ice cream in the freezer, and now it's gone."

Geez, who would have guessed it, Willy noticing these things about us! My God, had he always been so clued in, or had he changed this summer too? I felt a little uneasy about the whole thing, actually, I wasn't nearly as pleased with the new Willy as I thought I'd be, so I said, "How do you know Mom's the one who ate it?"

Willy shrugged again, as if to say I was entitled to my opinion even though he knew his opinion was right.

"Anyway, I'm sorry about last night," I said, "I'm sorry for not believing you. Sometimes, when a person has a reputation for lying, it's hard to believe them."

"I've changed, Jane. I swear. I do better away from here. At school."

"About that girl, Willy. She and Wayne Vecchio seemed pretty close. Maybe you shouldn't call her."

"I didn't like her, anyway," Willy said. "I wasn't going to call her, I just liked getting her phone number."

I felt kind of happy then, but kind of sad at the same time. On the one hand, it was sort of nice having what seemed like a "normal" brother for a change; on the other hand, I couldn't help feeling that I was losing something, something important to me, the little place I'd dug out for myself within my family. I guess the empty feeling that had engulfed me when Eddie backed up Willy's telephone-number story was proof of the fact that I'd always been more comfortable seeing Willy as the loser, since that was the only way I could see myself as the winner.

On my way back to my room, I stopped outside the room where Jonathan and Caroline were napping and listened hard. I'd heard somewhere that it was a mitzvah for married Jews to have sex on the Sabbath, and since the two of them had been in there all afternoon, I thought they might be performing a mitzvah. But I didn't hear any sounds coming out of their room.

I lay down on my bed and turned on an old Joni Mitchell record, *Blue*. It was still one of my all-time favorites, even if Caroline, the person who'd gotten me into Joni Mitchell in the first place, had given her up for Uncle Moishy and the Mitzvah Men. I must have fallen asleep, because when I woke up, the turntable was still going around but the record had been over, maybe for hours.

I looked at my digital clock radio: nine-thirteen. They hadn't even woken me for dinner. I started to get mad, but then I remembered that there probably hadn't been any dinner. Caroline once told me that she and Jonathan always skipped dinner on Saturday night, because they were so full from their big Sabbath lunch. Ha!

I raced downstairs to find everybody standing in the kitchen. Caroline was holding a big braided candle—she must have brought it with her from New York—over a section of the *Plain Dealer,* laid out on the kitchen table. Jonathan was holding a plastic foam cup full of wine.

After he'd said the prayer to end the Sabbath, and passed around my mother's jar of cinnamon for all of us to smell, the phone rang, and I knew it would be Lenny Levitsky. He wanted to know whether I'd go out for coffee with him, and would I like to bring along my sister and brother-in-law? Well, this is a first, I thought—using your old girlfriend to get to her Orthodox brother-in-law. Suddenly, Jonathan was a real commodity.

Caroline showered first, then Jonathan, then me. It was already ten o'clock by the time we were ready to leave, but I didn't care. I had to get out, my parents seemed barely able to sit in the same room with each other, and Willy looked longingly after us. I suppose we could have invited him along, but he was still the baby in our family, after all, even if some sixteen-year-old girl did have the hots for him.

Caroline sat in the back seat, I sat in front to give directions to Jonathan. It was sort of silly, considering that Caroline used to practically live at Arabica, the coffee house where we were meeting Lenny, but now that she was Orthodox, she'd all but erased that part of her life, so that she couldn't even remember how to get there.

I was feeling pretty depressed about my parents, about Eddie, about my job, and didn't even argue with Caroline when she started saying how little there was to do on a Saturday night in Cleveland. I don't even know what Caroline's point was, other than to make me feel bad; she wasn't the one who was stuck here, she and Jonathan were going back to New York the next day. Then I thought, perhaps Lenny will have changed, and I started to fantasize about a future with him. After all, if it worked for Caroline, why couldn't it work for me? Maybe we'd just forget about Cleveland and move to Israel.

Lenny looked funny without a beard, and I kept thinking of my mother asking if he still had a terrible chin. The outdoor café was crowded, and all the tables were taken, children and dogs running around and through people's legs.

We got a table inside the café next to the window, while around us all these intellectual types were playing chess and drinking espresso. Jonathan, Lenny and I went up to the counter to get coffee, and a muffin for me, Miss Rebel, while Caroline sat there, probably in fear of seeing someone she'd once had sex with. At some point, both Jonathan and Lenny had taken off their yarmulkes; the funny thing was, if Jonathan had taken off his pants, it wouldn't have been as strange as seeing the back of his naked head. Lenny, however, looked silly with one on— who did he think he was kidding? I really wanted to blow his cover, though, when we sat down at the table and I saw that all he was having was a glass of water. Even Jonathan was drinking a cup of coffee, and you couldn't get more kosher than him, I wanted to say.

"So what are you doing these days?" I said to Lenny.

"I'll be a sophomore at Oberlin in September," he said. "Not a lot of *Yiddishkeit* there, but a good education." He looked quickly at Jonathan, as if for confirmation that he'd used the right word.

Oberlin. That was where I'd wanted to go! My heart went crazy with envy. I still had their catalogues from the last three years, and each one looked as if it were a copy of a classic, the way the pages were worn out. I loved Oberlin, I had obsessed about Oberlin, I'd even been there twice, when I was sixteen, and I visited my friend Beverly Fisher, whom I'd met at Camp Ben-Gurion the summer before, when she and Lenny and I were all C.I.T.'s. Her mother was an Oberlin English professor, and Beverly took me to her lectures both times I was there. Their house was always freezing cold, in a really intellectual way, and I had to go around all the time with a blanket wrapped around me. We had spent hours in Beverly's room, painting, writing poetry, eating. The second time I was there, we went for a walk around the campus, and she told me what she'd discovered in bed one night the week before: you could give *yourself* an orgasm, you didn't need some guy like Lenny Levitsky to do it for you.

"Where did you go to college?" Lenny was asking Jonathan.

"Columbia."

"Good school."

"This isn't like a first date or anything," I said. "Jonathan's already married, Lenny, you don't have to compliment his alma mater." Lenny laughed, and I was relieved to see he had a sense of humor at least. I couldn't remember whether he used to have one; there was only one thing I could remember about him, and he certainly wasn't doing that at the table.

"I'm thinking of moving to New York," he said.

"Yeah? Me too," I said. I wasn't really thinking of moving to New York, but I was certainly interested in getting out of Cleveland, and I figured I'd tell Lenny I was. I mean, if he transferred out of Oberlin, maybe that would make a place there for me.

"You are not moving to New York, Jane," Caroline said.

"How do you know?"

"Why would you move to New York?"

"You think you're the only one who can live in New York?"

Caroline looked away, like she wasn't in the mood to get into anything with me, and then she asked Lenny why he wanted to move to New York. Lenny said something about wanting to meet the right kind of people, and he heard there was a college there specifically for Jewish girls. "Yeah," I said. "Shira goes there. Jonathan's sister. You and Shira might make a perfect couple. Just don't try any of your 'treats' on her on your first date."

On that note, I got up and walked out and left them there to talk about what a paranoid schizophrenic sex maniac I was.

I headed down old Coventry Road. Most of the shops were closed, but I looked in the store windows, at the imported wraparound skirts in Passport to Peru, at the funky stretch pants in the window of Record Revolution, at all the knickknacks in High Tide Rock Bottom, at the specials listed on the chalkboard inside Tommy's. On the street there were just me and some adolescents, who were dressed up to look like Rastafarians; didn't they know dreadlocks were passé? It was sort of depressing to think that Eddie, of all people, was about the only one left who wasn't trying to be anything other than what he was.

After I cooled off a little, I started walking back up the street. People were sitting on the grass in front of Arabica, imitating Neil Young on their guitars, singing "Helpless." They were probably all waiting for midnight, when the little theatre around the corner opened up to show *The Rocky Horror Picture Show*.

"You sure did a good job of rekindling that old romance," Caroline said when I sat back down in Arabica. She and Jonathan were sitting at the table, but Lenny had gone.

"What, old Lenny doesn't want to go out with me again?" I asked.

"He wanted to know what he'd said to upset you," Caroline said, "but frankly, I couldn't tell him, I had no idea myself. So he said to tell you he was sorry for whatever it was. He seemed pretty embarrassed about the whole thing."

"He should be embarrassed, he's a complete fraud," I said. "What a creep!"

"How do you know he's a creep? All he said was that he goes to Oberlin and he wants to move to New York."

"So he can meet the *right* kind of girl," I said. "Like he wasn't going around bopping every girl in sight three years ago."

"A lot can happen to a person in three years," Caroline said.

"Big deal," I said. "And, in case you forgot, I'm engaged. I don't need to rekindle any old romances."

Jonathan was turning red just listening to us fight. Caroline had told me he didn't like conflict, but this wasn't even his conflict, and here he was, practically breaking out in hives. Every so often he'd rub the back of his head, like he'd forgotten what it felt like not to have anything covering it. I couldn't believe I'd thought Lenny might be anything like Jonathan, just because Lenny was Orthodox now. Jonathan wasn't adorable because he was Orthodox; he was adorable because he was Jonathan.

On the way home, Caroline sat in front, though there was no way she could get the seat belt around her. Every day she grew about three inches more. We drove down Hampshire, and we were all pretty quiet, looking out the windows at the old houses. Nothing felt authentic to me anymore and I thought, if only my family still lived in one of these pre-1981 houses, with porches instead of patios, and dusty attics instead of finished basements, we'd have an authentic life. Everybody was going around turning into somebody else, and I just wanted to hold on to the way things used to be. Things were too damned pretty in Pepper Pike, too damned manicured, while everything inside was falling apart.

Monday morning I was all business; I could be that way when I wanted. Caroline and Jonathan left for New York, and

I got to my office determined not to have anything to do with anyone. Sitting on my typewriter were four little cassette tapes, and I knew they were from Dr. Stevens, since Dr. Rimer never put his there. At first it was hard to type, with Dr. Stevens's mouth so close to my ears. He kept clearing his throat and coughing and saying sexy things like "um," and I kept expecting him to say something like "it's okay to have sexual feelings." But after a while, his voice became like every other person's voice, his memos were as boring as Dr. Rimer's—all about getting funding for this hotline or that facility. Memos about the progress of the capital campaign, or about how social service cutbacks would impact on the agency's programs, etc., etc., etc. Money, money, money! Budget, budget, budget! There wasn't even one single memo about any of his patients or their sexual problems or anything like that.

The one thing I really liked about Dr. Stevens's letters, though, was the way he signed off on them. None of this "fondest regards" or "my best" stuff, those meaningless phrases that important men usually used. Instead, he used the word *sincerely*—in my opinion the only halfway-decent way to end a letter.

I didn't stop for lunch, and by five o'clock I had finished all four cassettes. It was five-thirty by the time I finally got up to give them to Dr. Stevens; I kept rereading them to be sure there were no typos. I knew he wasn't expecting to have them back before the end of the week, and I wondered what he would do when I handed them over. I thought he might put his arm around me or put his hand on my back or something, and then tell me he wanted to thank me for the favor by taking me out to dinner. I thought he might tell me he'd never seen such a good, hard worker before in his life; I thought he might tell me he was in love with me.

I looked in the mirror behind my office door, messing up

my hair a little so he wouldn't think I was trying to look good for him, and then I did something really ridiculous: I unbuttoned the top button of my blouse. Not that it mattered too much; I still showed about as much flesh as a nun.

"He's not there." Rena, the receptionist who always knew everyone else's business, was sitting there at her desk, like it wasn't five-thirty or something. "Are you going to Dr. Stevens's office?" she asked. "He's not there."

"Do you know when he'll be back?"

"He won't, not tonight anyway. He was in an awfully big hurry when he left," she said, and then as if it were some kind of afterthought, she added, "Oh, yeah, when he was waiting for the elevator, he said to tell you that if you finished any of the letters, you could give them to me to send off."

"But I need his signature," I said.

"I can sign them," she said. "His secretary Barbara always lets me forge his signature before I mail his letters out."

"I'm not sure they're right," I said. "I'm going to leave them on his desk, and he can sign them himself tomorrow."

"Suit yourself," she said.

The cleaning woman was in Dr. Stevens's office, dumping his wastebasket into a big green garbage bag, and vacuuming under his desk. She smiled at me, like we women were all in this taking-care-of-our-men thing together, and then lugged her equipment into the next office, the vacuum cord trailing behind her.

I sat down in the big leather chair behind Dr. Stevens's desk and tried to imagine what it felt like to be him, to hear everyone else's secrets and never have to divulge any of your own. It felt pretty good. I opened his desk drawers, but all they had were pencils, stationery (Michael M. Stevens, M.D.), some Band-Aids and a stapler. His top, middle drawer was locked, so I felt around in the other drawers for a key. There wasn't one, thank God, since who knew what devastating thing I would have found in there, a picture of his wife or a love letter from bitchy Dr. Lanz. I looked at his suit jacket, hanging there behind his office door, and then I got up and buried my face in it. It smelled like aftershave and deodorant and a wife, it smelled like leather briefcases and cigars and important business meetings, and all of a sudden I was bawling my eyes out. Why couldn't I have been somebody else? I kept crying into the suit jacket. Why did I have to be me? Why couldn't I have been him? Why couldn't I have at least been his wife? Why couldn't *I* be the person people looked up to? Why couldn't someone feel about me the way I felt about him?

I stood there a long time, crying and asking myself every humiliating question a person could ask herself, until finally, I was worn out. Then I sat back down in Dr. Stevens's chair and just sat and sat and sat. Then I had a brainstorm. I took out one of those little yellow sticky pads from his bottom drawer, and attached one to the blue folder I'd stuck the letters in. "Here are your letters," I wrote. "I hope you find them satisfactory." Then I put my initials underneath, real professional and everything. Then I took the whole pile of letters—folder and all—and tore it right in half. I did it pretty neatly, so if he were smart enough he could just tape them back together and then photocopy them. I didn't write that part in my note, though, because that would have pretty much defeated the purpose of the whole thing.

4

*C*aroline's baby was born the first week of September. Maybe if she hadn't been crying so much after the baby came, or at least if the baby hadn't been, Caroline would have noticed that my parents weren't talking to each other at the bris (or, as I liked to refer to it, the Circumcision of the Century, what with the tons of people who were there, not to mention the tons of food). As it was, Caroline didn't notice anything but the fact that her mother-in-law was running to every discount store in New York to buy things for her and the baby, and wasn't she wonderful and helpful, as if a person shouldn't have more important things on her mind than what kind of carriage to buy, as if it never occurred to her that a child could have *too* many outfits or toys.

Mrs. Klausner was telling the caterers where to put the smoked fish and Muenster cheese when my mother and father and I arrived at the Klausners' apartment. Once again, *we'd* come to *them*, this time to witness my first nephew entering into his covenant with God, a ritual that made me glad I was female.

It was already the middle of September, and Willy had gone back to school soon after the "August incident," the incident which proved in a most depressing way that Willy was still Willy. One day, not even a full month after he'd stood there in his bedroom doorway telling me he wasn't even going to call the miniature golf girl, a woman named Denise Trinetti called to ask my mother where exactly our vacation house in Chautauqua was located, and could she have the number there in case she needed to reach her daughter over Labor Day weekend. Of course, we didn't have a vacation house, not in Chautauqua or anywhere else, so my mother had to go and disinvite Carla, the sixteen-year-old who by now probably regretted having given Willy her phone number in the first place. Fortunately, my mother was able to think fast enough to spare both Willy and herself the embarrassment of explaining that there was no house. She simply said that our plans had suddenly changed. But then, as if all that weren't enough, Mrs. Trinetti went on to say that Willy had exquisite taste in jewelry, but that it certainly wasn't necessary for him to spend all his money on Carla. My mother thanked her for calling, said she'd pass the message on to Willy, and then ran to her jewelry box, only to discover that she was missing the jade earrings I'd said looked so nice on her back in April when Grandpa had died. Willy had changed, all right; in addition to being a liar, he had become a thief, too.

And so, in keeping with the family tradition of trying to avoid anything painful, we almost forgot to call Willy when Caroline's baby was born. As it was, he found out after even Eddie knew, who wasn't even part of the family yet. My mother told Willy he could come to New York for the bris if he wanted to, but he didn't come, and as usual nobody was dying of disappointment that he wasn't there. Only I was disappointed, having started to expect something from him and then finding myself all alone again.

Grandma didn't come to New York either; she said she didn't feel well enough to fly anymore, and of course that piece of information really impressed Caroline, who kept talking about Jonathan's heroic grandmother, *"aleha hashalom,"* who would have come back from the dead if she could have.

"Mazel tov," Mrs. Klausner said to us, pretending to kiss us and all that. She was wearing one of those miniskirts, like she was just dying for all the people in the room to come up to her and say she didn't look old enough to be a grandmother. Her legs weren't even that great—too thin. "The baby's eating," she said, "and Caroline's still a little embarrassed to nurse in front of people." People. We weren't just *people,* we were Caroline's family. Mrs. Klausner was acting like she was the only grandmother in the room. Like my mother didn't have feelings. Shira was eating a bagel and yelling at the caterer for forgetting the diet Coke.

Jonathan came over to us, smiling, and told us how glad he was to see us, how Caroline had been asking all morning for my mother and me, and I looked at Mrs. Klausner to make sure she'd gotten the message. But she hadn't, that was the thing about her, she never really saw us as existing at all.

And then something occurred to me, something that made me feel worse for Willy than I did for myself. The way Mrs. Klausner didn't notice us was exactly the way my family didn't notice Willy. Sure, I'd begun to interact with him over the summer, but even then I'd still been a little squeamish about getting close to him, and I'd carefully maintained my distance.

Was it possible, I wondered, that just as my family didn't

want to be reminded of our pain by noticing Willy, Mrs. Klausner didn't want to be reminded of hers by noticing us? Could it be that she sensed in my family a certain darkness lurking behind our genial facades, a darkness that threatened to call up her own painful feelings? I must say, it didn't seem as if Mrs. Klausner *had* any pain, but Caroline had told me something recently that made me stop and think. She said that after the baby was born, Jonathan confessed to her that he'd been worried sick during her entire pregnancy, because of what had happened to *his* mother when she was pregnant with her third child. According to Caroline, nobody ever talked about it, even Jonathan didn't know the details, but whatever it was that resulted from that pregnancy—it was said she had a stillborn—had prevented Mrs. Klausner from having any more children. Caroline said you could tell she was still suffering over it because every time she talked about her friends' children, she'd say how insecure they were, how there were too many children vying for the parents' attention.

"As soon as Caroline's done nursing, we're going to start," Jonathan said. He looked skinnier than ever, as if trying to please too many people was taking its toll. He brought chairs over for my parents and me and put them right in front of the bearded guy with the hat who was going to perform the circumcision. He gave my father a yarmulke, which my father graciously wore since it was Jonathan who gave it to him, and the three of us sat down and waited. A few people actually came over to congratulate us heathens, and my mother smiled and acted sociable. It made me mad the way she seemed to want these stupid religious hypocrites with their short skirts and their expensive nose jobs to like her, but for my father she hadn't smiled in months.

Caroline came out with the baby and handed him to Jonathan, who handed him to his father, and after that I didn't look. The smell of rubbing alcohol and A and D ointment was overwhelming, and I thought I was going to be sick. The baby was screaming the whole time so I never knew when they were actually doing it, you know, circumcising him, but I listened carefully to hear what they'd named him, and I nudged my mother when I heard the Hebrew equivalent of Samuel, Grandpa's name. I didn't know what I would have done if they'd named him after someone on Jonathan's side of the family! When the ceremony was over, everybody started singing some song about "Mazel Tov" and the circumciser carried the baby out of the room.

Mr. Klausner stood up and made one of his trademark speeches about how wonderful everything was, and how important tradition was, and how important family was, and how important love was, and I just about couldn't take any more of his unbridled warmth. The guy was *sincere,* that was the depressing part—why couldn't he have at least been a fake?

My father was wiping his eyes, but my mother wouldn't even look his way. "Dad's crying," I said.

"He's always been a sucker for a sentimental speech."

"That's not why he's crying, Mom," I said.

Jonathan came over to us and said Caroline wanted to see us. He said she and the baby were in the room that used to be his. The door was closed, so we knocked, but Mrs. Klausner, who was right behind us (God forbid we should get to see Caroline or the baby without her), just threw the door open as if she owned Caroline's life, as if it was *her* family, and she and Caroline didn't need any privacy from each other.

Jonathan's room, which when we'd been there in December had had his diplomas and posters hanging around, had been transformed into a baby's room, with rocking horse wallpaper on the walls and a blue sky with little white clouds painted on the ceiling. You would have thought the baby was going to live there with the Klausners, it was so permanent-looking.

"Could I hold him?" Mrs. Klausner said. It was a statement, not a question, and she kissed the baby's forehead, which was literally touching Caroline's naked breast. At that, even Caroline looked at her like she was crazy. Hadn't my family just come in from Cleveland to see the baby? Hadn't Mrs. Klausner spent every waking minute for the last eight days with him? I guess even she sensed she was out of line, and she sat down on the bed, pretending she hadn't said anything. "Why don't you hold him?" she said, gesturing to me, as if I'd been born yesterday, like I didn't know she was trying to make it up to me. "Just make sure to support his head."

"I know how to hold a baby," I said. "I used to hold Willy all the time when he was a baby."

"Yes, of course," she said, like that was okay for *Willy,* but not for *this* baby, The Little Messiah. I mean, I was sorry for her, I was sorry she'd lost a child, but it was hard to feel sympathy for someone so condescending.

Fortunately, Jonathan came in then and told his mother they needed more coffee, which left us alone with little Samuel. I was trying to get him to stop crying, by first holding him up over my shoulder, then cradling him in my arms. After a while, I said, "Maybe Mom and Dad want to look at him. You know, his other set of grandparents. The ones that are seeing him for the first time today." Caroline looked at me, like I was still just as impossible as ever. "You were the one who was hogging him," she said, and she took the baby from me and handed him over to my father. I could barely stand the look of pride on my father's face when he held him; I loved my father so much.

My mother took out a little gift-wrapped package, a pair of tie-dyed feet pajamas that she and I had gotten on Coventry. We thought they were the cutest things we'd ever seen. "This is for Samuel," she said, and she gave it to Caroline.

"Thanks, guys," she said, kissing my mother on the cheek. She opened the package and said she loved it and couldn't wait to put it on the baby.

"So go ahead," I said.

"Now? Well, okay." It took her forever to get his arms through the sleeves and his legs in the right place and all that. She didn't even bother to change his diaper; she was scared of the bandages from the circumcision and said she'd wait until Jonathan could help her. Never mind the fact that my mother was right there and could have helped; I mean, just because Willy didn't have a Bar Mitzvah didn't mean he hadn't had a bris, didn't mean my mother wouldn't know how to change a bandage, for heaven's sake.

The pajamas were a little big, but it didn't matter. You could tell how good it made my mom feel, having Samuel wear something we'd gotten him, even though Mrs. Klausner had made it virtually impossible for us to do anything that she hadn't done already. Later, when we took him back out to the living room, after all the Orthodox people in the city of New York were gone, Mrs. Klausner said to Caroline, "And where'd you get this little outfit?" I almost belted her one, but then I thought, anyone who's threatened by a pair of feet pajamas from the other grandmother is somebody you have to feel sorry for. Still, would it have killed her to say one nice thing about my family for a change?

Believe it or not, my father, who never cared about offending anyone in his life, didn't want to offend Jonathan's perfect family, and so when they invited us to stay at their apartment overnight instead of some anonymous hotel, he accepted the invitation. My mother gave him the dirtiest look I'd ever seen, not because she cared about where we stayed, but because if *she* had accepted the same invitation, he would have screamed his head off. It was disconcerting to see the way he kept changing for this family, as if they were so respectable, and we were just dirt or something.

I was even more annoyed with my father than my mother was. I mean, the Klausners had three bedrooms and a guest room, so guess how it was going to work out? Yep, that's right, Caroline and Jonathan and the baby in Jonathan's old room, Mr. and Mrs. Klausner in their room, and my parents in the guest room. Which left me with Shira.

There was hardly even a place to sit down in Shira's room, between all her clothes and shoes and prayer books and stuffed animals. I'm not even making it up; she still had stuffed animals around! The closest I'd ever come to having a stuffed animal was when I made something out of a sock in arts and crafts at Camp Ben-Gurion one summer, and even that seemed excessive.

At dinner that night, my father was giving compliments right and left. "Delicious chicken!" The pieces were so big you could barely even finish one. "Perfect asparagus!" I thought it was undercooked. "Caroline's got a tough act to follow!" Yeah, I thought, if all she wants to do in life is serve fat chickens and crunchy asparagus.

Jonathan kept jumping up from the table to take food in to Caroline, who was marooned in her room with the baby on her breast. Shira too kept running in there to offer to help. As if I was selfish or something because I felt like sitting there. I didn't even want to try to compete, and neither did my mother, who nibbled on her chicken and kept smiling. Mr. Klausner sat there like a king being served by his wife the queen, the two of them acting like they had just fallen in love, calling each other "honey" and other stupid names that didn't mean anything.

I wasn't feeling so well after dinner, all that food and the tension just made me feel sick, and I spent a certain amount of time in the bathroom. The baby's crying was beginning to get on my nerves, and it just about drove me crazy the way Mrs. Klausner kept carrying him around the apartment and telling him what a good baby he was. If it had been anyone else's grandson, I knew she would have been saying what an awful baby he was. In my opinion, a person had to call a spade a spade, or else a kid like Samuel ended up thinking he was better than everyone else.

My father was sitting on the Bloomingdale's Special (that's what I called that black leather couch in the Klausners' living room). He was having a conversation with Mr. Klausner about James Joyce, he was pretending he was Mr. Literature himself, when the truth was he barely had time to read anything but his hospital journals and *Forbes.* Mr. Klausner, on the other hand, was walking around his apartment with a paperback copy of *Ulysses,* for heaven's sake, pontificating on Joyce's real-life relationship with Nora Barnacle, the real-life Molly Bloom. We're the cultured ones, I wanted to scream out, we're the ones who are supposed to know about literature! I mean, I couldn't have taken it if it turned out that the Klausners not only had it over us in the hereafter but also in the here and now! I comforted myself by thinking that even if Mr. Klausner really was reading *Ulysses,* he certainly didn't understand it.

My mother was watching Mrs. Klausner walk around with the baby, and Caroline sat there saying she was so tired she didn't know what to do. Finally, Mrs. Klausner ordered her to bed and said she would take care of the baby until he needed to be nursed again, like she was the baby's mother.

It wasn't as if my presence was really adding much, so I said I was going to sleep, and everybody said good night as if they really liked me and were sorry I was leaving. Mrs. Klausner kept talking about how I shouldn't worry, there were fresh sheets on the top bunk in Shira's room, like I was some kind of princess or something and had never slept on used sheets. You should see the sheets that Eddie and I use, I wanted to say, but I restrained myself. She already thought we were wild people because we drove to temple on Yom Kippur.

I made myself comfortable in Shira's room, and even looked through her drawers and closets to see how someone like Shira lived. She had a built-in closet, with rows of shoes and dresses still in those plastic dry-cleaning bags. Other dresses still had store tags on them, like there weren't enough days in the year to wear everything she had. I guess there wasn't room for all her clothes in one closet, so I looked in the other, free-standing one, and sure enough, all her summer clothes were there, folded neatly on the shelves for next summer. It wasn't that I was jealous of her or anything, but I wouldn't have minded owning a few of her oversized cotton shirts. I even thought about putting two of them in my overnight bag to take home with me, since I was sure Shira would never miss them, but then I thought better of it. It was bad enough to have one thief in the family.

By the time I finally got around to turning off the light and getting in the top bunk, Shira came in, tiptoeing around like she was trying to be considerate. "I'm awake," I said. The truth was, I was dying of heat.

"Oh," she said. "I just have to wash up."

"Don't you ever go to sleep without washing up?"

"No," she said.

"You've never been so tired you just went to bed without brushing your teeth?"

"No," she said. She wore about two tons of mascara and eyeshadow, so I could see how it might have been gross for her to go to sleep without at least washing her face.

"I guess you wouldn't consider kissing your boyfriend after you gave him head, then, would you?"

This time she didn't even answer me, she just gathered up

her toiletries bag and went off to the bathroom. Imagine, a toiletries bag in your own house, like someone might use her toothbrush if she left it hanging in the bathroom. The truth is I felt kind of sorry for her. She seemed scared of me, like I could take away her virginity just by saying the word *head*.

When she came back in the room, she was wearing a big shirt that said *Nightshirt* across the front. I could just imagine what she'd have thought of what I wore to bed, a pair of bikini underpants. When I was little I wore nightgowns, but then one summer, the summer I was twelve, I went to camp and developed these breasts that were about three times bigger than my twenty-one-year-old counselor's. At first I tried to flatten my chest by wearing my nylon bathing suit under everything or smooshing my chest down with training bras that were too tight, but then I just ended up in the shower with all the other female campers and counselors, and someone would inevitably say something like "oo-la-la." That was the thing about girls; they could make you feel much worse about the way you looked than boys. I felt pretty terrible about myself and cried in bed every night just thinking about it, but eventually I saw that that didn't do me any good. Instead, I started walking around the cabin all the time without a shirt on, acting as if I felt good about myself, and people started to believe me. Now I sleep topless all the time, as if I'm daring someone like Shira to say something.

"Good night," I called down.

"Good night," she said.

"If you ever come to Cleveland, I'll let you sleep in my bed. It's queen-sized. Twin beds are no good for sex."

After a bit, she said, "Have you had sex with a lot of guys?"

"About ten," I said.

"Really?"

"Sure, haven't you?"

"No," she said, as if it were the most outrageous idea in the world to suggest that a nineteen-year-old might have had sex with ten guys. That was the thing about Orthodox people; they made you feel like *you* were the weird one. "I'm going to be a virgin until I'm married," Shira added.

"I used to be scared too," I said.

"I'm not scared. I just don't think it's right." Then Miss High and Mighty changed her tune. "Is it as good as everyone says it is?"

"Better," I said. "My fiancé and I can do it about ten times in a row and still want more."

"I read in *Cosmopolitan* that there are different ways you can do it. Different positions."

"Yeah, we've tried them all," I said, even though I thought *Cosmopolitan* was about the dumbest magazine I'd ever read.

"Do men prefer it missionary style?"

"It's not like I'm a sex expert or anything," I said. I was beginning to feel insulted, the way she was asking me all these questions with her innocent little voice, like I was some kind of prostitute or something. Like she was the normal one, being a virgin when you're nineteen, for God's sake. Of course, I was one too, technically, but she didn't know that.

We stopped talking then, and I started getting really depressed. I peered over the bed to see what Shira was doing down there, and saw that she'd fallen asleep with her arms around this big green Babar animal she had. I started sort of caressing my body, hoping I could do for myself what Babar had done for Shira, but I couldn't fall asleep no matter how close I held myself. I thought about masturbating, but I wasn't in the mood, lying there in that bed, my stupid tainted body with all its goddam feelings. I kept thinking of Dr. Stevens telling me how everyone masturbated, it was nothing to be ashamed of, as if he were going to get me to tell him *I* did. That was all he needed to hear about me to confirm his theory that I was a pervert.

I swung my feet over the edge and climbed down the little ladder, just like the one Willy used to have for his bunk beds. I put on the bathrobe that Shira had left hanging on her closet door in case she needed to cover herself on the way to the bathroom, like she was so sexy somebody'd get too turned on if they saw her in her nightshirt, and walked out into the living room.

Everybody had gone to bed, except for Caroline, who was nursing the baby, and my mother, who was sitting next to her on the couch, crying.

"What's the matter, Mom?" I said. I didn't even go over to her, I was so scared. My mother never cried, not even when her own father died, not even when everyone else cried at a sad movie, not even the way complete strangers did at my sister's wedding. I couldn't even have imagined the way her face would *look* with her crying. "What's wrong with Mom?" I said to Caroline.

Caroline shook her head, as if it wasn't her place to tell me why my mother was crying, as if all of a sudden she was Miss Mature Individual now that she was a mother. I went over to the Bloomingdale's Special and sat down, and waited for somebody to talk. Finally, my mother said, "I couldn't sleep."

"That's no reason to cry, Mom," I said.

Caroline snorted. "Could you be a little less literal, Jane?"

"All the thoughts, going through my head," my mom continued.

"What kind of thoughts?"

"About my life. My marriage."

Fortunately, Caroline stuck her pinky into the corner of The Little Messiah's mouth, detaching him from her right breast, and he started crying, loudly enough to change the focus of our attention. But then Caroline stuck him on the other side, and after about a hundred attempts to get a grasp, he started sucking, and we were back to my mother.

"Your life's good," I said. "What's wrong with your life?"

"You girls are all grown up now. Caroline's got a family of her own, and you will too, soon. I'm a grandmother. I don't have to stay married anymore."

"But what about Willy?" I said, as if somewhere I'd known all along she was going to be saying this to me one day and I'd have to have an answer ready. Finally, Willy was serving the purpose he'd been born for: keeping my parents together. I would stop hoping for love and harmony and understanding. My parents had to stay together, for Willy.

"Willy?" my mother said. "Can't you see what we've done to Willy? If it weren't for us, he might be on the honor roll at Randall Junior High instead of being on probation at Winthrop. Dad and I have been so busy fighting all these years, we've only had time for Willy when he was failing English or stealing my jewelry. He'll be better off with us apart."

"I can't believe you think you and Dad have anything to do with Willy's problems," I said. "Tell her, Caroline. Tell her it has nothing to do with them."

"I can't, Jane. I agree with her. Even someone like Willy, not the brainiest of kids, could do okay in school if other things weren't getting in the way."

Of course Caroline agreed with my mother; only *I* knew why Willy was at Winthrop. I couldn't believe I was going to be forced to divulge my secret, the thing that only Dr. Stevens knew, in order to save my parents' marriage. I wasn't going to divulge it now, though; I'd save it for right before they called the lawyers, if nothing else worked.

"You and Dad love each other, Mom. You can't live without each other."

"We may love each other, in some sick way, but we can't live with each other."

"But you like planting flowers together and you both like Brahms . . ." I said.

"Brahms isn't enough anymore."

"It's gotten better, though, hasn't it, Mom? Hasn't Dad gotten better?"

"Better!" she said.

"What does Dad say? Dad's not going to let this happen!"

"He says I have to do what I have to do."

"Of course he says that," I said, looking to Caroline to back me up, but all she cared about was the way her nurturing breast looked in her adorable baby's mouth. "He has too much pride to admit he'd be miserable without you."

"Well, then that's too bad," Caroline said. "He'll have to be less proud."

"Great advice, Caroline. You ought to go into marriage counseling."

"You ought to go find a life of your own and let Mom and Dad, and Eddie for that matter, have theirs back," she said. I would have hit her, but I did have a little compassion for Samuel, innocent bystander that he was.

"What happened, Mom?" I said. "Things are the same as they've always been. Why now?"

"I've put in my time," she said, not looking at me, but rather at her hands with their raggedy, bitten-off nails. She started to cry again. "I only feel bad that I didn't protect you kids more from Dad's tirades and put-downs when you were growing up. None of you has the self-confidence you should have, none of you has achieved what you're capable of."

I couldn't believe she was talking about my dad as if he were some kind of child abuser or wife beater or something! *She* was the one who was always telling us how it didn't mean anything when he flew off the handle, that it was just his way of blowing off steam, that it didn't bother her so it shouldn't bother us. Now she was saying that everything before now was a lie.

"You know this is going to be a shock to everyone," Caroline said. Typical. All she cared about was how the end of my parents' marriage would appear to the world. Or even worse, to her perfect in-laws with their perfect marriage.

"What's going to happen to our house?" I said.

"I guess we'll have to sell it," my mother said, and it was the first time I actually longed for Pepper Pike, for our neighbors, our house.

"You *can't* sell it," I said. "We live there!"

"You're getting married in two months," my mother said, "and I don't need such a big house to maintain, when Willy's only home in the summer anyway."

"Where will Dad go? How will he take care of himself?"

"He'll figure it out," my mother said. "He's not as helpless as he likes you to think."

"Yes he is!" I cried, and I started to sob then, picturing my father in some kind of bachelor pad, a place like Eddie's with a butcher-block breakfast table and chairs to match. He didn't know how to cook or clean or even make a bed. He *was* helpless. How could I go and marry Eddie if Dad was going to be all by himself?

"I'm not going to get married if you and Dad get divorced," I said, but my mother was already back to herself a little bit, unintimidated, strong. She wasn't crying anymore.

"That would be a shame," she said. "But that's not going to change my mind. I even thought of waiting until after the wedding to tell you, but I couldn't wait anymore."

"It's been twenty-five years, and you couldn't wait two more months?"

She had to admit that sounded pretty ridiculous, and in my stupid hopeful way I thought that if I had two more months before they told anybody else, I could get them to stay together. I just knew I could. Who ever heard of getting divorced after twenty-five years?

"I just want to be happy for however many years I have left—"

"What are you talking about, Mom?" I said. "You're not even fifty yet!" And then I thought, maybe this is just that old mid-life crisis thing that men usually go through when they're fifty. The thought actually made me feel better, like she was just going through a phase that would end.

"Why don't you take a sleeping pill?" Caroline said. "You need to get some sleep."

"Maybe I will," my mother said, standing up, as if we'd just had a nice little chat about nothing and now she was going to turn in. "I'm sorry about all this. I wasn't planning to say anything here. I hope I didn't put a damper on everything, Caroline." She didn't even seem all that interested in Samuel, something surely noticed by Caroline, who was moving farther and farther away from my family, especially now that my parents were splitting up. Orthodox people never split up, of course.

"I guess I'll try to put Samuel in bed now and see if I can get some sleep too," Caroline said. She stood up slowly, reminding me of the fact that a nine-pound boy had come out of her only eight days before. She hadn't gotten any pain medication or anesthesia, she'd delivered naturally, the way she'd learned in her childbirth class. She said it was a feminist thing to be in control of her body, not to let her male doctor take her autonomy away. If it had been me, you can be sure I would have begged that male doctor of mine to knock me out; Caroline always picked the wrong time to be a feminist.

"I can't believe you're going to sleep," I said. "How can anyone sleep now?"

"Have a baby," she said. "You'll see."

Maybe I wasn't being very sympathetic, but I was sick of everyone's excuses for being selfish. First it was that Caroline was getting married in December, so how could she possibly come to Cleveland for my high school graduation in June, almost six months before? Then, it was Passover, so how could she possibly spend more time in Cleveland after Grandpa died? Now, she just had a baby, so how could she possibly be expected to care that my parents were getting divorced?

So there I was, alone on a couch in a living room that looked like a department store. Why did Orthodox people have such unoriginal taste anyway? All they seemed to care about was buying things on sale; no one seemed to notice what the sale items actually *looked* like.

The only stuff that might not have been bought on sale was the Jewish stuff, and you better believe there was plenty of that. About a thousand mezuzahs hanging from every doorway, and Jewish books in the glass and chrome bookshelves, and records and cassette tapes by the Neginah Boys Orchestra or something, and even two pieces of art hanging on the living room walls, pictures of religious boys with those long sideburns.

It was sort of annoying the way the whole damned apartment was set up to make you feel you weren't Jewish enough. If I'd been the paranoid type, I might even have thought the Klausners purposely put all that spiritual stuff around just to prove to us how empty our lives were, with our antique bowls and our impressionist art; I might have thought they were trying to say that my parents' marriage could have worked out if they'd spent more time praying than buying oriental rugs.

I put my head down on the cool leather couch pillows, and tried to devise a plan to keep my parents together. Perhaps they could talk to Dr. Stevens, I thought, but then I broke out in a cold sweat. What if he told them about me? Perhaps Dr. Stevens could recommend another psychiatrist, one who specialized in mid-life crises. I had to find a way to convince my mother that no matter how my father acted, no one in the world would ever love her the way he did.

I sat there for a while, thinking up harebrained schemes that only worked on television sit-coms, not in real life. Things like trying to convince my father that my mother (Mrs. Sane, Level-Headed, Never Depressed a Day in Her Life) had temporarily lost her mind, and didn't he remember how there was a history of mental illness on my mother's side of the family? Or telling him how she'd said that thing about "being happy for however many years" she had left; maybe she was worried about her health? Finally, I heard a toilet flush somewhere in the apartment, so I put my ideas on hold.

"You're a middle-of-the-night waker too, huh?" It was Mr. Klausner, cheerful as ever, in his bathrobe and slippers. "I like to be the first one to get the *Times*."

"What time is it?" I said.

"Around two. Sometimes the delivery boy comes early."

I heard him unlock about a half dozen locks and pull open the apartment front door, and then he came back into the living room empty-handed. "I guess it's early even for the *Times*," he said. Was he always smiling, no matter what time of day, no matter what he was telling you?

"Don't let me get in your way," I said. "I was just sitting here because I couldn't sleep."

"You're probably getting excited about your *simcha,*" he said. "You know, your wedding."

"I guess that's it," I said.

"I wish Shira would get married."

"Why do you wish that?"

"I'd feel better if I knew she was going to be taken care of. Not that I'm going anywhere yet, but I'm not getting any younger."

"Maybe she could take care of herself," I said. Actually, I was just trying to be nice, give old Mr. Klausner a break. He was always giving everybody the benefit of the doubt, he was so damned optimistic about human nature I couldn't stand to see him worried about little Shira. But he was right. How could any nineteen-year-old who called her parents Mommy and Daddy take care of herself? I hadn't called my parents Mommy and Daddy since I was a fetus. "She seems very smart," I added.

"She's not independent, she's not like you or Caroline. She's still quite insecure."

"Insecure?" I said. "Shira doesn't strike me as being insecure."

"She is," he said. "I try to give her confidence, but I don't know if you can give someone confidence. It has to come from inside."

Like he was some kind of shrink. I mean, talk about simplistic. He may have known a lot of Hebrew words and Bible stories, he may even have known a little James Joyce, but still, he was no Dr. Stevens.

"Isn't it wonderful?" he said. "The new baby, little Samuel. Shmuel. And now your grandfather lives on in him, in the rituals that he'll perform one day."

"My grandfather didn't perform rituals," I said. "He didn't even believe in God."

"Oh," he said. I felt kind of bad then, like why'd I have to go and put a damper on his happiness just because I was so unhappy. But then I changed my mind. Grandpa was a good person; he was open-minded and tolerant, and what difference did it make if he didn't believe in God? I hoped Samuel would be just like him.

"Speak of the devil," Mr. Klausner said, as Caroline came into the living room, her eyes still closed, holding Samuel, who was, of course, screaming his head off.

"I can't take it anymore," Caroline cried. "I have to get some sleep." She sounded pretty desperate, and even I had to feel sorry for her despite her rotten attitude toward our parents. Maybe she had that postpartum depression everybody was always talking about.

"Let me take him," Mr. Klausner said.

"Why don't you wake Jonathan up?" I said.

"He can't nurse, can he?" she hissed.

"You don't have to yell at *me*," I said.

She sat down next to me and whipped out her left breast; which, even nursing, was no match for mine. Boy, for someone who used to lock her own mother and sister out of the dressing room, she sure didn't have a problem exposing herself in front of her father-in-law. I could never have seen myself doing that in front of Eddie's dad, not to mention my own. *My* dad might have thrown up, that's how much he hated breasts. I don't care *what* Dr. Stevens said, all that baloney about how hard it was for my father when I started developing, how my father was attracted to me or something and that's why he went around acting like my body disgusted him, how a lot of fathers went through that when their daughters became adolescents. Maybe some fathers, I said to Dr. Stevens, but not mine.

The only thing *my* father went through when I developed breasts was the need to tell me that I was too "old" to come downstairs in the morning without wearing a robe over my pajamas, and when we went on vacations, I was no longer to sit at the lunch table without first putting a shirt on over my bathing suit. I'd never heard him say those things to Caroline.

It was obvious that he didn't even want to look at me anymore, that he hated how sloppy I had become, and that he wanted me to cover myself up so he wouldn't have to see the awfulness of it for himself.

Mr. Klausner went over to Caroline and said, "Is there anything I can do to help? How about if I stay up with him when you're done feeding him?"

Caroline was just bawling away, while Samuel's little jaws were working. I started thinking maybe I'd been too hard on her, that maybe she was more troubled by what my mom had said than she let on. I sat there on the couch until Samuel finished eating, and then Mr. Klausner took him, singing some Hebrew lullaby or something to him, and I walked Caroline to her room before I tried going back to sleep.

"It's going to be okay," I said.

"The problem is that I can't fall asleep on demand," she said, like I'd been referring to her and the baby, like the only things that existed in the world were her and her messianic baby. "Just because Samuel wants to sleep now doesn't mean I can just fall back to sleep. And Jonathan just goes right on, snoring away."

"I'm sure you're upset about a lot of things," I said, "but I have a feeling things are going to look a lot better in the morning."

We said good night then, and I very quietly opened Shira's door so as not to wake her. There was something about her that made you want to protect her from people like me. I put her robe back on the door handle where I'd found it—I could just see her making a federal case out of it—and climbed back up the ladder. I fell asleep thinking about the way my mother's face looked when she cried and I knew that that couldn't have been my mother.

I woke up Friday morning at around ten to find Shira on

the floor below me, doing sit-ups. She was wearing a blue sweatsuit, like a person couldn't do sit-ups unless they were wearing a sweatsuit. I came down the ladder, and she did a sort of double take when she saw my naked chest, but then she went back to her sit-ups.

"I feel so gross," she said. "I ate so much at the bris yesterday, and tonight's Shabbos and then it's Sukkos."

"I didn't see you eat so much," I said, pulling on a clean pair of underpants and putting on my bra so that Shira could look at me again. Some people are so awkward.

"I did," she said.

"Coffee with Sweet'N Low couldn't be too fattening," I said.

"But did you see? They forgot the diet Coke, so I had to drink regular soda. All that sugar. And once I had all that sugar, I went and had a bagel on top of it."

"Well, I guess you'd better fast today."

"I know," she said. "I'm going upstairs to the health club for a real workout this afternoon, before Shabbos." I knew it! The Klausners just *had* to live in a building with a health club.

When I went to the bathroom, I noticed Caroline's door was closed, so I figured the baby must have finally gone to sleep, and so had Caroline. The apartment seemed sort of empty to me; I'd never been in it on a regular old weekday, when it wasn't the Sabbath or some kind of occasion such as the engagement or the bris. Jonathan had probably left for the hospital hours ago, not to mention Mr. Klausner, the early riser. He was probably at his fancy-schmancy law firm before the *Times* even arrived.

My mother was sitting at the kitchen table having coffee with, of all people, Mrs. Klausner. I certainly hoped she wasn't confiding in *her*. It wasn't like my mother to confide in people, but then again I'd never thought it was like my mother to divorce my father. That would have been just what Mrs. Klausner needed to hear, that my parents' marriage was in trouble, to confirm everything she already thought of us. But my mother wasn't confiding in her, she was just sitting there being friendly and cheerful and her usual self, and I was still hopeful that all she'd needed the night before was a good night's sleep. Mrs. Klausner was telling her some story about how the last time she went to the mikvah, the boiler had broken, and the water had been freezing.

"That's terrible!" my mother said. "You know, I have an Orthodox friend in Cleveland who goes to the mikvah."

"Uh-huh," Mrs. Klausner said. Why was my mother trying to fit in with this woman anyway? I mean, what did Mrs. Klausner care if my mother had an Orthodox friend in Cleveland? "Good morning, Jane," she said. "Sleep well?"

"Sure," I said.

"Joe told me you were up in the middle of the night with him," she said. "Too excited to sleep, huh?"

"Right."

"I wish Shira would get married already. You must be thrilled, Flip."

"What's so great about getting married?" I said. "Why would my mother be thrilled?"

"Every mother wants her daughter to get married," Mrs. Klausner said, like she, of all people, represented every mother.

"I want Jane to be happy," my mother said, and Mrs. Klausner smiled, as if to say being happy and being married were synonymous. She shoved a box of Entenmann's coffee cake across the table and then watched my mother and me eat it in that superior way people who are only drinking black coffee have.

My mother sort of looked down into her mug and hurriedly digested her cake when my father came in. He, of course, looked terrific, and I felt like telling him that if he didn't want my mother to leave him he'd better start looking a little tired and depressed, the way she did. Why wasn't he lying awake at night?

"Good morning," Mrs. Klausner said, and she got up to get him a cup of coffee. Not only was she *her* husband's perfect wife, now she was trying to show my mother up. Great.

The four of us went around the table and compared our night of sleep. Naturally, my father was Mr. Charming, talking about some dream he'd had wherein it was the morning of his Bar Mitzvah and he'd forgotten his portion. Of course, it just figured he'd had a Jewish dream in the Klausners' apartment. In certain ways, he was no better than Willy, the way he tried to fit in with these people by "talking Jewish," though at least my father knew better than to have a dream about the Holocaust. Mrs. Klausner laughed appreciatively; my mother didn't.

"I was going to invite you to stay through the weekend," Mrs. Klausner said, "but, you know, it's Sukkos, and we don't do much around here except go to shul and eat, so . . ."

She didn't fool me; she was only trying to make it all sound unappealing so we wouldn't stay. I couldn't stand it when people said they were *going* to invite you to something and then told you why they couldn't. We celebrated Sukkos too; we went to temple and ate sponge cake in the Sukkah the same way the Klausners did.

"I'm afraid we have to leave this afternoon," my father said, letting her off the hook. And then, as if he owed her an explanation for why we were leaving, when she didn't even want us to stay in the first place, he said, "Ever since Flip's father died, we don't like to leave her mother for long periods of time." I tried not to smile at my father's bold-faced lie. Grandma wouldn't have minded; she had a more active social life than the rest of us put together.

"Oh," Mrs. Klausner said and made one of those pretend pouty faces, with the downturned mouth and everything.

After my father finished his coffee and complimented it to death, he asked me if I wanted to take a walk with him. Shit. He was going to give me his side.

"Maybe Mom wants to come too," I said, hoping that if I could get the two of them to talk about the idea of divorce in front of me, they'd see how totally ridiculous the whole thing was. But my mother didn't seem to appreciate my thoughtfulness and said she was going to stick around and help Caroline with the baby. It seemed to me she said that last part, about the baby, for Mrs. Klausner's benefit.

I got dressed in Shira's room while Shira did her leg lifts to the music of the Beach Boys, of all the ridiculous groups in the world. Then I stood in front of her full-length mirror, trying to think of what else I could do to put off hearing what my father was going to tell me. Finally, when I could think of nothing else to do—how many more times could I brush my teeth or comb my hair?—my father and I walked across 86th Street toward Central Park. I tried to enjoy the perfect fall day—seventy degrees, no humidity—but under the circumstances I would have preferred rain.

"Mom told you?" he said. He didn't say it right away, though; he waited until we got into the park, like someone might overhear us on West 86th Street. He was a very private kind of person.

"I think she's having some kind of mid-life crisis or something," I said. "I wouldn't take it too seriously."

"No," he said. "She's serious."

"But you love each other, Dad! Don't you?"

We dodged some roller bladers and bicyclists. "We do, but you know how rough it's been," he said. "All the tension and fighting in our house all these years."

"But that's how it's *supposed* to be," I said. "You even told me that it's the people who call each other sweetheart and honey that you have to worry about."

My dad laughed, like I was some cute six-year-old who had said something adorable. "Did I say that? If I did, I didn't mean that you don't have to worry about the people who *don't* call each other sweetheart and honey." He was still chuckling. He didn't seem to understand how much stock I'd always held in the things he said, and here he was not even remembering saying them in the first place.

"I think this is a huge mistake," I said, "and if you do this I'll be totally disillusioned for the rest of my life."

"I'm sorry you feel that way," he said. "It's not as if we didn't try; I'd say twenty-five years is a pretty good effort."

"But this isn't supposed to happen to people like you! This happens to other people, not to people like you and Mom!"

"It happens to all kinds of people, Jane. You know that."

My father seemed so reconciled to my mother's decision that I would almost have believed he was, except for the fact that in one breath he'd say there was no point in dwelling on it, we'd all get through it just fine, and in the next breath he'd ask me how I thought he could prevent my mother from going through with it.

"I mean, do you see any other solution?" he said. For the first time in my life, my father was asking me for *my* advice instead of the other way around; it was enough to make me want to cry. I couldn't believe the hot dog and ice cream vendors were still going on about their business while my parents' marriage was dissolving. Nobody turned down their radios or their microphones or whatever was making so much noise, nobody stopped playing their electric guitars, not even out of respect for our conversation.

"Maybe you could see a marriage counselor," I said. "Remember when I was having all those problems? You sent *me* to talk to someone."

"No," he said. "I don't believe in it. I'm too old to change, and so's Mom."

We'd veered off into a wooded area, with little streams and paths. Not too far ahead of us a group of men and women in formal attire were standing around as if waiting for something to happen, and then I noticed a woman in a long white wedding gown emerge from the other direction. I couldn't believe that Caroline had gotten married in a hotel when she could have gotten married here; I guess it was that Orthodox unoriginal stuff again.

"Mom would love it here," I said. "Too bad you'll never be walking together again."

"We'll walk together again," he said. "It's not going to be a bitter separation. We'll still talk to each other; I mean, we have you kids."

"Where are you going to live?" I said.

"I'll find a nice little apartment on Coventry," he said. "Closer to the hospital. It's good to be alone. Nobody bothers you."

He was holding on to my arm as he said it was good to be alone, and it didn't take a brain surgeon to see that it wasn't going to be good at all.

"I'm going to move in with you," I said. "I'm not going to marry Eddie."

"Don't you ever say that," he said, turning to look at me. "You're not going to sit around taking care of me. If you don't want to marry Eddie, don't marry Eddie, but don't use me as an excuse. You're not moving in with me." If only Caroline could have seen him now, I thought, she'd remember all the things she used to admire about my father before she married Jonathan's family. Here his life was falling apart, and he was worried about mine. No matter how bad his temper was, he was still the best father a person could have.

"You know," he said. "There's a lesson in this for you. What's happening to Mom, it's partly because she never worked outside the house. This is what happens to a person who gives and gives and gives, raises children and then has nothing left when they're gone."

It was a little depressing to hear my father—the most insightful man in the universe, aside from Dr. Stevens—say something so dense. It wasn't because of *us* that she wanted a divorce; it was because of *him*! Besides, how could she have worked? She had to take care of three small children and one grown one!

After a while, we turned around and started walking west, back in the direction of the Klausners' apartment. We didn't talk about my parents anymore; instead, my father pointed out the azaleas or rhododendron or forsythia, things I couldn't have cared less about. My poor dad; he'd planted all those flowers and trees in our backyard, and if he moved to a little apartment on Coventry, he'd never see another azalea again.

"See this?" he said, pointing to a brownstone on 87th Street. We'd decided to take a different route home. "Now what would be so bad about living in an apartment like that?"

"Nothing, Dad," I said. I wasn't going to be the one to tell him that the apartments on Coventry bore little resemblance to the brownstone he was admiring.

When we got back to the apartment, everybody was in the baby's room, where Mrs. Klausner was talking to TLM (The Little Messiah) while she took him out of the pajamas we'd given him. "We can't have you wearing these filthy things all day, *boychik*," she was saying, like the kid would die from wearing drooled-on pjs or something. "Thatta boy, put your *kepuhle* down right there." *Kepuhle! Kepuhle!* Why couldn't she have just said head? I mean, in my opinion, if you're going to speak English, speak English! If you're going to speak Yiddish, speak Yiddish! Intermingling them, it's so affected!

The whole apartment smelled like chicken soup and brisket, and I could hardly hold back the tears as I realized I wouldn't have a house that smelled like that anymore. Lucky Caroline. Lucky lucky Caroline. She'd gotten herself a back-up family.

While Mrs. Klausner was undressing TLM, my mother was clipping his nails. "You do it like that?" Mrs. Klausner said, as if now she was going to find something wrong with the way my mother clipped fingernails. "See, I find it's easier to do it when the baby's sleeping. Oh well. Come on, everybody. It's time for Shmulik's bath."

Shmulik, for Christ's sake.

She carried him into the kitchen and held him over the sink while Caroline and I (and even my father, if you can believe it) hovered around to watch him getting a sponge bath. My mother turned on the faucet ("Don't you think that's too hot?" Mrs. Klausner said), and suggested it might be easier to put him down on the edge of the sink rather than holding him above it. Naturally, Mrs. Klausner held him above it, breaking her back rather than admitting that maybe my mother knew something about bathing a child too.

TLM, of course, was not very happy with the whole thing (he wasn't even happy when his face *wasn't* being smooshed with a wet washcloth!), so she'd barely even finished washing his hands before Mrs. Klausner wrapped him up in his little hooded towel and held him to her concave chest.

"May I?" my mother said, reaching out to take him.

"Be careful of his head," Mrs. Klausner said, and that was all it took to send me right over the old edge. I couldn't hold it in anymore. "Why don't you leave her alone already?" I said. "She's having a hard enough time as it is without you criticizing the way she clips his nails and the way she holds him and the way she turns on the water!"

Everybody fell silent, even the baby, who'd been wriggling around, of course.

"You've been insulting my family since the first day we met you," I said, "and I've had just about enough of your superior, condescending attitude. Who do you think you are, anyway?" Mrs. Klausner looked at me for a second with the most pathetic, pitiful look on her face (even *I* felt sorry for her) and then she left the room. Naturally, Shira followed, in her little blue sweatsuit.

"What'd you do that for?" Caroline said.

"If we'd waited for you to, we'd be dead."

Caroline didn't even argue with me, and my parents just stood there quietly, like I was some kind of mentally unbalanced freak or something. Like I was paranoid, and Mrs. Klausner really hadn't been treating us poorly all this time.

"You better pack up your bag," my mother said to me, as she bounced little Samuel in her arms. Poor Mom. I had embarrassed her, even though my intentions had been to do something on her behalf. "We're leaving in a half hour," she said.

I went into Shira's room and started packing. I took the dress I'd worn for the bris out of her closet and noticed that someone had replaced the wire hanger it had originally been hanging on with a wood one, as if my dress would have been ruined or something from hanging on a cheap wire hanger. Well, I certainly wasn't taking their wood hanger with me, I wasn't a charity case. I dug through the wastebasket and found the wire one, then replaced the wood hanger in the closet. Then I checked the bathroom to make sure I hadn't left anything, and what do I hear but my mother apologizing to Mrs. Klausner for my behavior.

"It's really been tough for her," she was saying. "She used

to be very close to Caroline, and now with the baby . . ." I couldn't believe my ears. My mother hated that kind of psychological bullshit!

"I understand," Mrs. Klausner was saying. I thought I heard a sniffle or two while she was talking, like she had to catch her breath from how hard I'd made her cry. "I understand it must be very hard for her. And she's so young; she doesn't understand yet how things change when you have a baby. You just don't have time for anyone else."

"Right," my mother said.

"I just hope you don't feel the way she does. That I've been insulting."

"Of course not," my mother said. "I couldn't be happier that Caroline's got another family who loves her so much."

"Oh, we do," Mrs. Klausner said. "We love her like she's our own daughter."

I couldn't listen anymore, I went back into Shira's room and slammed the door. That stupid New York accent, I was thinking. It wasn't even real, that was the thing; the woman was from *Berkeley* or something, she wasn't a New Yorker. Leave it to someone like her to want to sound like a New Yorker.

"Who is it?" I said, when someone knocked on the door.

"It's Caroline, can I come in?"

"I guess."

She was wearing a robe that only Mrs. Klausner could have gotten for her: polka dots. "Where's TLM?" I said.

"What?"

"The Little Messiah."

She actually laughed. "Is that what you call him?"

"Well, at first I was calling him The Little Prince, but that was too unoriginal."

"I have to admit," she said. "They do treat him pretty well, the little screaming brat." I suppose if I hadn't been such a self-absorbed asshole, I might have asked her whether she really felt as hostile toward her baby as she sounded, but I *was* a self-absorbed asshole.

"I'm sorry if I embarrassed you in front of your in-laws," I said.

"Don't worry about it," she said. "One thing I can say for my mother-in-law: she doesn't hear what she doesn't want to hear. She'll go to her grave thinking that *you're* the crazy one and that your jealousy drove you to say those things."

"*Am* I the crazy one?"

"Sort of," she said. "But not completely." We both laughed. I didn't even mind being called crazy when Caroline was the one calling me it.

"What are we going to do about Mom and Dad?" I said.

"Jane, you've got to let them do what they're going to do. You can't stop it."

"That's easy for you to say," I said. "They're my only family. I don't have another family when this one falls apart."

"But you're going to make a new family," she said. "With Eddie."

"Mom and Dad and you and Willy will still be my real family," I said.

"No," she said. "It changes. I think of Jonathan and Samuel as my real family."

How could she say such a thing? I knew I was going to cry if I opened my mouth, so I just sat there thinking how all alone I was in the world, how the only person who may have been more alone than I was was Willy. I didn't even have Dr. Stevens anymore, not as my shrink, and not as my colleague. Ever since that letter-shredding incident, he'd been treating me like some fragile kind of nut; it almost made me long for the days when he treated me like a typist. His secretary hadn't come back to work for another two weeks after the original week, but from then on he asked Rena the receptionist to type his letters for him, even though she was about twenty times slower than I.

At first, when he came back to his office and found the torn letters, he was really nice and caring. He buzzed me in my office and told me to come in, then he even shut the door behind me the way he used to when I was his patient. His voice was really nice and concerned, and he said he wanted to know why I was so angry. I told him that I didn't like being used for my typing skills and didn't he remember that I'd been the valedictorian of my class and why didn't he treat me the way he treated his other colleagues, like that bitchy psychiatrist Dr. Lanz he was always flirting with? "But you're a secretary here," he said, "you're not a psychiatrist." Maybe he thought he was being straight or honest with me, but I really resented the implications of what he said, and I started crying my head off and flew out of his office. He didn't come after me, and ever since, he'd been treating me like I might break. I tried to show him I was over it by acting normal and cheerful and funny, but he didn't seem to buy it. I even told him how he could just tape the letters back together and photocopy them so they'd look whole, and all he said was that the receptionist had already retyped them but he appreciated my suggestion.

When my parents and I boarded the plane to go back to Cleveland, I tried to organize it in such a way that they'd have to sit next to each other, but I guess they were more clever than I, and so I ended up in the middle. My father kept sitting forward and trying to strike up a conversation with my mother, but she just nodded or shook her head or gave one-word answers to his questions. He took out one of those airline magazines and asked her if he should clip the article about trips to the Thousand Islands, and she just looked at him like he was crazy, like didn't he understand, they weren't *going* on any more trips together. When the flight attendant came around to get our drink orders, my father ordered a Jack Daniel's and sat back in his seat like he was accepting defeat. It was three o'clock on a Friday afternoon, and he was ordering liquor! When he got up to go to the bathroom, I looked at my mother. "Do you have to be so mean to him?" I said.

"*Me* mean to *him?*" she said.

"Mom, he's trying to make up with you, don't you see?"

"He can't make up with me by suggesting a trip to the Thousand Islands," she said. "He thinks this is all superficial, that the problems will go away if he suggests a vacation. I don't want a nice vacation. I want a nice life. Or whatever's left of it."

"Whatever's left of it?" I said. "You're forty-eight years old, Mom! This is the second time you've said something about being on your death bed. Geez." I turned my Walkman on to listen to some Traveling Wilburys. Then I turned it off. "You're not sick, Ma, are you?" I said. "Ma, are you sick?"

"What?" she said, pretending like she hadn't heard me when I knew damn well she had.

"Something happened, didn't it, Mom? Tell me what happened."

"It's just a little cyst," she said. "It's nothing to worry about. I'll get it removed and everything will be fine."

"Where is this little cyst?"

"What difference does it make?" she said, and then my father came back from the bathroom and started talking to the guy in the row in front of us. He didn't know him or anything; he just saw that he was wearing a knit yarmulke with his name, Joshua, on it.

"My son-in-law wears a yarmulke," my father said.

"Is that right?" Joshua said, turning around just enough not to be rude.

"He's very Orthodox."

My mother sat there clucking her tongue and, even without looking at her, you knew she was giving my father a look.

"What do you have to eat there?" my father continued. "My son-in-law always orders the kosher snack, even if it's just a short flight like this one."

"Yep," Joshua said.

"Wilton Foods, right?" Like it was really going to impress the hell out of this guy that my father knew the name of the kosher airplane food!

"That's right," Josh said, but this time he didn't even turn around. My father reeked of Jack Daniel's, and Josh probably thought my father was a drunk. The one thing I'll give old Josh, though; he was pretty respectful. After all my father's harassing, he made a special point of saying good-bye to us when we were standing there in the aisle waiting for the people ahead of us to deplane. They were about the slowest people in the history of air travel.

The Cleveland Hopkins airport had one of those fancy people movers so that you didn't even have to move your legs and you were practically already in the middle of the parking lot. My father offered to carry my mother's bag, but that damned people mover made it so easy for you—you could just lay your bag down right next to your feet—it didn't even give a person like my father a chance to make it all up to my mother. I kept trying to pull over next to my father, tell him what my mother had told me, tell him this whole divorce thing had to do with my mother's mortality, for God's sake, but he was walking on ahead, like he didn't even realize you could stand still on a people mover and get to your destination.

The ride home from the airport was pretty quiet, except for me in the back seat, feeling sorry for myself, sniffling and crying like a baby, repeating in my head the same sentence over and over: my parents are getting divorced and my mother is dying of cancer. Finally, my mother turned around and said I should cut it out already, I wasn't doing anybody any good, and nobody was going to change their minds about anything because of my crying. She didn't even turn on the radio the way she usually did, trying to find a concerto or a sonata or something. She just sat there, looking straight ahead, like she wasn't even going to let herself look at my father and see how lovable he was, like she didn't even want to get divorced but she was too embarrassed to say she'd changed her mind.

I looked out the window as we drove down the highway, though there wasn't much to see. Unless you considered the Terminal Tower a tourist attraction. The Terminal Tower. It figured that Cleveland's one tall building would have a name like that. What a stupid place! There wasn't even a skyline, except for one tall building with a name that reminded you of your mother dying of cancer.

5

So, now I guess I can stand to tell what happened with Willy and me.

The summer I was twelve and Willy was six, I took his hand and put it on my breast. I had just finished reading *The Red Balloon* to him, and he was sitting on my lap in the yellow beanbag chair I had gotten for my Bat Mitzvah.

Earlier that day I had gone with my mother to Solomon's, the bra store, where an old woman with gefilte-fish breath told my mother that the training bra I was wearing was useless. She suggested a minimizer, like anyone so enormous couldn't possibly be attractive. I didn't say a word to my mother the whole way home, I was so furious with her for not sticking up for me, for not telling that old woman thank you very much but she doesn't need to be minimized, she's fine just the way she is. When we got home, I stormed up the stairs to my room and locked my door (I didn't care *what* my father said), and took that goddammed minimizer out of the bag, cutting it in half with a pair of nail scissors. It took a good half hour, what with all that wire I had to cut through.

I wasn't even wearing a bra when I had Willy sitting on my lap, which made the whole thing easier. I simply lifted up the black tanktop I was wearing, and stuck his hand inside. I had always been a very good girl before that, fighting with my conscience over this thing or that, but something about the way a hand felt on my breast loosed my inhibitions, and it was all I could do not to go any further than I had.

After that, Willy would just hang around me all the time, like I was going to make a habit of having him feel me up or something. "Could we read *The Red Balloon* again?" he'd say, and I'd know what he was asking for. At first I screamed at him, "No! I'm not reading to you anymore!" I knew it wasn't right to yell at him, but I was so mad at myself, so disgusted and depressed about what I'd done, that I acted like it was *his* fault.

One morning, about two weeks later, as I was coming out of the shower in my white terrycloth monogrammed bathrobe, another Bat Mitzvah gift, Willy was standing outside the bathroom door. That feeling came over me again, the one I'd had in the beanbag chair, a mixture of rage and desire, and I lay down on the floor in front of the bathroom and let him stick his hand inside the opening in my robe. This time he moved his hand around by himself, and if I hadn't been lying down I would have passed out from how good it felt. When I finally came to my senses, I stood up and went into my room, slamming the door behind me. Willy followed me, and I screamed at him to get out. Then I went crazy. I started throwing my 45 record collection around my room and knocking all the little stupid things on my dresser—old perfume bottles, fake jewelry, little ceramic penguins—onto the floor. We'd only just moved from our old house the week before, but I'd arranged my new room identically to my old one and had no trouble finding things to throw. Anyway, I must have been making a lot of noise, because my parents came running up the stairs like a bunch of firemen or something.

"What's going on in here?" my father said.

"She's going crazy," Willy said.

"Get out of here!" I screamed. "Everybody get out!"

My father told Willy to go to his room, and then my parents sat down on my bed with me while I cried my eyes out. My father put his arm around me and comforted me, while my mother, who didn't know what to do with someone so emotional, just sat there looking down at her nails. "I hate myself!" I cried. "I hate my fat disgusting revolting ugly stupid self!"

"You're beautiful, Jane. You're smart," my father said, the first and last time he said those things, thankfully, since I didn't know what to do with myself when he was being so nice. I knew he loved me and everything, but he'd been acting weird about me ever since my body had gotten so fat and out of control, and ever since I heard him in the kitchen saying to my mom one night, "What are these pills in the medicine cabinet? For Jane? For menstrual cramps?" He just *had* to go and read the label out loud, and there I was at the top of the stairs, having to hear my father read about my menstrual cramps, having to stand the awful fact that he knew I'd gotten my period. It just figured; every other female in the United States of America took Midol for cramps. *I* had to have a prescription, with my name on it no less.

Willy stopped asking me to read to him, and eventually things sort of went back to normal. Except for the fact that that was the year he started making up stories which, harmless as they may have been, were embarrassing and disturbing and made you wonder what was behind them. I mean, was it normal for Willy to tell Paul Caplan's mother that my mother was the mother in the Gatorade commercials, when my mother had never so much as heard of the stuff? Or how about the time he told his math teacher he hadn't done his homework because he was up all night packing for our move to California? We'd never even *visited* California, let alone planned to move there! Couldn't Willy even have made up lies that were less verifiable? Ones that couldn't be shot down with one simple phone call? Oh, the embarrassing phone calls! Mrs. Caplan, wondering whether my mother was in any *other* commercials; Willy's math teacher, wanting to know *when* we'd be moving!

That was also the year Willy started having problems at school; it was true that, the year before, his kindergarten teacher had called my mother a few times to say that Willy frequently seemed withdrawn in class. But first grade was when it became clear that he didn't have the skills he was supposed to have; anything that first graders were supposed to be able to do, words they were supposed to know, concepts they were supposed to understand, Willy didn't. I remember the school psychologist gave him a bunch of intelligence and psychological tests, tests with names I'll never forget because they sounded so funny: the Whisker, the Rat. Only later, when I took an introductory psychology class in high school did I learn that the Whisker was the WISC-R, the Rat was the WRAT. But at the time Willy was taking the tests, I was more interested in the results than anything else. Selfish as it sounds, I was praying that he had a learning disability, dyslexia, even mental retardation, anything with an organic name that wouldn't implicate me. So you can imagine how I felt when the psychologist wrote up his report saying that Willy's intellectual capacity was adequate, that his underachievement was "emotionally motivated," that Willy was so distracted by what was going on inside him that he couldn't concentrate on anything else. He said the good news was that Willy didn't have a psychiatric disorder; he had an academic problem with a psychological component, something, the psychologist said, which could be alleviated with therapy and tutoring.

But after three years of psychotherapy with a social worker whom Willy referred to as Mr. Nobody, and daily tutoring that took place in our living room, Willy was still too distracted by something to get satisfactory marks in school, and his lying had escalated into credit-card fraud. He'd dug up an old American Express card of my father's and tried to charge two hundred dollars' worth of record albums over the phone. Maybe if he hadn't had that academic problem of his, he would have been bright enough to see that the damned card had expired two years before.

My parents met with the therapist monthly, but usually, according to my mother, those meetings ended with my father walking out in a huff at some perceived insult. "I'm tired of being cast as the bad guy," I remember him screaming at dinner one night after a session. When Willy was nine years old and in the fourth grade (only having graduated from the third thanks to the ministrations of a kindly and lenient teacher), the therapist suggested that Willy's problems might be addressed more successfully away from home, and he went on to recommend the Winthrop School for Boys.

"But that's so extreme!" I remember crying to my parents when they told us. Caroline, naturally, didn't even bat an eyelash; she was never all that interested in things that weren't about her.

"We think it's the best thing for Willy," my father said, and I wondered if they knew what I'd done, I wondered if they'd told the therapist about me and that's why he said it was best for

Willy to be out of our house, like it was a house of *prostitution* or something.

It was a bad winter, after Willy left. I was sixteen, and I was going to all those sweet-sixteen parties, pretending to be just like all the other girls, talking about kissing and going to second base, when what I really felt like was a dirty old man who was so far beyond the innocence of second base that he could never go back. The week before I got my driver's license, I became so depressed I went into my mother's top dresser drawer and took out a bottle of Atarax. I stored the pills in my desk until I was brave enough to swallow them, and the next day I took out four library books about suicide. That's what a jerk I was; I had to *read* about killing myself before I did it. I stuck the books under my bed when I went to school the day after, but Rose, the maid, found them when she was vacuuming my room. She was pretty illiterate, so she just left them there, right on top of my bed where anyone who walked by my room could see them. That night my father sat on the edge of my bed and asked me if I wanted to talk to someone, he'd seen the books I'd checked out of the library.

I fell in love with Dr. Stevens pretty quickly. After everything I told him, he still didn't make me feel like a pervert, although he probably thought I was one. I mean maybe he had to say nice things to me, maybe he was scared I'd really kill myself and he'd get sued, so he said all sorts of things to make me feel better, things like how it wasn't my fault that Willy was in a special school, how plenty of people who have sexual experiences with their brothers or sisters go on to be perfectly fine, how there were so many things that affected a person you couldn't just isolate one thing and say that *that* was what did it. He kept saying how I had only been twelve, a little girl with the body of a woman, overstimulated by the way men, especially my father (right! like my father found cows really attractive!), started looking at me, even by the way girls, like the girls at camp, looked at me. He said I was attractive and bright and funny, and that I was very sensitive, the way I cared about Willy. Now can you see why I'm so in love with the guy?

I kept thinking of all this that Monday in October when my father moved out of our house, to his stupid little apartment on Euclid Heights Boulevard, right around the corner from Arabica, probably the same building where Alex Bevan and Michael Spiro and all those other Cleveland folksingers lived. How do you like that? My dad, in his three-piece Barneys suits and his wing-tip shoes, living with a bunch of folk singers.

He didn't take very much with him the day he left, said he'd come back when he was more settled in. He sat down next to me on my bed the way he had seven years before when I was twelve, to comfort me, the way he had then. I thought about telling him what had happened all those years ago; I was willing to do *anything* to keep my parents together, but then I thought, what if it doesn't do any good and all I end up doing is making it uncomfortable for us to look at each other again?

"Dad, what happened with Willy, you know, having to go to the Winthrop School and everything, that wasn't because of you and Mom."

"Who ever said it was?"

"Last month, when we were in New York for the bris, and I told Mom how bad it would be for Willy if you got divorced, she told me he would be better off with you two apart."

"She may be partially right," he said, "but we're not doing this for Willy's sake. This has to do with Mom and me and nothing else."

Nothing else except the fact that my mother had gone to the gynecologist in September—two weeks before the infamous bris—and he'd found a lump under her armpit. Her armpit, of all things. *That* was the body part she wouldn't name for me when we were on the plane back to Cleveland! Like I'd have been disillusioned to find out my mother had armpits! "I told you it was nothing to worry about," she'd said after the guy removed it. Like *she* wasn't the one who had been worried. Like *she* wasn't the one who was divorcing my dad because she'd thought she was dying. She didn't even tell my dad about the lump until the morning of the day she was going to the hospital. "I told you it would be benign," she said afterward, when the results came in. But then how come she was still divorcing my dad?

"I still think this whole thing happened because of that cyst," I said. "Mom probably started to feel really old or something, and then she just went crazy."

"Who knows?" my father said. "Who ever knows these things? Maybe Grandpa's death is what did it."

"Well, did you ever discuss that?" I said, as if it wasn't too late for this conversation, as if my father hadn't already paid a month's rent on his new place, as if my parents hadn't already met with a divorce lawyer.

"Listen, I don't blame Mom," he said. "It probably is for the best anyway. We'll both be happier this way."

Talk about defense mechanisms. Geez!

We sat like that for a long time, together on my bed, sometimes holding hands, sometimes not, talking about begonias and azaleas or anything that didn't hurt to talk about. Finally, my dad gave me a hard kiss on my forehead and stood up.

"I'll call you every day, Dad," I said. "We'll have lunch at Tommy's every Saturday. If you don't have other plans, that is." I said the "other plans" part because I knew if he thought I was just feeling sorry for him, he'd never have lunch with me. I didn't really think he'd *have* other plans.

"*You* may have other plans on Saturday, once you and

Eddie are married," he said. I hadn't told him yet that I wasn't going to marry Eddie. In fact, I hadn't even told Eddie, and the wedding invitations were supposed to go out the very next day. Mrs. Klausner, the wedding maven, told Caroline, who told me, that they should have gone out October 1 for a November 15 wedding, and here it was already October 10. I had told Eddie I was coming over that night to help him stuff the envelopes, but when I got there he was just wearing a towel, and he had that old horny look on his face.

"Come here," he said. Naturally, we had to go into his room and get into bed. Forget about the floor, the kitchen table, the couch. Mr. Spontaneous he wasn't, and you could tell he had to stop himself from hanging my clothes up after he had undressed me. I mean, don't get me wrong, it's not like I'm a slob or something, I just figured picking up a pair of underpants is something that can wait until afterward. And that's a pretty relaxed comment coming from me, Miss Hides Her Underpants in Her Shoes When She Goes to the Gynecologist.

Anyway, there we were naked, him on top of me, and it suddenly seemed ridiculous that we weren't just doing it, having sex. My parents were getting divorced, Dr. Stevens wasn't ever going to marry me, where in the world did I get my romantic ideas? What in the world was I saving myself for anyway?

"What are you doing?" Eddie said.

"What do you think?"

He hesitated for a minute and then said, "Well, I should at least put on a condom."

He opened up the drawer of his nightside table, and took out a condom. He put it on so expertly, I figured he must have been practicing up for our wedding night.

Well, all I can say is, it didn't hurt the way the magazines said it would, but it certainly didn't make me die of pleasure either. Frankly, I couldn't understand what all the fuss was about, having some organ which could just as well have been an elbow for all the difference it made, being shoved in and out, when you could have somebody's wet mouth right on the spot with all those amazing nerve endings.

Afterward, Eddie didn't even bother taking the rubber off; he just walked carefully over to the bathroom to dispose of it. Meanwhile, I sat on his bed and looked across the room at the picture of the two of us on his dresser. In the picture, I was sitting on his lap, my arms thrown around him, smiling. I wasn't that bad-looking, actually, when I smiled. Of course, that was what people had been telling me all my life—"You're so much prettier when you smile"—so it wasn't really a new thought or anything. It was just that it was such an idiotic thing to say. Like I could help it that the natural resting position of my face was a frown. Besides, my father liked the fact that I didn't smile so much; he said happy people were usually stupid too.

If I had to describe myself, I realized, I'd say that I was plain. But I mean that as a compliment, not an insult. I know that most people usually describe someone as plain if they're ugly, but I think of plain as meaning plain—simple, natural, not fancy. I have plain, simple features—small mouth, regular chin and teeth, straight nose, plain brown eyes, and skin that rarely breaks out. Contrast that with Julia Roberts, Miss Funny Mouth/Funny Nose/Big Forehead. I guess that's the deceptive thing about facial features, though; even if they're ugly individually, they sometimes come together to make a pretty face, and vice versa.

"We're not getting married, are we?" Eddie said from the bathroom. I think it was the most insightful thing he'd ever said to me, and it almost made me want to change my mind.

"No," I said. I thought about getting up and going over to him, putting my arms around him, like it would be a real comfort or something if I took my naked body and shoved it in his face, like I'd really want some asshole who broke *my* engagement to come over and pity *me*.

"I knew it," he said. "We wouldn't have had sex otherwise."

"I'm sorry," I said. "I'm sorry you won't be a virgin when you get married."

"No," he said. "I knew we weren't getting married, even before I put on the condom. But I wanted to anyway. I figured I ought to get something out of you."

He shut the bathroom door, and when he came out, he was dressed, and his hair was freshly combed. He walked out of the room then, sticking his wallet in his back pocket, like we hadn't just called the whole thing off. I took off my engagement ring and reluctantly put it in the drawer next to his condoms, wondering why I couldn't have loved Eddie as much as I loved his ring.

By the time I was dressed, he was sitting at his kitchen table, already halfway through the invitations, tearing them in half the way I'd torn those letters of Dr. Stevens. Luckily, there were only about fifty invitations, so it wouldn't take him too long; it was a good thing he hadn't been engaged to Caroline.

"Don't do that," I said.

"You can't save wedding invitations," he said. "Nobody else is going to use them. They'll make good scrap paper."

"I'm sorry, Eddie," I said again. The invitations were so pretty and simple and elegant—none of that pretentious Hebrew stuff on the inside, like Caroline's—I could hardly bear to see them being torn up.

"Just don't give me any bullshit about this having anything to do with your parents getting divorced," he said. "You never loved me, so don't blame this on them."

"I thought I loved you," I said, but even I wasn't convinced, and Eddie didn't bother to look up. "I'm sorry about the computer, you know, the way you figured out who should sit with who at the reception. You're very good at that stuff. Don't let anybody tell you you're not creative."

I couldn't think of anything else to say then, so I said good-bye. "See ya," he said, like we hadn't just had sex or something, like this were just any old ordinary night. I sort of stood there for a while, shifting my weight, waiting for something to happen, waiting for Eddie to say something. Finally, when he didn't, I fished my car keys out of my pocket and went down to the parking lot.

It seemed about a century ago that Grandpa had been alive and he and Grandma had lived in this same complex of apartment buildings. Grandpa had died only six months ago, and then Grandma'd moved to the apartment complex up the street where she became very friendly with her next-door neighbor Bill—The Locksmith, we called him (because he was always unjamming Grandma's faulty lock)—and now she was marrying him. Nothing fancy or anything, but a wedding nonetheless. Maybe someone would finally get married in our backyard, the way my father always wanted.

Anyway, the point was, what had *I* accomplished in the last six months? I'd become engaged and then I'd become unengaged.

When I got home, my mother was sitting at the kitchen table with two friends my father had always despised. One, because she had a loud laugh, and the other, because her teeth were too big. "Why does she have to have such big teeth?" he used to say, and my mother, before her Gloria Steinem days, would try to explain. Well, I hoped she was happy now; my father was gone, and she could have her stupid friends over to her heart's content.

"Joan's just finished her psychology dissertation," my mother said to me, like I was supposed to be interested because

I used to see a psychiatrist. My mother was always going around making these tenuous connections between me and her friends, like otherwise she and I had nothing in common.

"Congratulations," I said. "I just broke my engagement."

"What?" Mom said. She put down her iced coffee. "What happened?"

"I didn't want to be married," I said. "You can understand that, can't you?" Things got a little awkward and quiet then, until Mrs. Psychologist went and opened up her toothy mouth.

"You know," she said. "Your mother is not having an easy time of it. Maybe you ought not to be so hard on her."

Wow, what a brilliant insight, I thought. That's the thing about psychologists; they tell you things you've known since you were about two and then they act like they only know them because they have a Ph.D.

"I'm tired," I said. "I'm going to sleep. Good night, everyone." I went upstairs, giving Joan the freedom to psychoanalyze me to death, and called my father. I was ready to jump in my car when he didn't pick up the phone after three rings, but then he was there, his voice as great as ever. He started telling me how he loved his new place, how he could go out at ten o'clock at night and get a cup of coffee at Arabica if he wanted to, not like out in the suburbs where you had to drive everywhere. He told me how the commute to work took about fifteen minutes, not fifty, like it used to. Everything sounded just great, I told him, but I couldn't stop imagining him sitting there by himself at his kitchen table every morning, nobody to talk to, nobody to compliment the way he looked as he left for work.

"How's everything with you?" he said.

"I told Eddie I didn't want to get married," I said. "I know the invitations were expensive; I'll pay you back."

"Don't worry about the invitations, Jane," he said. He

didn't even seem very surprised to hear I wasn't marrying Eddie. "They're less expensive than a divorce."

"Yeah, but I could have told him *before* we ordered the invitations."

"Well," he said. "I'm sorry things worked out the way they did, but I think you know you did the mature, thoughtful thing."

"Thanks," I said. "I don't think Eddie would describe me as mature and thoughtful, though."

"He will, one day. In the meantime, you ought to get on with your life, do something with that brain of yours instead of letting it atrophy in a typing pool."

"You think I'm capable of more, huh?"

"Of course you are," he said. "You're one of the most capable people I know, and you care about things too, you're not just a lump. You need to push yourself, that's all."

"You mean, push myself to go to college?" I said, hoping he did.

"Yeah," he said. "Well, actually, I don't know, not necessarily. I mean, you can see all the good it did Caroline, sitting there in her apartment all day taking care of a baby."

"You're the one who always told Caroline that a college education was an end in itself," I said, "that she shouldn't think of it as a trade school, so why are you down on her now for not having a trade?"

"I'm not down on her any more than I'm down on you or Willy," my father said. "You're all disappointments."

"That's really nice, Dad," I said. I knew it. I knew it was too good to be true, I knew my father would have to go and ruin the first really serious conversation we'd ever had about my future.

"Hey, what happened to your sense of humor?" my father said. "You used to have such a good sense of humor."

"I guess I didn't think you were funny," I said.

My father kept me on the phone, then, for about a billion hours, the way he used to do to Caroline when she was at Barnard, when she still had time for him. He obviously felt bad for having told me what a failure I was, and I guess keeping me on the phone was his way of trying to make it up to me. Naturally, I let him go on, instead of hanging up on him the way any normal person with half an ounce of self-respect would have. I got my own sort of revenge, though, by proofreading my boss's paper on adolescent suicide while my father worked at getting back into my good graces.

I'd brought the paper home with me even though I could have proofed it at the office; I wanted it to be perfect, and I couldn't fully concentrate in an office where Dr. Stevens might walk by at any second. It's not like I hadn't read it and reread it a thousand times already, what with all of Dr. Rimer's additions and deletions and everything, but I still learned something new every time. For instance, while I was on the phone with my father, I learned that suicide was the third leading cause of death among male adolescents. My eyes usually glazed right over the statistics in a research paper and went right to the substance and anecdotal material, but this statistic interested me; I hadn't known any males who were as depressed as I was in high school, except for maybe Holden Caulfield, and I didn't really know him. And then there was that kid Conrad Jarrett from *Ordinary People,* but I didn't really know him either. The only males *I* knew in high school were anything but depressed, especially when they were out there on the football field or some other such inane place. What'd they have to be depressed about anyway? They weren't the ones whose bodies got misshapen and grotesque, they weren't the ones who started protruding all over the goddam place.

Finally, my father must have decided he'd been on the phone long enough. That's the thing about my father; when *he* wanted to get off the phone, you got off the phone. When *you* wanted to, you had to wait until he wanted to. "I have to go turn down my bed," he said. He just had to go and say it, he just had to go and remind me that my mother wasn't there to do it for him, like I wasn't depressed enough already.

"Wait, Dad," I said, just as he was about to hang up. "About college, if I wanted to go, would you be able to help me out?"

"Of course," he said, completely contradicting Caroline's theory about how my parents only spent money on frivolous things while Jonathan's parents spent money on important ones. "But it's a little early to start applying for next fall, isn't it?"

"I already applied, for this spring," I said. "When we got back from New York last month. I'm supposed to get the letter in December, and if I'm accepted, I'll be starting the first week of February."

"You applied last month?" he said. "But you were still engaged. You knew you were going to break your engagement a month ago?"

"I knew I was going to break my engagement the minute I got engaged," I said, even though I hadn't known I was going to say that. If my father hadn't hated psychobabble so much, I might have said I knew *unconsciously*.

So then he kept me on the phone for about another trillion hours, getting every last detail about when I applied, and how I must have given it a lot of thought, and why didn't I tell him before, and how did I come up with Oberlin, and was it really such a good idea to start college in the middle of a year and why didn't I wait until the fall, and then right before we finally said good-bye, he said how nice it would be to have me in Ohio even if Oberlin wasn't exactly around the corner. He sounded sort of proud, to tell you the truth, planning my brilliant future, telling me all the things I could do, go to medical school or journalism school or business school, and even though I didn't want to do any of those things, it felt pretty good to know that he thought I could. I even forgave him a little for having called me a disappointment.

The next day, I went looking for Dr. Stevens, like he was just sitting around waiting to hear that I'd lost my virginity and broken my engagement. I made a deal with myself, that I'd only let myself get up after I'd filed for a good fifteen minutes. I hated filing—my fingers were always getting squooshed between the too-tight Pendaflex folders, my back always ached from having to bend over, and there were always too many possibilities as to where to file a single piece of paper: did it belong in the B's for Budget, the F's for Fiscal Year or the S's for Special Donor? This way, I'd reward myself for a job I usually put off. So every fifteen minutes, I went trotting over to Dr. Stevens's office, like I just happened to be going that way, and each time I got there it looked as if he'd just gotten up and would be right back. His desk lamp was on, his briefcase was open and propped up on his chair, his glasses were sitting on his inkblotter. Finally, after running back and forth every fifteen minutes all morning, I came back from lunch to find his door closed. Oh well, I thought. At about five o'clock, I checked once more, found his door still closed, gave up and went home. Good, I thought. He doesn't need to know my every move, and I felt like I had one up on him because he didn't know I'd lost my virginity.

"Guess who's getting married?" my mother said when I got home. She was standing in the kitchen, making dinner for the two of us—fresh salmon steaks, baked potatoes and a salad.

Now that my father was gone, I never caught her nibbling while she cooked, I suppose because she didn't have to fill up before dinner the way she used to. I hated to admit it, but she was beginning to look really good, better than she ever had before.

"Besides Grandma?" I said.

"Shira Klausner."

"Shira Klausner! A month ago she didn't even have a boyfriend!" I couldn't believe it. Everyone was getting married except me, who was supposed to be!

"Caroline said she went out on a blind date, and then two more dates, and then they got engaged. The Klausners are thrilled."

"I hope he's not an ax-murderer or anything," I said, although to tell you the truth, I thought it would have served them right. Not that I wanted anything *that* bad to happen to Shira, but it wouldn't have killed her to see an alternative life-style.

"Far from it," she said. "Apparently his family is from the Five Towns, which Caroline says is *the* place to be from, in Mrs. Klausner's opinion."

"The Five Towns?" I said. My mother nodded and shrugged, like she'd never heard of them either.

"Do you think they're bragging to his family about where Caroline comes from?" I joked.

We got a good laugh out of that one, although to tell you the truth, I think my mom was just being a good sport; I don't think she was too crazy about being known as the in-law from Cleveland when she was used to being Miss Well Thought of by the World. "I can't wait to see the invitations for *that* wedding," she said.

"We're not going to be invited," I said.

"Sure we will." I didn't contradict her, I didn't want to be the one who broke it to her that the Klausners were embarrassed by us, that they didn't know what to do with people who ate shrimp and lobster. I could see it all in front of me: Mrs. Klausner saying to Caroline how she'd love to invite us to the wedding but she doesn't want to impose on us to come to New York and wouldn't we be uncomfortable at such an Orthodox wedding anyway? And then Caroline wouldn't know what to say, because she wouldn't want to tell Mrs. Klausner what to do, and Mrs. Klausner would walk away feeling good about herself, like we were the ones she was doing a favor by not inviting us to her daughter's wedding.

It was nice, having dinner, just my mother and me, even if I did miss my dad. I hate to admit it, but sometimes, even if you're crazy about your dad, you don't feel like having to watch every word you say for fear of starting a tantrum, you don't feel like watching everything you eat for fear of being called a pig. My mother and I just sat there, like two civilized people, eating our dinner, talking about our day, helping each other clean up the kitchen. Then we went into the living room and shared the couch and the *Plain Dealer*. It was nice to be able to read without having to worry about entertaining your father if he was bored.

6

The ground was thick with snow on the Sunday in December when Grandma and Bill were supposed to get married in our backyard. We had all prepared for the cold weather, and everybody liked the idea of having a wedding with our coats and hats on, but even the staunchest of the outdoor-wedding supporters gave in when it became obvious that the snow wasn't about to let up. My mother told Grandma that inside was just as good as outside, anyway, since there would only be six of us, hardly a suffocating crowd; and since Grandma always took my mother's advice as if she were *her* mother, the wedding took place in our foyer.

Grandma hadn't wanted a big wedding; whenever she was trying to explain how bad an affair was she always described it as "ostentatious," the worst insult she could think of. Even Caroline and Jonathan were discouraged from making the trip, and I don't know if anyone even bothered telling Willy about it. It was just me, my mother, my father, Grandma and Bill, and Rabbi Wax. Apparently, Bill wasn't an atheist like Grandpa, so Grandma didn't mind having Rabbi Wax officiate.

It was the first time since he'd left two months before that my father came back to the house. I was the one who talked him into coming, though I think my mom was glad I did. Besides, Grandma *had* been my father's mother-in-law for twenty-five years. I had very high hopes for a reconciliation between my parents that morning, and I did everything in my power to facilitate one. I was the only one with a camera, and I kept telling them to stand together for a picture, even though it was Grandma and Bill's wedding. At one point, Bill said, "How about one of me and your grandmother?" Grandma seemed embarrassed at the suggestion, like wanting to have a picture of yourself was beneath her, like Grandpa would never have made such a frivolous suggestion. Nevertheless, she posed, her arm around Bill's waist, his arm around her neck.

The ceremony was short, thank God. "It's not like this is a first marriage," Grandma said. "No need to drag it out." Rabbi Wax didn't object either; he was halfway out the door, with a breadstick in his hand, probably on his way to officiate at a more elaborate affair, someplace where he would have a *real* audience. Caroline was right about him; he was more like an actor than a rabbi. That's the thing about the Reform rabbis I've known, that and their movie-of-the-week sermons.

The dining-room table was set up buffet style, with some kind of exotic flower arrangement as the centerpiece. My mother served cold poached salmon and cucumber mousse, a watercress and Belgian endive salad and pistachio ice cream with fresh raspberries—a menu, I thought proudly, that would have totally gone over the Klausners' heads. I couldn't help noticing that these were all my father's favorite things, and that my mother was wearing a dress that he had always complimented. She looked great—even her fingernails were long and smooth.

It was sort of silly, the five of us standing around with our plates in our hands, like there weren't enough chairs for five people, so we finally sat down around the dining room table.

"Did everybody hear Jane's good news?" my father said. "Not bad, getting into Oberlin mid-year." I felt myself turn red. Why should it have occurred to my father that I'd intercepted the mail that morning before my mother could see it? Why should it have occurred to him that he was the only one I'd told? Most girls *did* confide in their mothers, after all.

"I didn't even know she'd applied," my mother said, but you could hardly hear her over Grandma's exclamations.

"How wonderful!" Grandma was saying. "I always wondered when you were going to leave that silly job and go to college, where you belong." Bill wasn't a big talker, but he smiled and held on to Grandma.

"I'm sure she was about to tell you, Flip," my father said. God, I loved him. He still cared about her feelings, even after she'd dumped him.

"I was going to tell you after lunch, Mom," I said. "I just got the acceptance letter this morning. I wanted to surprise you."

"It sure is a surprise," she said.

Stupid me, now she was going to be in a bad mood; not that I cared if she was mad at *me,* but I didn't want her to be mad at my father, like it was his fault that I told him things I didn't tell her, like he was to blame for being more interested in me than she was. "Where are you going to live?" she said.

"In a dormitory, I guess."

"So that gives me almost a year to sell the house, then."

"Didn't you hear what Dad said? I was accepted for the spring semester; I start college in February."

"Well then, I guess that gives me two months," she said, and she started clearing the table, even though we were still eating. First she took away the salmon, then the cucumber mousse. I sat there, all choked up, furious with myself for sabotaging everything. Then I started getting really angry with Dr. Stevens, imagining him saying in his analytical voice that I hadn't told my mother about Oberlin on purpose, like I was Miss Oedipus Complex or something, like I was trying to get back at my mother for being my father's wife, like I really *wanted* my parents to get a divorce so I could have my father to myself.

I'm not just paranoid either, thinking that Dr. Stevens would have implied all that, because once, when I was telling him some story, he practically came right out and *told* me I was in love with my father. What happened was I was telling him how the summer I was twelve, the summer I ruined my brother, the summer my family moved to Hazelnut Lane, my father had gotten promoted to the most important job at the hospital. He was the first non-M.D. in the history of Cleveland General to become president, and the hospital threw him a lavish party in a restaurant at the top of one of the tallest buildings in Cleveland. All these important people, like the mayor of Cleveland and the owner of the Cleveland Indians and even the two senators from Ohio were there. And at the end, after everybody got up to the podium and said how great my father was, and how important and distinguished and everything, and after my father thanked everybody for saying all those things, he called my mother up to the podium and kissed her and told everybody how he couldn't have done it without her, and I sat in the audience and cried because I thought he should have called *me* up to the podium and kissed *me*. So that's when Dr. Stevens practically accused me of wanting to have sex with him; like I'm the only girl in the history of the world who ever cried because she wanted to be in the spotlight, like wanting my father to kiss me in front of two United States senators made me a goddam sicko or something.

When my mother reached over my father's shoulder to take away the raspberries, he pushed her hand away. "What are you rushing everybody for?" my father said. "What's the big goddam rush?"

My mother let go of the bowl, and sat down again. Grandma was looking down at her plate, the way she always did when my father yelled at my mother in front of everyone. "Oh my," she said. I guess it must have been painful to hear someone else yell at your child, even if it was your child's husband. The Locksmith still had that silly smile on his face, like nothing had changed, like maybe he was deaf. Didn't he see that *everything* had changed?

"What do you have to yell at her for?" I said.

"You mind your own business," my father said. "Stop sticking your two cents into everything." Then he mimicked me saying "What do you have to yell at her for?"

When my father had eaten the last raspberry, he got up and slammed his napkin on the table. I wondered where he was going to go, considering all the snow outside, considering the fact that he didn't have a room here anymore, even if he was paying for all the rooms.

"He sure is mad," Grandma said.

"Fun, isn't it?" my mother said. She cleared the rest of the table, leaving me with Grandma and Bill.

"Delicious lunch," Bill said, "but I think we ought to be on our way, dear."

"Sorry we ruined your wedding reception," I said.

"Our wedding reception," Grandma said, practically guffawing. "Wedding receptions are for young brides, not for people like us." Bill helped her up, and the two of them thanked my mother for their beautiful wedding and lunch. "Beautiful!" my mother said, laughing. Bill went out to start the car, and I helped Grandma on with her boots. Her hands were so arthritic they didn't even look like hands anymore.

"Good-bye, sweetie," she said, reaching up to kiss me on the cheek. "I'm so glad about your going to college. You know, a seventy-one-year-old woman gets married for very different reasons than a nineteen-year-old woman." She winked at me then, like choosing Oberlin over Eddie had been the right decision. I supposed I agreed, but then why did I envy that she had someone to go home with?

Instead of reconciling with Dad, my mother went up to her room to lie down: my father went back to his little hippie apartment, and I got into bed and called Eddie to see if he wanted to go to a matinee. He wasn't home, and I didn't leave a message. I mean, I did have some pride; what if he was right there, having sex with some girl his mother's friends had fixed him up with, maybe even with one of his mother's friends? I was feeling so awful and lonely, though, I almost thought of calling Eddie's father. I wasn't feeling very particular about who wanted to grab my ass, as long as someone wanted to.

And then all of a sudden, I realized I was doing it again, I was trying to replace my angry feelings with sexual ones. I didn't want to have sex, though, I wanted to scream! At my father, for being so nasty, for yelling at my mother over nothing and then turning around and humiliating me. And at my mother, for clearing the table instead of saying what was really bothering her, the fact that, as usual, my father had let me undermine her and exclude her from our club. I mean, maybe Dr. Stevens was right, maybe I *did* have a thing for my father, maybe I did feel like I was his wife or something, but if I did, it was only because at home I'd been allowed to play the part. No, not allowed to, *forced* to. Between my mother, who tuned my father out whenever she became tired of him, and my father, who needed *someone's* attention since he wasn't getting hers, I didn't have much of a choice. Sometimes, I even felt as if my mother and I had traded places, me the wife, she the daughter, what with the way she never stuck up for herself, the way she always waited for me to step in and tell my father not to yell at her about this, not to insult her about that.

I'm not going to pretend I didn't enjoy being the one my father took walks with, or watched the news with, or ate chocolate sundaes with. And I suppose it made me feel kind of powerful and superior to stand up to my dad when he was mistreating my mom. But sometimes I wished they could have just taken care of themselves and left me out of it. Sometimes it just didn't seem fair the way they used me—my father, to build up the ego neglected by my mother; my mother, to protect the ego decimated by my father. What about me, I wanted to know, what about my ego?

I was still feeling angry and fired up and like I had something coming to me when I got up the next day for work, not a bad way to feel when you were planning to give your boss one month's notice that very morning. The alternative was to feel guilty and sheepish, and then you could easily be talked out of your decision to leave a job you felt safe in, only to go off to a strange college where no one knew you.

The funny thing was that when I finally told Dr. Rimer about Oberlin, before he left for lunch that day, he said he'd known all along that I wasn't going to work there forever, he said that he knew a smart woman like me would go off to college within the year. I was beginning to think I'd finally found the first entirely selfless person in the universe, letting me go like that, not making me feel guilty for leaving him in the lurch, when he said he thought I ought to consider starting college with the other freshmen in September. "Transfer students don't have an easy time of it," he said. "You know, the freshman mentality is to make friends the first few weeks of the first semester, and then to close the door, so to speak."

"That's what my dad says," I said. "But I'm going to take my chances."

"So I can't talk you into staying another nine months?"

"I don't think so," I said. Leave it to me to sound so sure of myself. So much for feeling fired up.

"Even if we raise your salary a bit?"

"No, thanks, not that it isn't tempting."

"Okay," he said, smiling. "Can't say I didn't try."

He picked up his desk calendar. "So your last day will be . . . ?"

"January 15," I said. "I'm planning a little trip before the semester starts in February."

"It's going to be hard to replace you, Jane," he said, and then I reverted to my old self again, I started to wonder whether this whole college thing even made sense. I mean, Dr. Rimer *liked* me, he thought I was a great secretary, he thought my typing was the best he'd ever seen, he thought my phone voice was extraordinarily professional, he said he'd never seen his files look the way they did after I was done with them. The other secretaries had even grown to like me, and sometimes they confided in me about their daughters who were my age, and how they wished they were as mature as I was. Ha! Dr. Stevens had finally started loosening up around me, like he'd forgotten about the letter-shredding incident, like he wasn't scared I was going to break into his house and boil a rabbit on his stove.

I was in a state of turmoil the whole day, thinking how much I liked it there, and wondering why I was going to make everything so hard for myself. Dr. Stevens was being real chummy (for him), smiling at me every time he passed by me in the hall, making small talk with me while he waited at my desk for Dr. Rimer to return from lunch. When I was getting ready to leave for the day, my phone rang, and it was Dr. Stevens asking me if I could stop in his office on my way out. It sounded as if he had something important to say to me, but I wasn't going to fall for that old trick again. He probably just wanted me to photocopy his Visa bill or something. I hadn't been in his office since that letter-shredding incident; I'd told him about my broken engagement in front of the restrooms.

"I hear you're going to be leaving us for Oberlin," he said. I wasn't even in his office yet; he ushered me in and told me to have a seat, the whole time smiling, probably because he was so relieved to be getting rid of me.

"You heard correctly," I said.

"That's terrific," he said, like I'd done something really impressive, like I wasn't just doing what most *eighteen*-year-olds do in their sleep, and here I was nineteen. "I know how hard it must have been for you to leave home."

"Home?" I said. "Home left me!"

"What do you mean?"

"My parents separated; they're getting divorced."

"Oh, I'm sorry," he said. "That must have been terrible for you."

"Terrible for me?" I said. "That's about the biggest understatement of the last twelve centuries! I mean, did I ever tell you anything that should have prepared me for this? Did I? I mean, did *you* see this coming? Am I the only one who's surprised by all this?"

"You never thought they had the happiest marriage," he offered, like it was really big of him to go out on such a limb.

"Happy, shmappy!" I said. "Don't you even care about them?"

"I care about *you*," he said.

"Well, you don't seem very shocked," I said. "My parents love each other! They've been married twenty-five years!"

Dr. Stevens just nodded, like he was anything but shocked, like he'd heard it all before, like my parents were just any old parents. "Well, you have to be a very strong person to do what you're doing then, picking up and leaving instead of hanging around and getting depressed," he said. "We'll miss you around here, though."

"*You* won't."

"Sure I will, Jane."

"You're so glad to see me go you can't stand it."

He had this sort of puzzled look on his face, like he was trying to decide which *DSM III* category I fit into. "I'm happy for you, Jane," he said. "Don't you see? I'm not your father. I *want* you to succeed."

"What? So does he."

"He may think he does," he said, as if he'd just been waiting for the perfect opportunity to spring his analysis on me. "But he's only human, you see, and it's very hard to allow, let alone encourage, his most devoted and loyal fan to leave him. I should know."

"What do you mean?"

"A year and a half ago, when you came in here to be Dr. Rimer's secretary, I should have discouraged you. I should have made it much more difficult for you to take a job which you were so overqualified for and which you were only taking so that you wouldn't have to leave me. But I didn't, because who wouldn't want someone like you around, someone who adores you and looks up to you and tries to please you."

"Oh, I get it," I said. "You're going to miss me because I'm good for your ego."

"I'm going to miss you because I like you, Jane."

He liked me! Dr. Stevens liked me!

"Well," I said calmly, as if I wasn't the most excited, happiest person in the world right then. "I could always defer my application."

He smiled, as if I was just being coy; actually, I wasn't. "You're capable of much more than pleasing men, don't you see? I'm not happy for myself that you're leaving; I'm happy for you."

"But I don't even see the point in living if a person can just let you go, just like that. What's it all for if you can just go on without me, like you never even knew me, like I didn't *mean* anything to you? I want to *mean* something to you."

"You mean something to me," he said, and on that note, I said I had an appointment, I had to be going. I mean, who knew what he might have said next? I didn't want to take any chances, and if he was anything like my father, he'd have had to say something insulting before I got too confident. I wanted to go to Oberlin remembering him saying "You mean something to me," even if they weren't his final words, even if he said something really mundane to me in the next four weeks before I left.

My mother sold the Hazelnut Lane house in record time, only two weeks after I dropped the Oberlin bombshell; she sold it to some other family just like mine who probably thought they were immune to divorce. Then she went and found a depressing little ranch-style house in Mayfield Heights, right near the old miniature golf place, and every day for the next week, she spent her time packing boxes, except when she was checking her underarm for lumps. She didn't know I knew she was checking, but it was pretty obvious; she'd developed this gesture where she'd prod her left underarm the way some people played with their hair, like they didn't even know they were doing it. She did it all the time.

When it was time for her three-month postsurgical checkup, I went with her and sat in the waiting room. I'd hated asking Dr. Rimer for an afternoon off during my last month of work, but I'd hated even more the idea of my mother going back to that doctor by herself.

We waited forever, of course, so that by the time she was called in, she'd become Lumpectomy of the Month, the way she was so friendly and everything with all the secretaries and technicians. They didn't even get annoyed with her going up to the window every five minutes and saying "Well?" That was the thing about her; she had a way of bugging people without making them mad. Everywhere you went—the grocery store, the hardware store, the bank—all you had to do was mention you were Flip Singer's daughter and the checkout girl or the bank teller would practically fall in love with you and do you all these special favors.

I sat there, looking up from my *Vogue* magazine every time the little bell rang and the office door opened. There were all these slightly familiar-looking suburban housewives parading in and out, the kind who probably even subscribed to *Vogue*. I was comfortable with them, with how they looked; they all reminded me of the mothers of my friends on our old, old street, where kids played with each other outside, where it was a *real* neighborhood, where somebody else's mother had just as much right to yell at you as your own mother. They were sweet and unsophisticated, their hair parted in the middle (the way Caroline's was before she moved to New York), and they wore sneakers with their pantsuits.

"Mrs. Graham?" I said. It was that eighth-grade English teacher of mine, the one whose son had died. I thought I recognized her when she walked in, but when I heard her talking to the receptionist, I was sure of it. She had this really nice voice, kind of low and calm. She came over to where I was sitting. "I was a student of yours about five years ago—"

"I remember," she said. "Jane Singer! How are you?"

"Good. I'm starting college next month."

"Wonderful," she said. "Terrific."

"I've been working in an office since graduation, but I finally decided I was ready for college."

"I'm glad," she said. "I think you'll appreciate it more than some students who go right away. Where are you going?"

"Oberlin."

She nodded. "You'll do well there," she said. "As long as you don't let that self-deprecating attitude of yours get in the way. You have a lot of good things to offer, if you could just be more sure of yourself."

"How have *you* been?" I said, changing the topic. Was everybody on to me? Leave it to an English teacher to use the phrase *self-deprecating attitude*. I always had hated when teachers told me what to do, how I could be more successful. Mrs. Graham had pushed my hair out of my face all the time, telling me how much prettier I'd be if you could see my face. I mean, if I'd wanted people to see my face, I would have worn my hair another way.

"I've been sick, actually," she said. "I stopped teaching in the spring."

"Oh," I said. "Those English students sure are missing out."

She sort of smiled, her eyes watery, and just then, my mother came out of the inner office, where she'd clearly gotten good news, and I reintroduced her to Mrs. Graham. They shook hands and said "nice to see you again" and all that. My mother had always gone to all those PTA meetings and open houses at school; of course, she was one of those mothers that all the teachers loved.

"Well, I'd like to write to you or something," I said to Mrs. Graham. "I could just write to you at school. I mean, you wouldn't even have to give me your home address or anything."

She laughed. "Oh, Jane, I'd love to hear from you," she said, and she opened up her purse and took out a pad of paper and a pen, just like an English teacher would. "I won't be going back to school," she said, "so why don't you write to me here?" She handed me the piece of paper with her home address on it, somewhere out in the Ohio boondocks.

My mother and I said good-bye to her then, though I felt sort of bad about leaving her there alone, her son being dead and her being so sick. We walked down the medical building corridor, passing X-ray labs and blood-drawing offices. "Everything's okay," my mother said. "You can stop worrying."

"Me?" I said. "What about you?"

"Dad and I were more concerned about you than we were about me."

"Really?" I said. It was nice to hear that my parents were worried about *me,* for a change, instead of the other way around. Nevertheless, I couldn't help plying my marriage counseling trade. "When did you talk to Dad?" I asked.

"I don't know, last week maybe."

"Was it a good conversation?"

"Jane—"

"Can't you just tell me if it was a good conversation?"

"It was fine," she said. We got on the elevator with some lady who had a broken ankle. Naturally, when we got to the lobby floor, my mother practically carried her across the snowy parking lot to her car, even though there were plenty of other people in the lobby who could have helped her. My mother wasn't about to give up an opportunity like that. I stood by my car in the parking lot and waited for her, even though we'd come in different cars and would go home in different cars.

Finally, after the broken-ankled lady thanked my mother about a thousand times and told her how wonderful she was, my mother came back. "I don't understand how she's going to drive," she said. "Oh well. I'll meet you at home."

"Ma, do you think Mrs. Graham is going to die?"

"I don't know, sweetheart. She didn't look very well."

"Why would she have to stop teaching?"

"Maybe she didn't feel well enough to get up in front of a bunch of kids every day."

"Ma, do you miss Grandpa?"

"Uh-huh."

"Do you miss Dad?"

She dug her keys out of her purse; she was very organized and even had a special compartment just for them. "Of course I do," she said, separating her keys and holding the ones for her car. "Now, are we going to go home or are we going to stand out here in the parking lot talking about life?"

I guess she was in a hurry to get home and continue packing up, or should I say, throwing out; I mean, how else do you go from a two-story house with a finished basement and four bedrooms to a one-story house with no basement and three bedrooms? And one of the bedrooms wasn't even going to be used as a bedroom, according to my mother. Instead, she was going to make it into a music room, where she could practice the violin. I never even knew she wanted to *play* the violin, for heaven's sake. All of a sudden, while she was packing up boxes and listening to her Brahms, she decided it was time to learn how to play a musical instrument.

"Why the violin, though?" I asked.

"Grandpa played the violin," she said.

I felt sort of guilty then, realizing that my mother really *did* think about Grandpa, that she really *was* in mourning when he died, even if she never cried and even if she appeared to be the strong one next to Grandma. Ever since that night in the Klausners' living room, I'd been finding out that my mother had all sorts of feelings I'd never given her credit for having.

One night while we still lived in our Hazelnut Lane house, the first night of Chanukah, Mom took advantage of her newly found independence and invited Rose, our cleaning lady, and her six children, for potato latkes. She could never have gotten away with something like that with my father around; he didn't like being bothered by people at home after a long day at the hospital. After dinner, Mom sent them off with three boxes of clothes that used to belong to Caroline, Willy, and me. At least they weren't clothes we wore anymore; when we were younger, she was always sending our things to Rose's family in Santo Domingo, but sometimes they were things we hadn't even worn much.

We lit the Chanukah candles all eight nights and even sang a few songs. I think she really missed my father then. I mean, my mother wasn't exactly the religious, ritualistic type; obviously she was still feeling something for him if she was lighting Chanukah candles. It was pretty depressing, though—Willy was staying up at school during intersession in order to repeat the math final he'd failed; Caroline was happily lighting candles in New York and probably eating the biggest, greasiest potato latkes ever made in the history of the Jewish people; and my father was most likely standing alone in front of his little disposable menorah every night. He had it sitting on the window ledge in his living room, so that all the bohemians strolling up and down the street could look up and see the miracle of the burning oil.

When I met him for lunch at Tommy's the Saturday after we moved, the day after the movers actually came and put all our furniture and boxes into their truck while I sat in my office and cried, he asked about my mother. I told him that her first violin lesson was to be that very afternoon, at the Cleveland Institute of Music. "Did you know Grandpa played?" I said.

"Sure," he said wistfully. "He was a wonderful violinist, and I'm sure Mom will be too. She's very musical, you know, I think she even has perfect pitch."

"You *think* she does? Of course she does, Dad. Her perfect pitch is her pride and joy!"

How depressing, I thought, that he didn't even know for sure! It was like the two of them hadn't talked to each other for years, like they'd told everybody but each other what things were important to them. Suddenly, I felt more sorry for their loss than for mine; even if I did feel I'd been poorly used by them sometimes, I'd also gotten to know each of them better than they had ever gotten to know each other. It seemed like such a waste—all those years my mother was in the kitchen broiling steaks for my father instead of playing the violin, all those years my father might have preferred to be married to a happy violinist than an angry steak broiler. Their marriage might have been saved if my mother had just done what she wanted to do in the first place.

I had the R.J. special—a toasted pita bread sandwich with melted Muenster cheese, green peppers, lettuce, tomatoes, and sunflower seeds—and a chocolate shake. My father had a salad and bottled water. It was a pretty quiet lunch. For some reason, we didn't have all that much to say to each other; my father wasn't being his usual nudgy self, asking me lots of personal questions which I always answered, prying into my innermost feelings and then asking me why I had to be so introspective all the time.

The waitress brought over the check while my father was eating his salad, and he gave her a dirty look, like why was everybody always rushing him, didn't she know his wife used to do the same goddam thing? I acted like I didn't notice—I do that sometimes, pretend I don't notice, when he engages in some embarrassingly antisocial behavior—and instead I looked away from him and around at the other tables. You had your regulars—women with long ceramic earrings and batik dresses, men with beards and Birkenstocks—but there were also quite a few people with bourgeois haircuts and clothing, eating earthy things like hummus and tahini. I even recognized these two girls from my class in high school—Stacy Jennings and Molly King. They were probably on Christmas break from Southern Methodist or Texas Christian or something. I sort of hid behind my father when I saw them so that they wouldn't see me; they'd be all friendly and everything if they saw me, and then they'd leave and talk about how I'm not so bad after all, considering I'm a Jew. One time, when we were in the seventh grade, I went to Stacy's house after school and when she introduced me to her mother, she said, "Jane's Jewish, but she doesn't act like it." Anyway, if Stacy and Molly were there, Coventry was obviously not only for hippies anymore. Maybe my father wasn't so out of place after all.

"Do you want to join me for a swim?" my father said when he'd finished his salad and was examining the check. I was still drinking my shake.

"Isn't it a little cold?"

"An indoor swim," he said.

"Since when do you swim?" I said.

"A few months now. It's the greatest. You really feel virtuous when you're done."

"No thanks." I hated those things that made you feel virtuous; it only made you feel bad when you stopped doing them. And besides, I hadn't worn anything even remotely resembling a bathing suit in front of my dad for about the last seven years, and I certainly wasn't about to start now. We got up from our table and walked over to the stairs. "I suppose you're trying to get in shape for that hot date of yours tonight!" I said. My dad smiled, but he didn't laugh. It was like I hadn't said something totally outrageous or anything, like he might actually *have* a date.

"Be careful on those stairs," my father said. He was always saying things like "be careful on those stairs." That's the thing about parents; they're always so worried about your physical safety they don't even think about the dangers lurking in your head. One time, when I was in the sixth grade, I had a slumber party in our living room. We'd only been living in the Hazelnut Lane house for a short time, and my father didn't trust the light fixture hanging from the living-room ceiling. All night long he was coming in, telling me and my friends not to forget to move our sleeping bags away from the center of the room before we went to sleep, as if having a chandelier fall on your head was really going to happen.

"Have a good swim," I said, shivering, when we were standing out in front of Tommy's. It was freezing outside, and all I had on was a little down vest.

My father kissed me on the forehead and headed up the street to his apartment, I suppose to change into his swim trunks. I watched him for a little while; he had this really adorable gait, kind of fast and furious. I couldn't bear going back to that awful Mayfield Heights house to unpack boxes while my father was going to work out for some woman who wasn't my mother, so I took a walk down Coventry instead, in the opposite direction from my father, and stopped into Record Revolution. I was flipping through the Roches when I heard Eddie's voice. He was talking to a skinny woman behind the counter that contained all the punky, garish earrings and things.

I came up from behind him and tapped him on the shoulder. "What are you doing in this neck of the woods?" I said.

"Hi, Jane."

"I thought you hated this whole scene."

"My girlfriend works here," he said, gesturing at the skinny woman. She had these tiny little breasts; she didn't even need to wear a bra, let alone be minimized. "Chelsea, this is Jane." Chelsea! What a name! She took my hand and shook it with her limp, ice-cold hand, but she didn't seem too interested. She turned to wait on a woman with red and blue hair, and Eddie and I moved away from the counter.

"I'm going to college in February," I said. "Oberlin."

"That's great," he said. He was wearing one of those big fluffy cotton sweaters, white, to contrast with his dark hair, and he looked really handsome. I kept thinking of Caroline, and how in the old days she would have been really impressed by the way Eddie dressed, but now she was married to someone who didn't even know the difference between acrylic and wool.

Eddie looked at his watch. "Do you want to get a cup of coffee?"

"Sure," I said.

He was parked in a lot across the street from the record store, and it was pretty awkward, the way neither of us said anything the whole way there. That's the thing about deciding you're going to have sex with someone you broke up with; you're afraid if you have a conversation with them you'll remember everything you didn't like about them in the first place.

When we finally got to his car and Eddie had adjusted all his mirrors and his seat and turned on his lights (it was one of those dark winter days where you needed your lights at two o'clock in the afternoon), he drove out of the parking lot and made a left onto Euclid Heights. Then he asked me where I wanted to go. I kept hemming and hawing, saying I didn't know, where did he want to go, I wasn't really hungry, was he, I didn't have much money with me, did he, and by the time I suggested Corky & Lenny's, we were parked in front of his apartment building. Of course, his apartment building wasn't exactly around the corner from Coventry—it was about six miles away, to tell the truth—but I swear to God, I hadn't suggested it.

His apartment looked the same as it had the night we broke up, except for the fact that the wedding invitations were just scrap paper now, sitting next to the kitchen telephone. He had a bottle of Scotchgard on the butcher block table, like if I hadn't come back here with him, he would have been spraying the seats of his chairs.

"Are you serious about Chelsea?" I asked. I felt silly even saying her name, especially while Eddie was lifting my shirt off over my head. We were sitting on his living-room couch.

"No," he said.

Maybe I'd gotten more mature or something, but I didn't even want to fool around or have oral sex, I just wanted to get right to the intercourse part. I kept redirecting Eddie until he finally understood that I wanted to get right to it, and he went to get a condom from his bedroom. It was better this time, and I was beginning to see its appeal. It was deeper than everything else; I could even see how if you loved someone, sex could be about more than just nerve endings, although it still didn't seem totally fair that Eddie could have both whether he loved the person or not. I started to cry at one point near the end, but Eddie wasn't looking at my face so I don't think he noticed. I wasn't even sure he cared it was me down there underneath him, as long as I was female.

I don't mean to say Eddie didn't like me or anything, just that he didn't like me for the reasons a person *should* like me. He liked me because he was comfortable with me, because it didn't take much effort to be together, because he was used to me. But I wanted to be special to someone, irreplaceable, loved because I was *Jane,* specifically and uniquely Jane, not just because we'd been going out for a year and a half. That was the depressing part; I wanted to *mean* something to someone.

Not fifteen seconds after Eddie and I were finished, he blurted out, "I haven't called you in over a month now," like he'd been counting the days or something, like each day he'd managed not to call me was a small achievement in self-discipline. I understood what he was saying; it was something I'd often experienced with Dr. Stevens, that each feeling I withheld from him was my own private victory. The thing was, though, that it wouldn't have been a victory if Dr. Stevens had known how much effort it took, if he'd thought my self-containment was anything but a breeze. And here Eddie had gone and given himself away; he'd gone to all that effort not to call me, and then in one small sentence he'd made it so that he might just as well have.

"How did you meet Chelsea?" I said.

"At a bar."

"What bar?"

"Peabody's."

"I like Peabody's," I said.

"Yeah," he said. "My parents miss you."

"They said that?"

"My mother's always going on about you. She loves you."

"I really like your mom too," I said, and then I had that feeling again, the one I'd had when I was standing in Dr. Rimer's office and he was telling me how tough I'd be to replace, like why was I going around leaving people who liked me, why was I going to a college where I didn't know a single soul? Even Lenny Levitsky, who could have been the one person I knew, was transferring to another college, probably Ye-shiva University, he was so religious. And Beverly Fisher, my Camp Ben-Gurion friend from Oberlin, probably went to Bryn Mawr or Sarah Lawrence or some other place where there were girls who weren't embarrassed to tell each other they mastur-bated.

I went into Eddie's bathroom to wash up and get dressed. For some reason, it's easier to have sex with old boyfriends than it is to get dressed in front of them. The bathroom floor was carpeted with the same lime green stuff that carpeted the rest of the apartment, and while it was soft and comfortable to stand on, it sure was ugly. I kept thinking, This is what you would have been standing on every day for the rest of your life while you were getting ready to go to your secretarial job down the hall from Dr. Stevens.

After I was all dressed and everything, I stood and looked in the mirror for a while, and maybe it was like after you've looked at a word on a page too long, you no longer recognize it, because I sort of couldn't recognize myself after a while. I wasn't too scared; it had happened before. Dr. Stevens told me it was called disassociation or something, when you looked at yourself in the mirror and saw someone you'd never seen before. Actually, he was probably just making up some fancy word so I wouldn't feel like that woman with twelve different personalities, Sybil. Like I really needed to be told I wasn't crazy or something, like I really needed Dr. Stevens to tell me I was sane.

Eddie was standing outside the bathroom door when I came out. "I just want you to know," he said. "That was the last time." He said it really fast, as if he'd been standing there preparing those exact words the whole time I was in the bath-room and wouldn't have been able to get them out if he'd said them any slower. He was sort of looking down at the lime green carpeting, there in the skinny hallway opposite the bathroom. "We're just using each other," he said.

"I know."

"I don't want to be used. And I don't want to use you."

"But you're the one who drove us—"

"I know. I don't care."

"Okay," I said. "You're right."

"I don't want you calling me between now and the time you go to Oberlin, just because you're scared or lonely."

"I won't."

"I don't want to start running into you all over the place either—"

"I mean, Eddie, that's a little ridiculous."

"No," he said. "No it's not. I know all you think I am is a computer, with no feelings. You think you're the only one with feelings. But you're not."

"I never said—"

"It doesn't matter what you said; from the very beginning you just used me to make you feel better, from the time you didn't get that part in *Gypsy* to right now."

"I'm sorry," I said. I tried to hug him, but he pulled my arms off him and led me to the door. He practically double-locked the thing with me still walking through it, Miss Asshole of the Year. I got on the elevator in a kind of numb way, pushed the button for the first floor, and ran through the lobby as fast as I could.

I was thinking about how I wanted to call Dr. Stevens's office as soon as I got home, just to hear his voice on the answering machine, just to be reminded that there was someone out there who would talk to me no matter what an awful person I was; sometimes I did that when I was feeling bad, called his office when I knew he wouldn't be there—on the weekend, or late at night—just to hear his voice and then hang up before the sound of the tone. Sometimes just hearing a person's voice is all you need, even if you have no message to leave.

But when I got out to the parking lot, I remembered that I didn't have my car there, that I'd left it at a meter spot on Coventry when I'd come back with Eddie to his apartment. At first I was really annoyed—with myself, with Eddie (*he* surely remembered how I'd gotten to his apartment)—but then I thought about it, and I decided it served me right. If I walked, it would be at least an hour before I could hear Dr. Stevens's lovely voice, perfect punishment for the whore I was. Not that I would have refused a ride had someone offered me one; I mean, I'm not that much of a martyr. I looked around the parking lot once more, considered my options, and even thought about going back up to Eddie's apartment to use his phone, before I finally committed myself to my harsh decree. When I realized I had no choice, that I didn't even have anyone to call if I did use Eddie's phone—my father was swimming, my mother was playing the violin, Grandma and Bill were at Bill's daughter's house in Akron—I zipped up my vest and started out on the long walk home. With my luck, some Cleveland Heights cop was probably at that very moment sticking a parking ticket on the windshield of my Olds.

7

By the time my mother and I had thrown away the last of the moving boxes and found a place in the new house for all the miscellaneous odds and ends we'd avoided looking at—decks of cards, place mats, half a box of Sabbath candles, rubber bands and paper clips—it was time for me to pack up again for Oberlin. Besides clothes and shampoo and *The Catcher in the Rye,* I couldn't think of anything else to bring, and yet I remembered Caroline's room at Barnard, how she and her roommate had made it look homey with posters on the walls and little African violets on the windowsill and one of those futon couches for their friends to sit on when they visited. I even slept on it once, when Caroline was a sophomore and I came for a weekend that spring. It was the greatest weekend I'd ever had; during the day we sat on the steps in front of the Columbia library, or walked up and down Broadway or through Riverside Park. Then Friday night Caroline took me to this outdoor café in Greenwich Village at the corner of Bleecker and MacDougal, and Saturday night she took me to a party in John Jay, this really run-down dormitory at Columbia. I felt so grown-up and sophisticated and so relieved to be away from all the sweet-sixteen parties in Cleveland. It was the first time it had ever occurred to me that I didn't have to live on Hazelnut Lane the rest of my life, that I would graduate from Randall High School and never have to look at it again if I didn't want to.

I put aside my beanbag chair, but I didn't have any posters except this one Caroline had sent me from Barnard. It said "New York Is Book Country," and underneath was a picture of a girl reading a book. Naturally, the girl was wearing glasses. I don't wear glasses, but Caroline said the girl reminded her of me, the way I was always reading, the way I took better care of my books than of my clothes. Not that I mind being thought of as a bookworm, but maybe I'd want to change my image at Oberlin; after all, for the first time in my life, I could be whoever I wanted to be.

So what I did was I took this old photo collage that used to hang in our kitchen (two houses ago!), one of the odds and ends my mother didn't know what to do with, and stuck it in my suitcase. I figured it might make my room sort of homey, hanging there above my bed. It had pictures of my family from about a billion years ago when we still looked like a normal family, having picnics, on bicycles, on sleds in Cain Park. Pictures of me when I was at my skinny athletic stage, doing cartwheels or handstands or diving into a swimming pool. There's this one picture where my parents are dancing, at a wedding or Bar Mitzvah or something, and you can't believe from looking at it that they aren't the happiest, most well-suited, most attractive couple in the entire world. My father's looking at my mother with this admiring look he sometimes bestowed on her, and my mother's looking over his shoulder, with the confidence of someone who knows her husband thinks she's wonderful. You can almost hear the Frank Sinatra music playing in the background. My parents may not have had many happy moments in their marriage, but this picture had caught one of them.

I had everything packed up for Oberlin before I left for my trip to New York, so that as soon as I got back, we could just load up the car and go. Both my parents were going to drive me, and I can't say I wasn't still hoping that after they dropped me off, they'd reconsider the divorce on the trip back to Cleveland. I didn't really think they would, but I guess there was still a part of me that wanted to cling to the way I used to see my parents and my family, as the perfect parents, the perfect family.

In the meantime, I was off to New York to see Caroline and Jonathan and The Little Messiah. On the plane I kept going over and over in my head the good-bye party Dr. Rimer had given for me that afternoon in the office. In front of about a million people, he made a speech about how great I was and how he'd never find someone like me again, how I'd even managed to make revising a paper on adolescent suicide pleasurable (that got a big laugh). The other secretaries said I'd been a joy to have in the office (they sounded like my elementary school teachers), and they'd even gotten me a going-away present, an overnight bag like the one Caroline had. Dr. Stevens just stood in the back, smiling, like he was glad to see that people actually *liked* me, like maybe I wasn't such a psychotic lunatic after all. Later, he came up to me and practically had sex with me, the way he kissed me good-bye and everything, and then he said I should call him if I ever wanted to talk. He even gave me his private number, not the office number with the machine, but his real private number, the one that probably hooked into his phone at home, the phone that was probably sitting right next to his bed! I started to cry a little then, so he just sort of patted me on the shoulder and walked away, as if he wanted to let me have a little dignity. Before I left for good, at around four-fifty-five, after I watered Dr. Rimer's plants for the last time, I peeked into Dr. Stevens's office to make sure he wasn't sitting there, and then I hurriedly dropped a note into his in-box before he came back. It was one of those mushy notes, about how much he meant to me and how often I'd think about him and everything, the kind of note you don't want someone reading while you're still on the premises. I can be pretty mushy when I want to be.

I took a cab from La Guardia to Caroline's little studio apartment on West 82nd Street, the same block as the old mikvah if you can believe it. The cabbie was listening to such nice classical music, I almost didn't want to get out—I kept thinking of that Greek cabbie who'd been so nice to my mother the year before, I kept thinking how little it took to make my mother feel good and wondering why my father couldn't just have been as nice to her as that cabbie was.

Caroline's building was a real dump, if you ask me—a thousand dollars a month for a dingy lobby and an old, creaky elevator? I mean, call me antiseptic, but I'd take Cleveland any old day over this. When I finally made it to the third floor, Caroline was standing in her doorway holding The Little Messiah. The sun had been set for hours already, so I guess she was trying to prevent me from ringing the bell.

"Hi," she said.

"Did I ruin the Sabbath? I forgot how early it starts in the winter, but I couldn't take an earlier flight, I couldn't leave work early on my last day."

"That's okay. Sometimes it gets so lonely I just stand out here and hope someone will get off on my floor."

I kissed the baby's little blond head, which was warm and smelled great. He wasn't even four months old yet, but you could tell no matter how much Mrs. Klausner spoiled him, he wasn't going to care about materialistic things. His mind was on other, more serious matters. He even looked a little like Grandpa, his namesake, and you couldn't get any less materialistic than Grandpa was. I decided I wouldn't call him The Little Messiah anymore.

"Where's Jonathan?" I said.

"At the hospital." She didn't seem very warm or friendly, considering I'd just come from halfway around the world to see her. Well, maybe not halfway around the world, but still. She put Samuel in this swing contraption that you had to wind up every twenty seconds or something, and I followed her into her little kitchen, where her cupboards and silverware drawers were divided into "dairy" and "meat." Blue for dairy; red for meat. She had two sets of everything: dishes, silverware, pots and pans, even potholders, of all things. Her kitchen wasn't even big enough for one set, so she had things sitting on the stovetop, as if they were being used even when they weren't.

"Nice kitchen," I said. "It's almost as big as Dad's."

"It's as big as kitchens get in New York," she said.

Caroline filled up two glasses with ice and then poured us some Coke. That's how I liked Coke, real diluted, and I was glad to see she still did too. I was also glad to see it wasn't *diet* Coke. "Wait till you hear about Shira's fiancé and his family," Caroline said, like I'd just traveled five hundred miles to hear about Shira. Not that I wasn't interested, but it seemed to me that Shira was about the last thing I wanted to talk about, even if the big wedding *was* only three months away, even if Caroline assured me my parents *would* be invited. I wanted to talk about me. I had just left my job, our parents were in the middle of a divorce, and I was about to start college.

We took our Cokes and sat on the fold-out couch, watching Samuel as he fell asleep in the swing. The apartment looked like it had been decorated by Fisher-Price or something. There wasn't one inch of floor not taken up by a toy or some other baby paraphernalia. The rattle that my mother had sent looked tiny and insignificant among all the fancy, modern toys that must have come from Mrs. Klausner. I played around with the corn popper a little; it wasn't such a bad toy, really. "I wanted to tell you something interesting about Mom and Dad," I said while I popped some corn, "something that I think has a lot to do with why their marriage was so turbulent."

"Jane—"

"I know, I know, you think I ought to get on with my own life, my own family. But just listen to this." Then I went on to tell her all about my mother's violin lessons and how if only they had communicated with each other from the beginning, my mother would have seen that my father didn't want her to be his slave, he wanted an equal partner.

"Yeah, right. He wanted an equal partner."

"He did."

"Dad may be a great guy in a lot of ways," Caroline said, like she was just talking about any old father, "but a women's-libber he's not. He *did* want a slave, Jane."

"Nobody understands him," I said.

"Except for you, right?"

"I'm willing to look below the surface," I said.

"Mom's tired, Jane. Just let things alone. Stop looking below the surface all the time."

"You know, you're only religious when it's convenient. Who gives a shit if you use the same dish for an ice cream sundae and a scoop of chicken salad? Don't you think God would have rather you helped your parents stay married when you could have than gone out to purchase two sets of pots and pans?"

"You're so naïve, Jane," she said, and then she went and stopped the swing from swinging. She lifted Samuel out, like he wasn't perfectly content to be where he was, just so she could have an excuse to stop the conversation. She put him into his state-of-the-art crib, surely purchased by You-Know-Who, and said we could eat now. I noticed Samuel was wearing one of those plastic diapers, Pampers or whatever, and it was all I could do to stop myself from asking her what had happened to Caroline the Environmentalist Who Would Only Use Cloth.

She poured the wine and said the blessing. "Do you want to wash?" she said. "You don't have to."

"I think I'll just wait here."

She went into the kitchen and came back to say the blessing over the bread. "You really do all this when Jonathan's not here?" I said.

"Of course. I'm not just religious because he is."

"You're not?"

"Well, maybe, a little." She laughed. Thank God she still had a bit of a sense of humor left. She served big pieces of chicken with this very rich sauce I was sure I'd eaten at her mother-in-law's, plus about twelve side dishes the recipes for which could also have come from only one source. Everything tasted good, but you sort of had the same feeling you had after you ate at a fast-food restaurant. I mean, there was this really good garlicky taste in the chicken sauce, but you just knew it came out of one of those yellow garlic powder bottles, you *knew* she hadn't chopped a clove of fresh garlic. And the corn in the spinach/corn casserole definitely came from a can. What ever happened to the person who came home from a date at two in the morning and started grating fresh cheddar because she would only eat "real" macaroni and cheese, not Kraft? What ever happened to the person who yelled at *me* for eating Stouffer's potatoes au gratin instead of tempeh fingers?

"I remember when you used to think Mom was the best cook in the world," I said. "Remember?"

"You act like I don't love Mom anymore because I like my mother-in-law's cooking."

"No, but that's the thing," I said. "The old you *wouldn't* have liked it. The old you would have said it was too rich and artificial, that it looked better than it tasted, that more isn't necessarily better. Everything about you is different than it used to be. I mean, where'd you learn to cook? You used to think a good grilled cheese sandwich was the perfect meal—fresh sourdough bread, fresh Muenster cheese, a slice of tomato."

"People grow up," she said. "I'm a mother now; people can't live on grilled cheese."

She sounded sort of tired and resigned, like she was just saying what her mother-in-law had told her, even though she didn't really agree, even though deep down she still thought people *could* live on grilled cheese.

I sat quietly and ate while Caroline told me all about Shira's future husband and in-laws and how the wedding was going to cost hundreds of thousands of dollars, like Caroline's wedding had been cheap or something. She said she was sure Shira didn't even love Daniel, how could anybody love such a fanatic, that she just thought she *had* to get married because she was almost twenty, and that Mrs. Klausner was trying to become best friends with Daniel's parents because they were from the Five Towns. She said the two mothers went shopping together and out to lunch and how they were just hitting it off like old friends.

"It sounds like you're jealous," I said.

"Jealous? Of what?"

"Of all the attention Shira's getting."

"That's ridiculous."

"And of the fact that you don't come from a family that Mrs. Klausner wants to be friends with."

"Christ, Jane, I don't know why I bother telling you anything," she said. "No matter what I say, you think I'm slighting Mom and Dad."

Caroline got up and cleared the table. She brought out a tin of chocolate chip cookies, with nuts of all things. I guess Mrs. Klausner made hers with nuts.

Samuel started to cry then, and I knew just how he felt, waking up when it was dark out, after a nap, all nauseated and depressed. "Can I pick him up?" I asked.

"Sure," she said. "Just stall him a little; then we can give him his last bottle before bed."

"You're not nursing anymore?" I said.

"My mother-in-law said she only nursed Jonathan and Shira for two months."

"So who's your mother-in-law," I said, "Dr. Spock?"

I cradled Samuel in my arms until Caroline laughed at the way I was holding him and said "He's not a newborn, you know." Then I shifted him around and held him up over my shoulder. I walked back and forth over the rug between his crib and the fold-out couch, until he finally stopped crying and just looked around. The truth is, he didn't look like Grandpa. He looked the way Willy had looked as a baby, cute and innocent and not at all damaged. I wished I could have told Caroline what I'd done to Willy, just so she could tell me it wasn't that bad, but I was afraid she'd think I was some kind of child molester and never let me hold Samuel again.

Caroline opened up the couch and put a fitted sheet on the mattress and pillow cases on the pillows. "I'm going to sleep on Jonathan's side?" I said.

"Yeah," she said. "What's wrong with that?"

"Could you imagine Dad letting another person sleep in his bed if he were away?"

"You talk about Dad as if he represents the norm," Caroline said. "When are you going to realize that he doesn't?"

"Oh, and you do." That's what I hated about Orthodox people; they thought *they* represented the norm, of all things, they thought *my* family was weird because we didn't want other people sleeping in our beds when we weren't home.

Caroline sat next to me on the bed while I fed Samuel his bottle. He kept rubbing my fingers and holding them while he guzzled his formula, and when there was nothing left, he started crying.

"But he wants more," I said, as Caroline took him from me, patted him on the back until he burped, changed his diaper like an old pro, and then put him back in his crib, which was so close to the opened-up couch I could have touched it with my feet.

"Well, he's not getting more," she said. "There's a reason why bottles only hold eight ounces—a baby doesn't need more than that. That's what the pediatrician says, anyway." The pediatrician, the Talmud, her mother-in-law. Didn't she have one independent thought left in her head?

Caroline went to the bathroom to put on her nightgown. Meanwhile, I stripped down to my underpants and got in bed, and about five minutes later, the light miraculously went out. "The timer," Caroline called from the bathroom. Like God would have been really mad if she'd turned the light off on the Sabbath herself. I mean, what did the Jews do before they had timers?

"The thing that burns me up about the whole thing," Caroline said, sliding in next to me, "is that Daniel isn't even *nice* to my in-laws—he's always saying nasty things about the building they live in, how his house in Lawrence, Long Island, is the only place to live, how Manhattan is no place to raise religious kids. Even Jonathan, who never says a bad word about anyone, admits that Daniel's not a very charitable guy. Anyway, it just seems unfair that because he comes from the *right* family, everybody worships the ground he walks on."

Suddenly I felt sort of sorry for Caroline. I wanted her to know that even though she'd snubbed us and taken us for granted and everything, we'd still take her back into our family whenever she wanted to come back.

"They're crazy about you," I said.

"But they don't *respect* me," she said. "No matter what I become, I'll never be the genuine article."

I turned over on my side to get a good look at my nutcase sister, wondering what it was that was *really* bothering her, wondering why she was obsessing about whether the Klausners respected her, wondering why she gave a damn what they thought of her.

"What are you wearing?" Caroline said, as if her eyes had just adjusted to the dark, as if she just noticed I had no shirt on.

"Underpants," I said. "That's what I wear to bed."

"Holy cow," she said, laughing. "What knockers!"

"Shut up!" I said, punching her in the arm. "I hate that stupid word."

"Put on a shirt if you don't like it!" she said, punching me back.

It was a pretty ridiculous sight, if you want to know the truth, two grown women, one topless, punching each other while an innocent little baby slept two feet away from us. Mostly, Caroline did the punching, since I was practically paralyzed from her first punch to my right shoulder. Nevertheless, I got a few good ones in; I even pinched her upper arm hard enough to bring tears to her eyes.

"Boy," Caroline said, laughing and crying and breathless,

after we'd finally finished beating each other up. "It's been about a thousand years since I felt sexy enough to go around without a shirt. I wonder what it's like to feel sexy enough to go around without a shirt." She said it like it was a good thing to feel sexy, like a person actually *wanted* to feel sexy, like being sexy wasn't depraved or disgusting or anything. "You used to have a real hang-up about your boobs, you know that?" she said. "I mean, you used to cry if you thought someone was even *looking* below your neck. You sure have gotten over that, you topless wonder, you."

"I never cried about people looking at my boobs," I said.

"Yes, you did. Sometimes Dad would make a crude joke, and you'd go running off to your room, crying. And the sad part is, you weren't even that big. It was just fun to tease you because you were so sensitive."

"Dad never made a crude joke about *me*," I said.

"Oh, I forgot," she said. "You're like his P.R. department; I didn't mean to offend you by defaming his character."

"I'm not his P.R. department, Caroline, it's just that—"

"Face it, Jane. Dad wasn't all that great to be around a lot of the time. And you and I didn't even get the worst of it; poor Willy never had a chance."

"Dad *loves* Willy. He loves all of us, he wants only good things for us."

"I didn't say he doesn't love us, or that he did anything on purpose. He couldn't help himself, in my opinion; he was obviously so fragile that the only way he could feel powerful was by undercutting all of us. Especially Willy, being the only other male in the family. But did you ever see such a bunch of losers in your life? None of us has fulfilled our potential. It's sort of sad, really."

I didn't say anything then, I didn't want to gang up on Dad, and besides, I didn't see what good it did to blame your problems on someone else. Every so often, while we were growing up, my father would make an oblique reference to how critical his father had been of *him,* how painful a childhood *he'd* had, and because of that, it was as if we were supposed to excuse him for doing the same things to us. Now Caroline was repeating the pattern, using my father as her excuse for not achieving whatever it was she wanted to achieve.

And then it hit me: I was on my own. I had only myself to depend on, not my father and not Dr. Stevens. Nobody else could take the credit if I made something of myself, and nobody else could take the blame if I didn't. For the first time, I realized I was responsible for me, and I was kind of glad for the responsibility.

It didn't take me long to fall asleep—I can usually fall asleep pretty fast if I think about something nice, like graduating from Oberlin and doing something really important with my life and maybe even getting my picture in the *Plain Dealer*—but then I woke up in the middle of the night, all disoriented and wondering where I was. Caroline wasn't in bed next to me, and then I realized that the reason I'd woken up was because of the sound of someone crying. I got up and looked in Samuel's crib, like I couldn't tell the difference between a baby's cry and an adult's. He was fast asleep, his little jaws sucking away at nothing. I put on a shirt and went over to the bathroom. The door was locked, but I could hear Caroline making these awful moaning sounds. "Oh, God," she kept saying.

I knocked. "Caroline?"

"Don't come in!" she screamed.

"What's the matter?" I said. "Are you sick? Let me in!"

After about a thousand hours, she finally opened the door, and pointed to the sink. She had one of those home-pregnancy tests sitting there, the kind that turns pink if you are. It was pink.

"They say first-morning urine," she said, sniffling. "Is

three o'clock too early?" She sat down on the toilet seat, and I stood there by the sink, trying not to look shocked.

"Geez," I said. "Don't you guys believe in birth control?"

"Oh, that's great!" Caroline said. "That's really helpful, Miss Jane Sensitivity!"

"I'm sorry," I said. I went over to her and put my arms around her while she sat there on the toilet seat, sobbing.

"What am I going to do?" she said. "I can't have another one yet! I'll die if I do! I'll have a nervous breakdown!"

"Does Jonathan know you might be?"

"Jonathan!" she said. "Jonathan doesn't keep track of my period, unless he's in the mood. Why should he? He's not the one who has to go into labor or stay up all night with a colicky baby!"

Poor Caroline. No wonder she was so worried about the Klausners, about the fact that they'd never think she was the "genuine article." She wasn't! I mean, Orthodox women *wanted* to be fruitful and multiply, didn't they? They were supposed to *rejoice* when their pregnancy tests turned pink, not cry! Her own mother-in-law's deepest source of pain was the fact that she hadn't been fruitful enough!

My sister wasn't one of them, no matter how hard she tried to be, no matter how many chickens she cooked, no matter how many Friday night candles she lit, no matter how many mikvahs she dunked in! She was still the person who'd had sex with twelve thousand men, still the person who'd gone to Barnard so she could be "in charge of her own fate," still the person who thought women could be whatever they wanted to be. I was so glad!

"What am I going to do?" she said, and I tried to contain my joy that she was still one of us while I comforted her.

"There's nothing you *can* do, is there?" I said.

"They haven't overturned Roe v. Wade yet," she said.

"Orthodox people don't have abortions!" I said.

"Jesus Christ, Jane," she said. "Do Orthodox Jews say 'Jesus Christ'? I mean, everything is so black and white with you! You go around with all your generalizations and all your stereotypes so that you can't even see what goes on in the real world. You act like you're so tough and so streetwise, but you're really just Daddy's little girl, spouting off *his* theories and *his* philosophies."

"Fine," I said. "Get your mother-in-law to take you to the abortion clinic this time."

I stormed out of the bathroom and got back into bed. I was pretty much fuming. Here I was, the only person she could even confide in, and she had to go and yell at me. Here I was, the sister she'd all but forgotten about until she was in trouble, and she had to go and be mean to me. I sat there in the bed, my arms folded across my chest, until I couldn't take it anymore, at which point I went back into the bathroom. Someone had to be the bigger person, after all.

"I'm sorry," I said. Caroline was sitting on the toilet seat still, picking her fingernails. If *I* had been doing that she would have pulled my hands apart and said I was annoying her, but I figured she was entitled to do whatever she wanted at a time like this. Besides, younger sisters never got to say to their older sisters what their older sisters got to say to them.

"Okay, let's see," I said. "The one thing I know is that you have to tell Jonathan. You can't just decide by yourself."

"But I know what he'll say; there's no question what he'll say."

I tried to imagine Jonathan's response to Caroline's news. She was right; there was no way he'd be anything but thrilled to hear they were going to have another baby. That's the thing about men; they can afford to be thrilled because they're not the ones who sit around all day being bored to death.

"It's not that I don't like being a mother," Caroline said. "I don't know what it is."

"Maybe you could get a babysitter, so you could get a job or something."

"What kind of job? I majored in English, don't forget."

"There are jobs," I said. "I mean, if you thought you wouldn't have to be in the house all the time with two babies, would you be happier about this pregnancy?"

"Yes," she said, with no hesitation. "But then what's the point of having babies if you don't want to be home with them?"

"They grow up," I said.

Caroline sat there, biting her nails. I could tell she was mulling the whole thing over, and I felt pretty good about the advice I'd given her. I'd even reminded myself a little of Dr. Stevens, all rational and wise and everything.

"You know, the thing is," Caroline said, "I could get an abortion now and not even feel so bad about it. I guess that says something pretty rotten about me, doesn't it?"

"You felt bad about it when you were eighteen," I said.

"Not really," she said. "Back then, I was just scared to death, scared of Mom and Dad finding out, scared the doctor who did it would ruin my insides."

"He didn't."

"That's for sure," she said. "But the actual abortion itself, I didn't believe it was a baby, and I knew whatever it was, it was better off not being born, because I couldn't have taken care of it. And that's how I feel now too; there's no baby inside me, just a bunch of cells."

And I thought *I* was liberal; next to Caroline, I was about as pro-choice as Jerry Falwell! I mean, I couldn't stand those activist pro-lifers who went around blocking the entrances to abortion clinics or setting fire to anyplace that gave a woman the option, but Caroline, on the other hand, was being a little bit too blasé about the whole thing, as if a sperm and an egg were just any old cells instead of the ones that united to create a life. Suddenly, I, of all people, was becoming the voice of reason. "There are people to help you, Caroline," I said. "You have Jonathan, your in-laws."

"No," she said. "You'll see. When I tell Jonathan what it's like taking caring of Samuel, he says it sounds exactly like being on call, but all the time. There are no laws, like the ones for doctors, limiting the number of hours you can work."

"Well," I said, rubbing my eyes, "there's nothing you can do now. We may as well go back to bed, since I do have to get up with Samuel in a little while."

Caroline flashed me a grateful smile, and the two of us walked out of the bathroom. I almost turned off the bathroom light, but then I remembered the Sabbath. I left my shirt on, and we got back in bed.

It seemed like I'd just fallen asleep again when Samuel started moving around, although my watch said six-forty-five so we had been asleep about another three hours. I'm a pretty light sleeper, and I could hear the sound of his plastic diaper rubbing against the crib sheet. Caroline was snoring, so I jumped out of bed and got a bottle of formula from the refrigerator. It seemed to me you were supposed to warm up a baby's bottle, but Samuel was starting to cry, and I didn't want him to wake up Caroline. I was afraid she might kill him, in her current state of mind.

He didn't have much of a problem with the ice-cold bottle, after all, and when he was done, I patted him on the back, just the way Caroline had done the night before. He gave this great burp, which, stupid as it might sound, made me really proud of myself.

It was only seven o'clock by the time Samuel was fed and

burped, which meant there were about five hours to kill before we went to Caroline's mother-in-law's for lunch. I lay down on my back next to Caroline and placed the baby on my stomach. Then I sort of played with him, as much as a person can play with a four-month-old. I played Pat-a-Cake, and This Little Piggy Went to Market, and Ring Around the Rosy. After about a year, he finally let out this big yawn and I decided I could put him back in his crib for a nap. He made a few sounds, lying there in his crib on his stomach, but then he found his thumb and that was the end of that, he was out. I got back in bed.

The next time I woke up, Caroline was dressed and putting the baby in his snowsuit, an Oscar de la Renta or something. Maybe I wasn't such a light sleeper after all.

"What time is it?" I said.

"Eleven-thirty," Caroline said. She sounded a little better than she had eight hours earlier. "You better get dressed."

I put on this white turtleneck and black wool jumper I'd had since I was about fifteen. Even Mrs. Klausner would approve of what I'm wearing, I thought, as I looked in Caroline's bathroom mirror. Not that it was stylish or fashionable or anything like that, but at least it was modest. Not only was my neck covered, my arms and legs were too; you couldn't get more modest than that, unless you completely eliminated my chest.

Caroline put the baby in the carriage, I pushed the elevator button, and the two of us walked the two blocks over in the snow—if you could call dirty yellow slush snow—to the Klausners' for lunch. I kept trying to bring up what we'd discussed the night before, but Caroline kept changing the subject. That's what I hated about people; first they confided in you, then they wanted to shut you out.

When we got there, the two of us carried Samuel in the carriage up three flights of stairs to the Klausners' apartment, even though I told Caroline I didn't think she should be lifting heavy things, and after all, what's a doorman for if not to push the elevator button for religious Jews? She got really mad then, like she was sorry she'd told me anything in the first place. I wanted to tell her I thought God would forgive a pregnant woman for taking the elevator in her in-laws' apartment building (forget about the fact that we'd already taken the elevator in *her* building; I'd given up trying to figure out the way religious people made up rules for themselves), but I got the feeling she didn't want to think of herself as pregnant. Then it occurred to me, Albert Einstein that I was: maybe she wanted nature to take care of her problem instead of an abortion clinic.

Shira opened the apartment door and started cooing at the baby and acting all excited like she always did. She leaned over the carriage to kiss him and she practically toppled over from the weight of all the gold hanging around her neck.

"This is Daniel," she said when we entered the living room. They made a great couple, she with her fancy black dress and jewels, he with his baggy designer suit. "My fiancé. I can't believe I have a fiancé!"

Well, the guy clearly hated my guts from the get-go. He didn't even bother getting up from the couch when we came in, like I was Miss Non-Jew because I pushed Caroline's elevator button on the Sabbath. He barely even mumbled hello, and then I thought, maybe he doesn't even know I'm not Orthodox, maybe he's just mad at me because I'm taking some of Mrs. Klausner's attention away from him. She kept complimenting how I looked, saying did I lose weight or something. I could have been obnoxious and said only idiots weighed themselves, but instead I was really friendly and nice and said I didn't know. She really was staring at my chest the whole time, I wasn't just imagining it, and I could practically hear her saying to Shira after I'd left, "She could be such an attractive girl if she just had a little breast reduction."

Mr. Klausner called everyone to the table. After he said all the prayers and everyone went into the kitchen to wash their hands and he finished telling us all how wonderful everything was, and how fortunate he felt to have his growing family around him, we sat down to eat. He was a pretty nice guy, I have to give him that; he remembered where I was going to college and asked me all about the campus, and he didn't even imply that I was an idiot for rejecting the only marriage proposal I'd probably ever get.

Jonathan straggled in from the hospital in the middle of the chopped liver, his knapsack slung over one shoulder. "My religious son," Mrs. Klausner said, like she was embarrassed in front of her new about-to-be son-in-law. Then she started explaining about doctors, and how there are special exceptions for doctors to work on the Sabbath, like somebody was accusing her of raising an atheist. Like Daniel might run home and tell his parents on her. The truth is, he looked like he might.

It was another one of those lunches, with a ton of food and singing and rituals, but what did I care? It took too much energy to hate everything all the time, so I just sat there and ate and listened politely to Daniel's sermon about the biblical proscription against homosexuality. And I didn't even bark at Mrs. Klausner when she asked me in this really condescending way, "How are your parents doing?" like she had some kind of perfect marriage or something. Maybe I'd grown up in the last year but I just didn't feel like saying, "If you really gave a shit about them, you'd pick up the phone and ask them yourself." Instead I said they were fine, great, wonderful, couldn't be better. I didn't want her to think they were waiting around for her to call. I was very pleasant, and you could just tell that on the basis of the way I answered her two questions—had I lost weight and how were my parents—Mrs. Klausner was going to pull Caroline aside later and say how pleased she was that I'd finally matured, like it was her business to be pleased or not pleased.

Meanwhile, she hardly had the time of day for me, the way she was running circles around Daniel, bringing him the salt when he said *his* mother's soup was saltier, bringing him the entire ice bucket when he noted that in *his* house they always served water with ice. She was so intent on Daniel, she didn't even seem to notice the baby, if you can believe that, nor did she seem to pick up on the fact that Caroline was practically in a clinical depression. After lunch, when we were saying the grace after meals, Daniel looked like he was having some kind of attack, the way he was rocking back and forth and singing with all this emotion. I suppose I should have been impressed with his devotion to God, but I had a hard time admiring the piety of someone who only minutes before had said that the AIDS epidemic was God's divine retribution on the faggots. I swear to God, that's exactly what he said. Not that that bothered Shira, though; her admiration for Daniel didn't seem at all compromised by what he'd said; if anything she looked even more proud of her catch than when we first walked in. I guess old Lenny Levitsky was out of luck.

At about two-thirty, after we'd helped Mrs. Klausner clear the table, and after Daniel had run off to the bathroom without saying good-bye to us, Jonathan, Caroline and I took the baby and walked back to their apartment. I loved Jonathan, the way he wanted to push the carriage and the way he worried that the baby's hands would be cold. "That's just how Dad always was," I said to Caroline. "You probably don't remember, though. You only remember the things he did wrong." She'd pretty much started ignoring me when I said things like that, and that was okay with me, as long as I could say what was on my mind.

We trudged up the stairs, the three of us carrying the

carriage with Samuel in it. I gave Caroline a look, but she pretended she didn't notice.

"We usually take a nap Saturday afternoon," Caroline said when we got inside the apartment. "Even Samuel seems to know it's Shabbos." She pointed at the baby, sacked out in his carriage. Jonathan had already collapsed onto my side of the bed, which I guess was really his side of the bed, but I didn't want to take a nap anyway, I wanted to go out. I figured I ought to give Caroline and Jonathan a chance to be alone when she gave him the word.

"No nap for me," I said. "I'm going to take a walk."

"Here, take my key," Caroline said, like she wasn't *too* glad I was leaving. "Be careful."

I walked for a long time. It was cold but sunny, and eventually I had to unbutton my coat I got so warm. I walked from Caroline's apartment over to Central Park West, and then through Central Park, maybe even where my father and I had walked that day he told me I shouldn't hold so much stock in the things he said. It was the heart of winter, fortunately, so I didn't have to be reminded of my father pointing out every kind of shrub and flower that ever lived: "How about that pachysandra over there? How about that ivy?" It was such a huge park, with bridges and gazebos and lawns and creeks and skating arenas and baseball diamonds, I almost started feeling sorry for little old one-mile-long Cain Park sitting there in Cleveland Heights, Ohio. Then I thought of Grandma and smiled. She would have said Central Park was pretentious and ostentatious and like an Orthodox wedding with too much food and too much to choose from. Who needed so many choices? she would have said.

When I came out of the park, I was standing across from the Plaza Hotel, some guy offering me a horse and buggy ride, as if I was just some naïve first-time visitor to New York he could swindle. I shook my head and continued walking down Fifth Avenue, which was kind of depressing in its post-Christmas bleakness. I remembered how different the mood had been the year before, when my family had been in New York during the pre-Christmas excitement, with the big snowflake on 57th Street, the windows at Saks, the tree at Rockefeller Center.

Caroline never would have taken a walk like this by herself in a city she didn't live in, but I'd always been more daring than she was anyway. She would have wanted to go into all the stores or something lame like that. I didn't go inside any of them, but I did stand in front of the Doubleday bookstore for a long time. Bookstores were so warm and had such a nice smell to them, and they had all those books, just copies and copies of them with all those great sentences inside. Sometimes I thought books were the only things you could depend on in life.

It took me forever to get from one block to the next, the streets were so crowded with people. When I finally got to 42nd Street, I made a left and walked over to Lexington, and stood in front of Grand Central. I thought about going on over to the Waldorf, just for old times' sake, since it reminded me of my dad, and of my mom and dad being married, but I decided what the hell, did I really want to be reminded?

Instead, I went inside Grand Central and stepped over the homeless people. I didn't want to embarrass them or anything by doing something obvious like pinching my nose shut, but the whole damn place smelled like urine, so I tried breathing through my mouth until I'd made my way over to the information booth.

"I was just wondering," I said to the guy in the booth, "do any of these trains go to Fairfield, Connecticut?" Fairfield was where the Winthrop School for Boys was, and the idea of going to see Willy had been brewing in my mind ever since I'd planned my New York trip.

"Next one's at four-thirty-four," the guy said, and handed me a little red and white schedule. "Ticket counter's over there."

I still wasn't sure I was going to go through with it, but I bought a ticket anyway, and then I sort of strolled over to one of the eateries to get a cheese Danish and a lemonade. I chuckled to myself thinking about Mrs. Klausner catching me at Grand Central on the Sabbath, eating a dairy product less than an hour after I'd eaten chopped liver, not to mention the fact that I was thinking about getting on a train.

I walked over to track 40 on the upper level and stood around the platform for a while, eating my Danish and wondering whether I was really doing the right thing by going to Willy's. Was I going because he needed me, or because I needed him? Was I thinking only of what was in my best interest or was I thinking of him too? Could anything good come out of my visit or would things always be the same? Maybe I should just forget the whole thing and go back to Caroline's.

Finally, there was an announcement that the train was going to depart. I tossed my lemonade cup into a garbage can, went to the nonsmoking car closest to me, and got on. I could always change my mind when I got to Connecticut, after all.

It took me a while to choose a seat then; it seemed like practically all the seats were facing the wrong way, and I didn't want to get car sick from riding backward. When I did find one facing forward and next to a window, I sat down and put my coat on the seat next to me, but naturally I had to move it so some guy could sit there. He was one of those businessman types, with just a trace of cologne or aftershave that reminded me of Dr. Stevens's smell. He took off his suit jacket and laid it flat on the rack above us, and you could sort of smell a combination of Mitchum deodorant, Bounce fabric softener and that cologne I mentioned. It was very attractive.

A female conductor came around to get our tickets. I wasn't too crazy about female conductors, though I wouldn't tell that to just anybody. One time, I told Dr. Stevens how I felt safer flying in a plane with a male pilot or having my teeth filled by a male dentist. He kept telling me how that was because *I* was a woman, and I couldn't imagine *myself* doing anything that mattered. Like *he* didn't prefer a male president of the United States or something, Mr. Feminist.

The seats weren't very comfortable, and you could tell I was sort of getting on the businessman's nerves, the way I was shifting around, sitting straight up, then slouching. I hate getting on people's nerves, so I looked at all the stops listed on my little red and white train schedule and tried to make rules for myself for how often I could change position. Like, between 125th and Fordham, I could only change once, and between Fordham and Mount Vernon, I could change again, and so on. Then I saw, when we sailed right by the old Fordham station, that the train wasn't even *making* local stops; according to the schedule, it wouldn't be stopping again until Stamford, about forty-five minutes later, so I told myself I could shift around as often as I needed to, I was there first after all. The businessman didn't care anyway; he was sitting very still, staring intently at the Yankees and Blue Jays box scores in some sports paper. He was sort of holding the paper in one hand and playing with the end of his nose with the other. It's funny how important-looking men can get away with doing something like that without grossing you out.

So there I was, distracting myself with all sorts of inconsequentials, when I suddenly remembered what I was doing on that damned train in the first place. I wasn't just going for a ride,

I wasn't just there to observe the foibles of a middle-aged businessman: I was on my way to see Willy. And what was I going to say to him when I got there? Why was I going?

Somehow, I guess I wanted to let Willy know that he wasn't alone, that the fact that Mom and Dad were getting divorced didn't mean they were divorcing him, didn't mean he was without a family. I was still uneasy with Willy, with the way I felt about myself when I was with him, but I knew he needed me now, and that I'd have to get over my self-consciousness for his sake.

But there was something else, too, something I needed Willy to do for me. I wanted to let go of the past already, I wanted to get on with my life, and I didn't think I'd be able to until I told Willy what had happened between us all those years before, until he let me off the hook, until I heard him say, "I remember" or "Big deal" or even "You did what?" I realized that it didn't particularly matter *what* he said, that just telling him would take away some of the power I'd given the whole experience by keeping it such a secret from everyone but Dr. Stevens.

I still wasn't sure why the whole thing had happened in the first place, whether I'd been overwhelmed with sexual feelings, the way Dr. Stevens said, whether I'd been acting out with Willy something that was actually going on between my father and me. Or maybe it had something to do with trying to distract myself from being angry, kind of like what I'd done with Eddie when we were fooling around. Maybe I'd wanted to go roller skating with my friends sometimes instead of babysitting for Willy. Maybe I'd wanted my parents to take care of him instead of asking me to. For that matter, maybe I'd wanted my parents to take care of me.

I loved my parents, I admired their values and what they stood for, I admired them as *people,* and all in all, I thought we kids had turned out to be decent human beings. But lately it had occurred to me that, as parents, my mother and father had been a little selfish. It seemed as if my mother mostly wanted to give to people outside the family, people who would heap praise and gratitude upon her in return for her caring. And my father, who had no problem giving criticism, only seemed willing to give compliments if he could immediately take them back, like otherwise he would have been left with nothing.

I was thinking about all these things while I looked out the train windows, at the clotheslines and run-down apartment buildings and cemeteries, but I must have dozed off after a while, because the next thing I knew, we were in Westport. I mean, I hadn't even heard them *announce* Stamford a half-hour before, that's how out I was. I woke up with a start, when I felt the guy next to me getting up. It just figured a guy like him would live in a place called Westport; he probably had this really respectable-looking wife and 32B daughter, and a really classy-looking house. He was sort of tucking in his shirt and taking down his suit jacket from the rack by the time I figured out what was going on.

"We're in Westport already?" I said to him while I dug out my train schedule.

"Sure are," he said. He was pretty friendly, considering I didn't look like someone he'd have the time of day for. "Where are you headed?"

"Fairfield," I said.

"Heads up," he said. "That's three more stops. You've got Green's Farms, Southport and then Fairfield."

"Thanks," I said. He smiled before he walked over to the doors, but he walked over to the doors nevertheless. I mean, it's not like the guy was going to have an *affair* with me or something just because he *smiled* at me.

The doors closed, after letting out all the Westportians, and I started getting really nervous. It was dark out and Caroline would be wondering where I was. Forget about Willy, who didn't even know I was coming. He might not even be there; after all, it was almost Saturday night, even thirteen-year-olds had plans on Saturday night. I didn't even know where his school was, exactly. All I knew was it was right up the street from the Fairfield train station, probably some hoity-toity neighborhood like Pepper Pike.

Okay, I thought, I can still change my mind if I want. I can just cross the tracks and get right on the train going back to New York City, or I can stay right here on this train and go to the end of the line; I can just forget the whole thing if I want to. I reminded myself of Caroline, when she was going through that postpartum depression after Samuel was born, and all she did was cry; one time, she told me that she was able to comfort herself by thinking, okay, I can always give him up for adoption, if worse comes to worst, I can always give him up for adoption.

Poor Caroline. She hadn't even wanted one, let alone two. She was probably right at that moment sitting there at her little kitchen table with Jonathan, crying, telling him she couldn't go through with it, telling him she'd have a nervous breakdown, telling him she was afraid she'd lose her mind. Jonathan would probably be all sensitive and everything, looking at her and listening patiently, maybe even caressing her hand, letting Caroline think she had some kind of say or something, even though we all knew in the end that he would get his way. That's the thing about people like Jonathan; don't let their quiet gentleness fool you: they always get their way.

And then I thought of something really incredible: for all of Caroline's condemning the inequity of our parents' marriage, it turned out she had entered one even more inequitable. Jonathan didn't yell at her or insult her or burst out with obscenities at the dinner table, but he definitely held the reins in their marriage, more so than my father ever had. And right then I knew that Caroline would have her baby, and probably many more, whether she wanted to or not.

"Fairfield!" the female train conductor announced. I still thought I might just stay on the train and go to the end of the line, but at last I got up and stood by the doors, and when they opened, I just stepped off onto the platform and started walking, as if I belonged there or something.

The people walking briskly ahead of me weren't like me; they didn't need to pretend they knew what they were doing or had a lot of self-confidence. They *did* know what they were doing; they *did* have self-confidence. Women in wool slacks and long coats, with shopping bags from New York, teenagers in faded blue jeans and down jackets, carrying bags from Tower Records—they were all headed over to the station's parking lot. I guess I could have asked someone where the Winthrop School was, but the truth was, I was afraid to find out, I was afraid someone might offer me a ride, and then I'd have no way out, I'd have to see Willy and his depressing little room with all the little knickknacks he'd saved and then posted on his bulletin board—birthday cards with hastily scribbled messages that meant the world to him, movie ticket stubs from a thousand years ago.

I walked through the parking lot and out one of the exits, which I picked totally at random, onto one of those windy types of streets. It was cold, but it was an uphill walk so I warmed up pretty fast. I passed a little street on my right which reminded me of old Hazelnut Lane, what with its fancy mailboxes and their little red flags. I passed a condominium development and a little nature museum, and then I saw a lighted track at the top of the hill. My heart started beating sort of fast. Even I, Miss Non-Sports Fan, knew the presence of a track meant a school was probably nearby.

When I got to the top of the hill, I stood in front of the

track for a while, watching a man a little younger than my father walking and then running and then walking and then running, like he was going to live longer if he followed some stupid exercise plan. I must have watched him do fifteen laps when I noticed he was heading over to me.

"Can I help you with something?" he said through the fence. It was so cold, you could see his breath.

"I was just watching," I said, worried that he was going to point to a NO TRESPASSING sign. "My brother's a student at Winthrop."

"Oh, yeah? Who's your brother?"

"William Singer."

"Willy," he said, smiling. "What is this, Family Week? Willy's other sister was here a few days ago."

"Caroline was here?"

"Caroline, that's right."

"Caroline? Blond? Pretty?"

The man nodded, but he looked amused, like describing Caroline as pretty was a fairly big understatement, coming from someone like me. "She was carrying her baby in one of those pouches the mothers wear these days," he said. "My wife could have used one, when our kids were small."

"I can't believe Caroline was here with The Little Messiah," I said, thinking out loud. "I mean, with Samuel."

"She sat right up there in those bleachers," the man said, pointing. "I had the boys out here doing laps. It was good for Willy, having an audience. He didn't give up after two laps, the way he usually does."

"So, you're the gym teacher."

"Physical education," he said, and he reached over the fence to shake my hand. "Dave Hamilton."

"Jane Singer," I said. I was tempted to ask him whether Winthrop really did have a junior varsity basketball team, the way Willy had once said they did, but I restrained myself. I figured I had to let the poor kid off the hook sometime, especially if I expected him to do the same for me.

"The boys usually go out for pizza on Saturday night, Jane, but they probably haven't left yet."

"Oh," I said, "thanks for telling me." I'd almost forgotten that the purpose of my visit was to see Willy, I was so stunned to hear about Caroline. "I guess I ought to get going, then."

"Me, too," Mr. Hamilton said, running in place. "It was nice to meet you. And by the way, you're not so bad yourself. Not everyone prefers blondes."

He took off around the track then, and I just stood there, trying to absorb the fact that this guy Hamilton had talked about my looks and Caroline's in the same breath. That was almost as shocking as the other stuff he'd said, about how Caroline had come to visit Willy too. So much for the originality of my idea. Suddenly, I remembered the way Caroline had looked the day before, holding Samuel there in her doorway, waiting for me when I stepped off the elevator in front of her apartment. Then I remembered her saying how she sometimes got so lonely, she'd just stand there, hoping somebody would get off on her floor. I realized now that I hadn't believed her, I hadn't taken her seriously. How could she be lonely, I'd thought, she's married, she has a husband and a baby, she has a mother-in-law who buys Oscar de la Renta snowsuits.

But she must have been telling the truth, or why else would she have come up here? Maybe she'd had a confession of her own to make, though I doubted it; she'd barely even talked to Willy when we were growing up, let alone stuck his hand up her shirt. No, Caroline must have come because she felt alone, as alone as I often felt, and maybe she thought she'd feel better if she saw someone who reminded her of home. Boy, if Caroline felt as alone as I did, maybe everyone did. Maybe even Mrs.

Klausner did, all the while cooking or going to the mikvah or lighting the Sabbath candles.

Right beyond the track was Winthrop, and when I could put it off no longer, I pulled up my coat collar and started off in that direction. I couldn't stop thinking about Caroline, though, about how close I'd thought we were, yet how little I knew about her, and how little she knew about me. Maybe that was why we'd both come here; maybe people spent their lives going around trying to feel close to someone.

And then, as I made my way over to the spooky-looking mansion that was Willy's school, I started to feel pretty good. As proud of myself as I was for breaking up with Eddie, for leaving a job down the hall from Dr. Stevens, for hauling myself off to Oberlin, I felt that what I was doing now, seeking out Willy, confronting him and the pain we caused each other, was going a step further. For the first time in my life, I wasn't worried about me, I was worried about Willy—about what was going to become of him, about whether he'd ever be able to make it on his own, about whether it wasn't too late for him to get on with a normal life. As far as my life was concerned, I felt that it was starting to mean something, including to me. I guess I knew I was going to be okay, even if my father did something sickening like get remarried, even if my mother moved away from Cleveland one day, to join the Boston Symphony Orchestra or something.

ABOUT THE AUTHOR

EVE HOROWITZ was born in 1963 and grew up in Cleveland, Ohio. She is a graduate of Barnard College. She lives in New York City with her husband and their son.